Sunny Paradise

Also by Lisa Herrington

The Renaissance Lake Series

The Fix

Fall Again

Million Reasons

Mistletoe in Maisonville

The Pursuit

Sunny Paradise

Chasing Love

Standalone Books

One Starry Night

Sunny Paradise

Lisa Herrington

Writerly House Publishing

SUNNY PARADISE

Published by Writerly House Publishing
www.WriterlyHouse.com
www.LisaHerrington.com

This is a work of fiction. Characters, names, places, and events are products of the author's imagination. Any similarity to events or places, or real persons, living or dead, is purely coincidental.

Copyright © 2023 Lisa Herrington
First Published April 2023

All rights reserved. No part of this book may be reproduced or transmitted in any form or by any means, electronic, mechanical, photocopying, recording, or otherwise, without written permission.

ISBN: 978-0-9990626-4-7

10 9 8 7 6 5 4 3 2 1

For James

Chapter One

Growing up on the island of Maui where there were an average of 276 sunny days a year made Nalani Kahale have a different outlook than most.

Born into a family of overachievers, it had never occurred to her that she could fail at anything. It made the blow back that much harder.

It seemed that when things began going downhill figuratively, they picked up speed literally too.

At least that had been her experience.

She was kidnapped three weeks ago.

When she didn't give her captors the information they wanted, they pushed her out of a moving vehicle on the interstate.

That was the last clear thought she could remember as she kept slowly going in and out of consciousness.

There had been a guardian angel with her. He had blue-green eyes and a bit of stubble on his jawline. But he promised he wouldn't leave her side.

It helped her hang on for the last few hours.

PATRICK MORALES PACED the hospital hallway outside of where the doctors were x-raying the woman, he'd climbed down a ravine to rescue.

He'd only been there by chance. He was at a cookout in a nearby town with some of his law enforcement friends. His buddy always kept his police scanner on and when the call came through about a kidnapping, he jumped into the car with him.

After all, Patrick had spent 8 years in the military as a marine, 9 years as a police officer, and for the past 3 years he was the chief of police in New Orleans.

Speeding down interstate 12, they were only seconds behind the incident. Flagged down by an older man who had stopped his pick up truck in the middle of the highway.

He was beside himself trying to tell them that someone had thrown what looked like a body out of the back of an SUV.

Patrick barely heard the words. He took off down that steep hill where the little woman was fighting to get free of the bloody blanket taped tightly around her.

He would never forget the wild in her eyes. She was injured but you wouldn't know it with the way she kept moving. There was no way he could leave her there.

Trying to be gentle, he carried her up the steep incline. An ambulance would arrive soon, but she was scrappy and trying to get disentangled from the material stuck to her skin.

He knew not to move someone with severe unknown injuries, but she wouldn't lie down and wait for anything.

Focusing on her helped Patrick not to think about the animals that did this to her. It was unthinkable, and he wanted to go after them himself. He would make sure they never did this to another woman.

Instead, he focused on easing her mind. She had to be terrified because her arm was clearly broken and possibly her shoulder, but the pain didn't seem to faze her. That could only mean she was in shock, or adrenaline was masking the pain.

Easing her down into the pickup truck bed where the older man had placed several blankets, she gripped Patrick's arm.

Another pickup truck and an SUV came screeching to a halt in the middle of the highway, and two big men ran toward them. Patrick instantly put his body in front of her to protect her until he saw the larger man's face.

Patrick's heart pounded in his chest as he saw the anguish in his eyes. "That's not her. That's not Tenille. It must be her friend from Hawaii, Nalani Kahale. She's been missing for three weeks."

The men ran back to their truck and sped off down the highway again, and Patrick turned all his attention toward the woman he'd just carried to safety. Did the large man say she'd been missing from Hawaii for three weeks? What had Nalani Kahale been through, and how was she still alive? She was thousands of miles away from home. He hoped she didn't have life-threatening injuries, but in his experience, cases like hers never ended well.

He leaned down and assured Nalani. "You're going to be just fine, sunshine. I promise. My name is Patrick Morales, and I'm the chief of police in New Orleans. No one is going to hurt you again. I'll see to it."

When she squeezed his hand, that was it. He refused to let her go in an ambulance. If she had internal bleeding, she needed the best trauma center around.

Still, she clung to him as she fell in and out of consciousness. And when they arrived at the hospital, Patrick followed her through every x-ray and test, even when he had to stand outside the door.

One doctor told him that she wasn't conscious and wouldn't know if he was there or not. Patrick Morales shook his head. "Doesn't matter. I'm not unconscious, and that is the only way I'm letting her out of my sight. You got me?"

After that, no one questioned the chief again.

It was a long night as the doctor fixed her dislocated shoulder, set her broken arm and ankle, and x-rayed her torso, finding three broken ribs. A strict older nurse kicked him to the hallway so she and tech could bathe Nalani and wash her hair.

When he returned, she had tears in her eyes and more intravenous fluids to help get her hydrated. The bastards hadn't fed her or given her water in days, and he understood they meant to kill her when they were done.

Patrick Morales was friends with the New Orleans Mayor, who informed him that the former Navy SEALs whom he'd met briefly on the highway had caught up to the men responsible, and they were no longer a threat. But they'd taken Nalani because she'd helped another woman, their intended target, escape not once but twice.

She was a hero.

Surveying all her injuries and her shiny dark hair piled on top of her head in a messy bun, he smiled. Of course, she was a warrior. Who else could have survived what she'd been through? And he didn't even know the half of it.

Watching him as he approached her bed, Nalani wasn't afraid. The handsome man, she'd been sure was her guardian angel, was six feet tall with light brown hair, but those eyes were pulling her in. He had an athletic build which must have come in handy as he hauled her up that hill. She remembered him talking calmly to her but couldn't remember his words.

Her memory was everywhere as she tried to piece together what had happened. She recalled struggling to escape the bindings around her body, and that man was there carefully removing them, trying not to hurt her.

Had she been in a helicopter? If so, he was there too. Holding her hand and telling her to hang on, they were almost there. She could only assume there was the hospital where she was now.

At some point, she'd clung to him and rambled about her captors and her home. He used his deep calming voice on her. He promised she had nothing to worry about because he would stay beside her.

She'd stared at him for the longest time as if he wasn't real.

"Who are you?" she asked, and the way she looked at him made him feel ten feet tall.

"Patrick Morales."

"Thank you, Patrick." She had so much more to say to him, but all she could manage was to stare into his eyes as he came closer and held her hand with both of his. His hands were warm, and her comfort when he was near didn't make sense, but she couldn't deny it.

When he looked like he was going to move away, she held his hand a little tighter. Patrick reassured her. "I'm just going to pull the chair a little closer, sunshine."

She watched as he picked up the solid wooden chair and set it next to her hospital bed. After he sat down, he reached over and held her uninjured hand again. "Now, that's better," he said, and she smiled at him as she slipped back into the darkness.

When Nalani woke up again, a doctor was standing over

her left side, examining her shoulder, but still, Patrick held her right hand. He nodded at her reassuringly and explained that she would need a sling for the shoulder she had dislocated.

Nalani's entire body felt like it had been through a cement mixer with gravel, but she didn't remember having a dislocated shoulder. She wasn't sure what specific injuries she'd sustained and waited for the doctor to finish. Once he left, she looked at Patrick.

She had a cast on the same arm as the dislocated shoulder and a brace on her ankle and foot. She could see scratches and felt skinned areas all over her body. "How bad?" she asked.

Patrick kept the same adoring expression as he'd had earlier. "Amazingly well, considering. Broken arm and ankle. A dislocated shoulder that the orthopedic doc manipulated back into place, but he doesn't think you will need surgery for the ligaments." He grimaced before adding, "But the three broken ribs will be rough for the next six weeks or so."

That didn't sound so bad, considering what she'd been through. Three weeks with psycho Peter Miller was no joke, and yet, she'd lived through it and now was somehow in New Orleans?

"Did you say I was in New Orleans? How?"

"I talked to Detective Ghee from Maui, and he said Peter Miller kidnaped you. Do you know him?"

Nalani nodded her head, but it made her eyes feel heavy. Still, she pushed through the dizziness. "He was stalking my friend, and I helped her escape. Something happened at my family's restaurant early in the morning. One of my brothers called me, and I threw on some clothes to meet them there, but before I could get to the restaurant, Peter Miller and his men ran me off the road-- is my father okay?" She sat up straighter in her bed as worry enveloped her.

She was naturally beautiful with large dark eyes and full lips. The dimples on her cheeks when she smiled got to Patrick. The little Hawaiian woman looked sweet but had a fiery nature about her. He leaned in closer to reassure her. "He's good, sunshine. I'm sorry to tell you that those bad men burned down your family restaurant, though. Your father was inside, but your brothers busted through a wall and got him out. They've been worried sick over you."

Nalani knew there was an emergency but hadn't known it was a fire at the restaurant. No doubt, her brothers didn't want to tell her until she got there that morning. The Island Fish Company had been in her family for fifty years. She couldn't imagine how much the fire devastated her father and the rest of her family.

Her mind skipped to random events. She thought about how grateful she'd been when her father bought her the white SUV when she moved home from college. She proudly drove around the island in her Nissan Rogue, but the men in that large SUV ran her off the road that morning like her car weighed nothing. The bigger vehicle shoved her car past some trees and almost into the ocean.

"I tried to run, but they caught me and dragged me into their car. My car-- it was the first new car I've ever had, is probably totaled. I think they drugged me because I don't remember anything else until I woke up tied to a chair in some kind of storage building. I guess I thought I was still in Hawaii."

Patrick could see the concern on her face, and he wanted to ease her mind. "You don't have to worry about any of that right now. Just focus on healing."

"Do you think I could call my family?"

Locking onto her, Patrick gave her that warm smile again. "Of course," he said, handing over his cell phone.

Nalani looked at the phone and then at him. Her hand with the cast was swollen, and she couldn't type in her parents' phone number without some help.

Patrick gently took the phone and asked her for their number. "I only know the house phone number."

He nodded and then dialed it for her.

"Hello, Mama," Nalani said, and he shouldn't have been surprised when her voice cracked, but it got to him. Patrick leaned over and kissed the top of her head. Then he stepped out of the room to give her privacy to talk to her family.

Chapter Two

Victims always broke down when they saw or talked to their mothers. It was the way of the world, and Patrick had seen the biggest men reduced to children in those moments. Nalani Kahale had been taken from her hometown, not knowing whether she would ever see her family again.

Yet, even after the torture those evil men had put her through, the moment she was conscious in that muddy ravine, she tried to get up and fight.

That woman had a fire in her veins and wouldn't give up. She had tearfully talked to him in the helicopter before she fell unconscious. She told him about her captors and was terrified for her friend, Tenille.

But once he told her that Tenille had been rescued and was safe, Nalani calmed down and held his hand as she blacked out again. He felt protective over her and immediately considered his counseling sessions with new police officers, men, and women, over the savior complex or white night syndrome, but he wasn't a rookie.

Patrick Morales was the chief of the police department, and

he had to pull himself together. He didn't have a complex where he fell for a woman that he rescued. But she'd been through something traumatic and was alone. He'd given Nalani his word that he would stay with her until her family got there. But then he would have to leave.

He had to get back to the office and let her return to her life which he presumed was in Maui, Hawaii. It would help if he didn't feel like he was connected to her somehow. And it would doubly help if she didn't look at him like he was more than a new acquaintance.

Patrick wasn't a betting man, but if he were, he'd bet he was at least ten or fifteen years older than Nalani. He wiped his face with his hands. There wasn't anything between them. She just needed someone to watch over her until her family got there.

He could do that and then go back to his regularly scheduled program of work and casually date random women. It was a simple life. But he'd never asked for more.

When he was younger, he'd tried dating but had never met a woman that could handle the fact Patrick wasn't the marrying kind.

He didn't hide that truth from anyone, but still, a few women thought they could change him. Those relationships had crashed and burned. He'd outgrown the drama. Patrick had finally learned never to go out with a woman more than a few times. A few dates usually led to sex, and he was happy with that arrangement. And honestly, he had no problem ending things before a discussion about exclusively dating came up.

That dark-haired beauty was not a three-dates-and-we're-done-kind-of-girl. Patrick was getting ahead of himself, but she called to him in a primal way. The last six hours had been intense, and the way she clung to him was screwing with his head.

He couldn't be with her and move on quickly. It would hurt her, and he refused to be that man after she'd already been through too much. Instead, they would be friends. He would stay with her until her family showed up. That was it. Then he would return to the life he'd carved out for himself.

Besides, what did he know about her? Detective Ghee gave him as much information as he could, and his friend, the mayor, explained everything his people had found out about the Kahale Family. They were great folks. She was a good person. She'd attended college in California, which included a master's degree and two years toward her doctorate in History. But for the last year and eight months, she'd been back home and working in the family restaurant business.

He didn't know much else about her, and she certainly didn't know him. They didn't have a connection beyond the rescue. He should return to work, and she had to go home. He kept reminding himself of all those things as he paced outside her hospital room.

But when Nalani called his name, those thoughts went out of Patrick's head, and he immediately went to her.

As he walked into Nalani's hospital room, he could see she was tangled in her bed linens from trying to get out of bed on her own. Her hair had fallen out of the clips the nurses used, billowing around her shoulders, framing her gorgeous face.

Patrick rushed to her side with a grin. "Making a run for it, sunshine?"

As Nalani sunk her teeth into her bottom lip to keep from laughing at him teasing her, he wanted to pull her closer.

What had he been telling himself out in the hallway? He

couldn't remember. At that moment, she needed him, and no one had ever depended on him personally.

He untwisted the blankets and sheet she had tangled around the lower half of her body. And then he gently lifted her free of the bed and onto her good foot, partially holding her upright. "Bathroom?" he asked before he helped her in that direction.

A minute later, she stared into his eyes, "I've got it from here," she said. He liked the spark he saw in her.

Giving her a nod, he closed the door between them so she could do her business. After he helped her settle back into bed, the nurse told her about the additional tests ordered for her head injuries. Next, the male nurse gently scolded her about eating. He'd brought her some juice, a sandwich, and crackers through the night, but she hadn't touched any of it. She needed to eat something to take the medicine the doctor had prescribed, or it would upset her stomach.

Nalani wasn't a great patient, and she questioned everything the nurse said to her. Once they were alone again, he leaned in close. "They are just looking out for you, sunshine. If you want to get out of here, let's follow the plan."

"Are you a plan follower?"

Patrick grinned. "Sure. When I'm the one that comes up with the plan."

"Exactly." She nodded. "Who knows how many tests they will put me through? I don't think I need another MRI. I just have a headache."

"And broken ribs, a broken arm, broken foot, and numerous lacerations, including the one on the back and side of your head," he said matter of fact as he handed her the remote to adjust her bed.

She lowered it to lay on her less injured side, facing him.

"Are you from here? Originally?" Nalani seemed to need to talk about something other than her injuries and what happened to her.

"No. I grew up in the northern part of the state."

She nodded and watched him expectantly, and he grinned because no one asked him personal questions. "I grew up in a rural town and joined the Marines after high school."

"The military? Hmm. It fits." Nalani stared at him, and he stared back at her. "How long did you serve?"

"Eight years."

She pulled the blankets up higher and seemed to snuggle in as she continued watching him and waiting for more answers. He wasn't much of a talker, but something about the way she kept looking at him made him explain himself.

"When I got out, I immediately joined the police force and went to college at night."

"Your family must be proud of you."

"No family to speak of, but I'm okay with that. I did it so I could help people."

"To protect people?"

He grinned again, but that wasn't exactly the truth.

Nalani pressed the button to move her bed again, this time to sit up. She had difficulty getting comfortable, and he was sure it was because she hadn't taken more pain medicine. The nurse told her to call when she needed it, but that stubborn Hawaiian girl wouldn't ask.

"You alright?"

She nodded. Her eyes looked darker and more prominent in the low-lit room. "I was just thinking about why you went into law enforcement."

Nalani winced as she tried to sit up a little straighter, and Patrick stood to see if he could do something, anything, to help her. She favored her shoulder and left side, so he grabbed a pillow and gently put it behind her injured body.

"You know, you could call the nurse and get some medicine. It's been a long time since you had anything."

Nalani adjusted her blanket again. "I was trying to see if I could go without it. I don't like how it knocks me out."

It was refreshing, especially in his line of work, to hear someone dislike drugs. But Nalani clearly needed something. "You could probably use more rest. Besides, you know when you sleep, that is when your body heals itself?"

Nalani grinned at him, trying to take care of her. Sure, he'd explained that he went into law enforcement to help people, but it felt like his staying with her meant more. She wasn't going to read anything into it. She'd grown up with four brothers and a ton of male cousins, and they taught her that most men said what they meant and meant what they said. He was there because of his job, and then he'd be gone.

She just needed to enjoy his company for the short time he was there. Especially since two of her brothers were already on the way, she loved Jensen and Noa, but they were a lot to take, even on their best days. No doubt, when they arrived, the entire hospital would be in chaos, and the handsome police chief would be on his way.

Chapter Three

The nurse did a great job of explaining to Nalani that she would never rest if she didn't take at least a low dose of the pain medication offered. "Honey, you have to rest so your body will heal. Trust me, it will take much longer if you try and do it without anything, and it isn't worth it."

Finally, she agreed.

As she slowly relaxed, Patrick told her stories about New Orleans and some historically relevant events.

He sounded like one of those tour guides that showed people around Maui. But she loved history and listening to his deep voice.

Once the medicine hit her system, she felt much better and told Patrick about her huge family and their restaurant business.

Her father was a native Hawaiian and had a lot of brothers. Her mother was born in Mexico, but her parents moved her and her siblings to Hawaii when she was a young girl. All her aunts and uncles had loads of kids, and her entire family still lived there today. Her father had a famous restaurant, and lots of her relatives worked there, but they also did other jobs like accounting that still benefited the family. No one ever left Hawaii. "It sounds wonderful, and on many levels, it was a great way to grow up."

"And on other levels."

She rolled her eyes and held her head afterward as if that had hurt her. "My dad is the oldest and sort of the leader of the whole family. It's not the easiest place when you're the youngest and only daughter of the family patriarch. And when your four older brothers watch over you even more than your father."

"High expectations?"

"I'm an overachiever. Just my interests are not in the same realm as all of them."

Patrick nodded. "Are you saying that the restaurant business isn't your thing?"

Nalani laughed, but it sounded hollow. "I love my family. I do. But they don't understand that I don't want to marry a nice Hawaiian boy and have lots of Hawaiian babies." Looking annoyed, she added, "If I have to hear how Maui is a sunny paradise and how lucky I am to have grown up there. Or how fortunate I am to get to live there now, then I might scream."

"That bad, sunshine?"

Nalani suddenly realized that she had admitted what she hadn't been able to admit to anyone until now. "It isn't bad. I shouldn't complain. I--"

Patrick rubbed his thumb over the back of her hand in soothing circles. "Want something different."

Nalani stared at him. Why did she admit all of that to him? Especially since she couldn't tell her family. Her family had supported her through everything, and Nalani couldn't admit to them that she didn't want to live on the picturesque island that housed every single member of the Kahale Family, including extended members.

Her father indulged her academic dreams and paid for her higher education. She was lucky. She was truly lucky to have the support, emotional and financial, that they'd given her, but when she gave it all up and moved back home, her mother cried happy tears.

After finishing her undergraduate degree and master's degree and halfway through her doctorate, she quit and moved back home. No one asked why. Sure, she'd offered up that it wasn't what she thought it would be, and after failing a class, she couldn't let her father continue to financially support her in a career her heart wasn't in. But that wasn't the truth.

The family that adored her acted as if that was normal. She wasn't a skilled liar, yet they didn't question her whatsoever. She'd decided it was because they didn't want to know. They were just so relieved to have her back home, and now she owed it to them to live the life they expected of her.

So, she moved in with her folks and began working full-time at the restaurant. She even dutifully dated all the appropriate boys her age, and all was right in the Kahale Family's world.

She saw the concern on Patrick's face. It was time she turned this conversation around and stopped whining. "Everyone wants to live in Hawaii. Maui is voted one of the most desirable locations in the world every year, according to most travel magazines. I sound ungrateful."

Patrick watched as Nalani put a mask over her true feelings. For a good half hour, she'd been honest and listened to him and offered truths about herself. But what she was saying now was the excuse she told everyone, and she had memorized the words. But he was skilled at knowing when someone said what they thought he wanted to hear. He just couldn't figure out why she felt she had to live a life she didn't want.

"I've been to Hawaii once. Didn't make it to the island of Maui. I think it's a great place to vacation, but I wouldn't want to live there. It's not for everyone, sunshine."

Nalani shrugged and then winced. A recently repaired dislocated shoulder in a sling was tender and shrugging hurt like crazy. Patrick stood up and kissed the top of her head.

Kissing her and being kissed by him felt so natural but afterward, they both stared at each other. It wasn't until his phone beeped that they looked away.

Patrick looked at his phone, and Nalani watched his face. Her stomach tightened because he might leave. He'd probably stayed too long and either needed to go back to work or--worse, had a family waiting on him.

"Are you married?" she blurted out, and then instead of shrinking from asking him a personal question that she should have probably asked from the beginning, she locked eyes with him.

He shook his head, but the look he gave her was serious.

"I know that's none of my business."

"It's fine. I'm not married, and I haven't been on a date in months. I work too much."

"When your phone went off, I figured it was either work or a woman."

Patrick laughed. "How about you, sunshine? You have someone waiting on you at home?"

Nalani shook her head. She hadn't been serious with anyone in years, but her family expected her home immediately. Before she could get distracted into that rabbit hole of thought again, Patrick reached over and held her hand, making her look up at him.

"It was my office. The federal agents who were looking for you have some questions to wrap up the case. I can tell them it's too soon, or if you are up to it, I'll sit here with you so we can get this over with now."

Who was this man, and how did she luck out into him finding her before anyone else?

"You don't mind staying here with me?"

"I wouldn't rather be anywhere else."

Nalani couldn't help but stare at him. He seemed so serious when he said that, and it meant more to her than she could say at that moment.

"Okay. I want to get it over with before my brothers get here."

Patrick sent a text and then nodded at her. "There's some good news too. Your friend, Tenille, wants to come by this afternoon too."

Nalani teared up when he said Tenille's name, but the smile on her face told him that they were happy tears. He reached out to hold her hand and reviewed what he expected the agents to ask her so she would be ready.

It was less than a half hour when the two FBI agents knocked on Nalani's hospital room door. Patrick greeted them and shook their hands before he sat back down next to Nalani and held her hand reassuringly.

Patrick and Nalani had talked about many things but not what had happened to her after she'd been abducted. But Nalani didn't shy away from any of the details when the agents showed up.

"Are you alright to talk to us, Ms. Kahale?" the older agent, Rothe, asked.

The younger female agent, Agent Tolliver, looked annoyed at him and stepped forward. "We know that Peter Miller and his accomplices ran your SUV off the road in Maui."

Nalani took over from there. "It took me a second before I realized what was happening. I thought it was just a driver not paying attention when they bumped into my car. But as soon as I ran off the road, they spun around and were behind me."

"They had weapons?" Tolliver asked.

Nalani thought about it for a minute. "I can't remember if I saw a gun then or not. But I recognized Peter Miller and tried to run, but someone caught up to me from behind and put something over my face."

"So they drugged you?" Tolliver asked.

Patrick stood up to look at the agent, who was more aggressive than the situation warranted. "Perhaps you could let her explain in her own words what happened instead of talking over her with your questions."

Agent Rothe nodded and told Nalani to go ahead. Agent Tolliver was annoyed at all three of them, and Patrick could see she was unsure of herself, which caused her to act so abruptly. She probably hadn't worked too many cases yet, and he could let it slide if she checked her attitude for the rest of the interview.

When he wrapped his hand around Nalani's, she picked up her story again. "They put a bag over my head, and I kicked and screamed until they hit me in the head with something. It must have knocked me out because I woke up in the back of a car, the trunk and my hands and feet were tied. My head hurt, and I was sure how long I was in there because I was going in and out of consciousness. At some point, someone gave me water, but it must have been drugged because I think I was out for a really long time."

Nalani looked uncomfortable as she readjusted her bed linens and tried to pile all her dark hair back on her head. She had a hard time lifting her injured arm, and without speaking, Patrick reached over and clipped all her silky tresses into place so she would continue.

"I woke up in a room with only a mattress on the floor and a metal toilet and a sink attached to the wall. There wasn't a window, and I couldn't see any light from the outside. Honestly, I had no sense of time and felt like I'd been there for a month or more. Every day, someone cracked the door enough to slide food and a bottle of water inside, but I didn't see anyone or talk to anyone.

"I felt like I would lose my mind. When I thought it couldn't get any worse, Peter Miller showed up. He asked me if I had helped his girlfriend run away that night at the restaurant, and I told him I didn't. He hit me so hard that my ears rang, and my vision blurred."

Nalani took a deep breath and then admitted, "I'm pretty sure he caused the concussion and broke my ribs--because he questioned me like that for several days. When my answers weren't what he wanted, he hit me."

Patrick held her hand a little tighter. He figured it wouldn't be easy for Nalani to talk about what had happened. Strangely, it seemed to be easier for her to talk about it than it was for him to listen to what she'd been through.

"It was crazy to me that he wanted her so badly when he didn't know her. He would ask me questions that a boyfriend would know, but he didn't. He didn't know her likes or dislikes and would ask me random things about her. I didn't think he deserved to know anything about her. So, I didn't tell him anything. Tenille and I had been close and lived together at my parents' house and then in our own apartment for the ten months she was in Hawaii. I wouldn't betray her. I guess he finally figured that out because he slapped me to the floor one last time, and then they locked me back in that room. But at that time, no one brought me any food or anything to drink. It felt like a few days, but I'm unsure how long I waited.

"I was weak, and when I woke up the next time, someone had wrapped me in a comforter, and they'd used duct tape to seal it around my body. I think they planned to dump me all along and waited until they found the right spot. Thankfully, it was the highway where I was found."

Agent Rothe explained that they tracked Miller's plane, and he'd taken her out of Hawaii the same day he took her. They were pretty sure he'd held her someplace in Texas near Houston.

Agent Tolliver didn't ask any questions. She only nodded when Agent Rothe thanked Nalani for her time and wished her well.

As soon as they left, Nalani seemed lighter. Patrick had to work at keeping his anger in check because he wanted to resurrect Peter Miller and make him pay for hurting the sweet woman in front of him. He pulled her hand to his mouth and gently kissed it.

"You know that nurse is going to be back in here soon. He said you need to take those antibiotics and the only way to keep them down is if you eat something. What about a smoothie? I know a great little place close by. What's your favorite flavor?"

Why was there so much comfort being around this man? He was virtually a stranger and yet, he soothed her with kisses on her hand or the top of her head. It was such a loving gesture and Nalani couldn't get over how a sweet kiss like that was so underrated.

"Chocolate and peanut butter," she responded, and he winked at her.

"I'll be back in ten minutes. Try and rest. Okay?"

Nodding, Nalani lowered the bed again as he turned out the lamp above her head as she closed her eyes.

Chapter Four

Seeing Nalani's face when Tenille came to visit was going to do Patrick in. She'd talked to the Federal Agents as if she were telling a story of something that happened to someone else, but seeing her dear sweet friend who didn't look much better than Nalani was difficult for both women.

Tenille didn't spend much time with Nalani because they both needed rest from the ordeal they'd been through, and Nalani had to go have another MRI. But there was no doubt that she'd be back and if their body language said anything, it was that they cared deeply for each other and would be lifelong friends.

As soon as Tenille and her boyfriend, Reaper, the Navy SEAL from the highway left, Patrick asked the hospital tech if he could give them a few minutes before taking her off for another MRI. The tech agreed and as soon as they were left alone, Patrick kissed her forehead. She had tears in her big brown eyes and he wanted to hold her and tell her that everything would be okay now. Nalani and Tenille would never have to worry about Miller or his men hurting them again.

But Tenille had bruises around her neck and wrists. The white part of one of her eyes was completely red, proving her short time with Peter Miller had almost been deadly.

Seeing her friend that way had been overwhelming.

"How are you doing, Sunshine? You know she's going to be okay. And so are you."

Nalani nodded. "I just never thought I would see her again."

"I'm sorry for what you went through."

Nalani stared into his eyes but shrugged as if being tortured wasn't a big deal. "I know this is going to sound weird, but I wasn't worried for myself or whether or not I would make it. But that guy was pure evil. There was no way, Tenille was going to walk away from him again."

When her tears fell that time, he knew they were tears of joy for her friend. But why had Nalani's life not mattered more to her? Patrick carefully wrapped his arms around Nalani, and she leaned against him. It was exactly what they both needed and the connection between them was undeniable until the hospital room door opened, and two Hawaiian guys bounded into the room.

"Who are you?" one of them asked as the other one aggressively walked over to stand on the other side of Nalani.

"Calm down, Noa. She looked up at her other brother standing close. "You too, Jensen. This is my friend, Patrick Morales."

Patrick stood up and held out his hand to shake hands with Noa and then Jensen. They shook his hand and then hugged their sister. They were even more protective when they really noticed how injured she was and then asked who Patrick was again.

Instead of letting Nalani explain things, Patrick spoke up.

"I was nearby when the call went out and was on the scene first."

Nalani knew her brothers would need more, and she couldn't let Patrick deal with them alone. "He's the Chief of Police, guys. He also climbed down into a ravine and carried me up the steep hill to make sure I was okay. His friend the mayor sent a helicopter so they could get me looked at as soon as possible."

Noa looked at Patrick with respect, but Jensen still had questions. "We were told you were dumped on the highway outside of the city of Baton Rouge not New Orleans?"

"She was in-between the two cities and the helicopter from NOLA was already in the air. It was the best choice." Patrick said in that voice Nalani was just getting to know that expressed his words were indisputable.

Her brother Jensen wasn't so sure. He looked at his little sister and how battered and bruised she was, and his eyes locked onto hers. "How are you feeling, kid?"

Jensen still acted as if Nalani was in high school. She wasn't a kid and she'd almost finished her doctorate degree. Almost. Still, she couldn't help but slide back into her designated role within their family. "I'm good. A few bumps and bruises but I'll be fine."

Patrick held her hand and agreed. "You will be fine." He reiterated what her injuries were and then added how she needed another MRI and that the hospital worker would be back to get her any minute.

"We'll get you home and mom will tend to you along with dad. Everything is going to be fine as soon as we can get you out of here," Noa added.

Patrick watched as Nalani lowered her head instead of responding to her brother. The doctor had told her several times that she needed to rest and couldn't travel for at least a few weeks. The results of the MRI would determine when they would discharge her too.

Before anyone spoke again, the tech came back to collect her. Patrick smiled at her and pointedly told her that he would be there when she returned. Nalani gave him a short nod and then half smiled at her brothers as they wheeled her off to her next test.

As soon as she was out of sight, both of her brothers turned to glare at him. But Patrick had dealt with difficult family members before, and he wasn't someone who backed down from an uncomfortable conversation.

They clearly loved their sister, but she wasn't explaining what she needed. He would. He sat down in the chair he'd occupied for most of the night and leaned back to look at them. "I'm glad we have some time alone to talk," he said and both brothers looked at each other and then back at him.

"Why don't you two have a seat so we can talk?"

Jensen sat on the large leather couch on the far side of the small room, but Noa sat on the end of the hospital bed.

"Exactly what are you doing here with our sister and what are your intentions?" Noa asked.

Jensen nodded. "Because I have to say that I don't like the way this looks. Not one bit."

"I have to tell you both that when I ran up on the scene of where she'd been pushed out of a moving vehicle bound in a bedspread and wrapped in duct tape, I wasn't prepared. According to the eyewitness, her body rolled across the highway and down into that ravine. It was a fifty foot drop off and I didn't expect to find her alive. I was down there next to her before I even thought about it, and she was fighting to get loose. There was some mud and a huge pile of ants nearby. I didn't think I should move her, but I couldn't leave her there. She was ready to start swinging on anyone that got close. I told her who I was and that I was there to help her. She must have believed me because she relaxed and let me carry her up that hill.

"At first, I thought she was Tenille because that was who we were looking for but then we quickly found out it was Nalani. She must have been in shock because her left shoulder was clearly dislocated, and her left arm was broken. She was bruised and bloody but still trying to make sure we knew that the men who had dumped her still had Tenille."

"Sounds like her," Noa admitted.

"She must have trusted me when I told her that help was on the way for Tenille because she finally succumbed to her injuries and was in and out of consciousness through the helicopter ride. The few minutes of consciousness, she begged me not to leave her and I promised to stay with her until her family got here."

Jensen watched knowing there was more to it. He saw the way the man looked at his sister.

"Nalani acts strong but I'm telling you both, she's been through a literal hell on Earth for the past three weeks and those men planned on her not making it. Peter Miller tortured her and in the end they stopped giving her food and water."

Noa stood up and paced the floor. The anger on his face was unmistakable. "It's a good thing he's dead."

"Exactly the way I feel," Patrick admitted. "I won't go into the details because I think that's up to her discretion. I do want you both to know there was no sexual assault."

Jensen nodded. The entire Kahale Family saw Tenille after she'd gotten away from Peter Miller the first time. It was obvious she'd been through it all with that despicable excuse for a man and it had worried them even more for Nalani. She was the baby of the family and precious to them. Letting her go to college in California at eighteen had been the hardest thing. If Jensen hadn't spent a month following her around that campus without her knowing it, of course, then none of the Kahale Family could have let her go in the first place.

Nalani had always been studious, and they tried to support her dreams of one day becoming a history professor. However, the moment she quit in the middle of her doctorate program, they all celebrated her permanent return. All was right in their world with his baby sister working at the restaurant and dating local guys on the island. This event had shaken them to their core, and he wouldn't let anyone get to her again. He and Noa made a pact that they would keep an even closer eye on her than ever before but now he had a burning question for Patrick Morales.

"We appreciate what you did for our sister, but we can take it from here."

"No offense, Jensen, but this happened on your watch. I think I'll stay around a bit longer." Patrick said and stood up to make his point.

Jensen and Noa both stood too.

"Offense taken," Noa replied. "We don't need you here."

"I'm not leaving unless Nalani asks me to."

"Don't you worry, Police Chief Morales. She will relieve you of your duty when she returns," Jensen said through gritted teeth and that was when the nurse wheeled Nalani back into the room and witnessed the men squaring off.

"What is going on here?" Nalani asked. She'd worried she shouldn't leave her brothers alone with Patrick. She'd felt the pull toward him the moment he climbed the hill with her in his arms and it had only felt stronger as they spent the last twelve hours together. No doubt her brothers wouldn't approve, and she had to find a way to tell them it was none of their business. She just wasn't sure if Patrick needed her to let him off the hook.

The look he gave her made her believe that he was where he wanted to be but she sure could use the words. He stepped toward her and reached out for her hand. "It's okay, sunshine. We were just talking."

Nalani stared into his eyes, but she couldn't trust her own judgment. "It sounded like you were disagreeing and that maybe you were leaving. Do you want to go?"

She hadn't had a proper night's rest in so long and right now couldn't make any big decisions. But if it was her choice, she wanted Patrick nearby.

"I'll be here as long as you want me to stay. You have my word." Patrick watched as she seemed to relax. He helped Nalani out of the wheelchair and into her hospital bed.

"How did the test go?" Noa asked abruptly, trying to change the subject. He knew his little sister was going to let them have it and he didn't think she needed that kind of stress right now. She looked smaller than usual and a bit defeated.

"The doctor said he would read it and come talk to me in a few minutes. Apparently, he was waiting for the results before he left the hospital." She avoided Noa's eyes as she spoke. She never did that and he worried her condition was worse than they'd originally thought.

Chapter Five

Half an hour after Nalani returned to her hospital room, her doctor walked in. He introduced himself to her brothers and shook Patrick's hand again. They'd spoken multiple times when Nalani was brought in and then once since all the tests began.

The doctor turned the overhead light on and then examined Nalani's head where she was bruised and then her vision. "The good news is there doesn't seem to be any permanent damage. But there has been some head trauma and I feel certain that the headache, and eye strain you are experiencing is due to that trauma."

"So she does have a concussion, Doc?" Noa asked.

"It's a little harder to pinpoint without having a baseline established before the accident. But I would say that it's highly possible and we need to watch her for another twenty-four hours." He said looking directly at Nalani and not Noa.

Nalani looked discouraged. She didn't necessarily want to leave New Orleans yet, but she desperately didn't want to be in the hospital any longer.

Patrick held her hand a bit tighter. "It's just another day, sunshine. Better safe than sorry. Right?"

"You're right," she agreed.

Then the doctor added, "But even if we agree to release you in twenty-four hours, Ms. Kahale, you won't be cleared to travel back home to Hawaii for several weeks or longer."

Both of her brothers stood up. "Why not?" Noa asked.

The doctor looked annoyed but turned toward Nalani's brothers. "Your sister's external injuries are bad, and she'll need physical therapy under a doctor's supervision. But her internal injuries could be very dangerous if she isn't careful and doesn't rest properly. I won't clear her to fly until I believe it's safe." The doctor looked at Nalani again. "Those injuries are very painful. You need time to heal before you put that much stress on your body. Flying from here to Hawaii would physically be too much."

The Kahale Brothers looked at one another and then finally agreed. Nalani rolled her eyes because although they thought they were running this program; it wasn't up to them. Thankfully, she didn't have to be the one to tell them.

The doctor promised to come back by in the morning and tomorrow night. But also encouraged Nalani to take the pain medicine so she could rest. He assured her that was the quickest way to heal and to get him to release her from the hospital.

Before he left, he told Nalani to hang in there and to get some sleep. Five minutes after he walked out the door, the male nurse returned. "Okay. The doc says Ms. Kahale can only have one visitor at a time. She needs her rest, fellas."

"We're her family. We'd planned to stay with her until she's released."

"I was unaware that she was still in danger." The nurse said, looking at Police Chief Morales for confirmation.

"She's not in danger," Patrick said. "But she does need to rest."

"Well, we don't care who stays with her, but two of you have to go." The nurse said it one more time and then leaned against the wall as if he was giving them privacy.

"We don't even have a hotel yet," Jensen said and pulled out his phone.

"It's carnival time. Mardi Gras is early this year. It'll be hard to find a place at a reasonable cost. My place isn't huge but you're both welcome to stay with me," Patrick offered

Noa didn't seem keen on that idea and Nalani didn't want them to impose on the police chief either. "Tenille told me there is room at the boarding house where she lived in Maisonville. She offered it to me when I got out of the hospital too. I'm sure she could set it up for you guys.

Patrick gently squeezed Nalani's hand. "Maisonville is across the lake and will take you over a half hour to cross one way. I'm afraid it will be too much for you to travel that far especially if you have to do physical therapy, sunshine."

"But the guys would be comfortable, right?" Nalani asked sweetly and Patrick wanted to pull her into his arms again. What was wrong with him? Had he ever been so ruined over a woman he'd just met?

Jensen cleared his throat since Nalani and Patrick were still staring into each other's eyes. He was irritated at how familiar the police chief acted with his little sister. She was too young for him and when he got Morales alone again, he would tell him in no uncertain terms that he needed to leave her alone.

For now, he would play nicely and try not to upset Nalani. Patrick Morales was right in saying she'd had been through hell and he wanted her to heal properly, so he could get her safely home where she belonged.

"Do you have Tenille's phone number?" Jensen asked. "I'll text her and see if we can get set up."

Patrick Morales sent Jensen and Noa the phone number so they could contact Tenille and watched as both stood around not wanting to say goodbye to Nalani yet. "I can step out and give you guys a few minutes if you want?" he said, asking Nalani more than Jensen and Noa.

She smiled warmly at him and as much as he didn't want to leave her, he stepped into the hallway. When the nurse came back to kick two of the three men out, Patrick stalled him with questions to give the brothers a few extra minutes.

When he followed the nurse into Nalani's hospital room, he could see she'd been emotional from talking with them. It made his gut hurt to see her upset and he used all of his professional training to keep his temper in check.

"You both have my number if you need to call," Patrick said, with the tone of it's time for you both to go. He hadn't noticed until that moment how upset Noa and Jensen looked too, and he felt brash for not considering how close the siblings were and what they had been through over the past month. "And I'll call if there are any changes, okay?" He leaned in, "I'm certain she'll feel much better tomorrow and they will allow us all to be here with her."

Noa looked hopeful and Jensen appreciative as they each kissed their sister and said goodbye. As they were leaving, dinner was brought in, and Nalani seemed overwhelmed with the idea she now had to eat something. "Why doesn't anyone around here ask me what I want. I swear this is like a prison and they keep shuffling me to and from without any regard to how I feel."

He knew she was upset over her brothers and tried to ease her pain. "You tell me what you want and I'll do my best to make it happen."

"I want this all to be over," she said hastily and the way she pouted was sexy as hell.

Patrick sat on the side of her bed and looked into her eyes as he gently tucked the hair that had fallen out of her messy bun back into the hair clip. "The good news is that Peter Miller is gone. Tenille is on the mend. You are safe and healing here at the hospital. And two of your brothers are in town and ready to whisk you home as soon as you are able to go."

Nalani lowered her eyes at him. "Then why don't I feel better?"

"Probably because you haven't had your antibiotics or any pain medicine in hours and your shoulder, broken arm, fractured foot and various scrapes, burns, and bruises must be singing by now."

"Has anyone ever told you, chief, that you don't have to fix everything? I know all those things. I just want to be mad. None of this should have happened. Tenille didn't deserve any of it and my family didn't either."

"I wish none of it had ever happened to you, Tenille, or your family."

Nalani pouted some more. She was being rude to Patrick, and she didn't understand why, but he was an understanding and sweet man who held her hand through some scary moments over the past twenty-four hours. "Thank you, Patrick."

He winked at her, and she leaned back in her bed and stared at him. "Were my brothers really difficult? They truly mean well."

"Sunshine, your brothers were worried sick about you and

I'm a stranger. I understand they were just being protective over you."

"You know that isn't an answer, right?"

Patrick grinned and began opening the items on her food tray. Nalani reached over and held his hand. "Thank you so much."

"You're welcome." He handed her a saltine cracker as he took the lid off her covered plate to reveal a rice dish with chicken and some green beans.

She took a few bites and then looked at him. "Patrick? What are you going to eat?"

"I'll get something. Don't worry about me."

She reached over and held his hand. "You've been up all night and day with me. Aren't you exhausted?"

He smiled at her but didn't give her an answer.

Her heart hurt but she needed to let him go if that's what he wanted. "I'm okay, you know. I could stay here alone tonight so you can go home and get some rest."

"If you want me to go then I'll go," he said and the look in her eyes told him what he already knew.

"I don't want you to go."

He leaned over and kissed her forehead. They both looked up to see the nurse coming in with a tray for him. "We all noticed you haven't eaten Chief Morales and we can't have you malnourished in a New Orleans Hospital on our watch. Could you imagine the press?"

Nalani and Patrick both laughed at the nurse who had a dry sense of humor but was funny. "Thanks. You didn't have to do that, but I appreciate you."

"My pleasure. You seem to be the only one she'll listen to around here and you've made my job easier getting her to eat and take her meds."

Nalani laughed but it was true. She did listen to Patrick more than she would anyone else and she wasn't even sure why. But the way he looked at her was exciting and if she didn't feel so battered, she would pull him into her body and kiss him like crazy. She licked her lips and then saw how he stared at her.

The desire she felt when he was near was off the charts and she couldn't remember ever being that attracted to anyone at home. She liked older men and Patrick had to be near the same age as her oldest brother, Keanu. No one ten years older than her, who all went to school with her brothers and cousins would look her way. And if they did, her family would let them know immediately that she was off limits. It had always been that way and she'd been treated like everyone's little sister.

But Nalani didn't have anything in common with boys her age. Even as she got older it hadn't changed. Patrick looked over to see her watching him as he unwrapped his sandwich and began to eat. "Do you need something, sunshine?"

Nalani bit her bottom lip and smiled at him.

"You better stop looking at me like that or we're going to get into a lot of trouble with that nurse."

Nalani laughed and then challenged him. "What kind of trouble?"

Chapter Six

Patrick Morales had dated more than his share of women and he wasn't shy when it came to desire or sex talk. But the adorable, injured little Hawaiian woman lying in the hospital bed in front of him was going to be his undoing. And she knew it. She was teasing him and he couldn't help his reactions toward her.

"You know exactly the kind of trouble I'm talking about, and you are too injured for us to try and fool around in that little hospital bed."

Nalani was suddenly hotter than the sun. "You underestimate me, Patrick Morales. And this bed isn't that small."

He loved to hear her say his name and he would like to hear her say it while he made love to her, but things were already out of control between them.

The truth was, he was exhausted and not thinking clearly. This woman had to be in her twenties and lived thousands of miles away in Hawaii. She belonged to some kind of giant Hawaiian clan. He'd just met two of her brothers and they were every bit as big as him if not bigger. They would have his head roasting on a stick over an open fire if he even looked at their little Hawaiian princess and he wanted to do more than just look at her.

Sitting his sandwich down, he closed the space between them and leaned down, so they were just a breathe apart. "I would never do anything but praise you, sunshine. But this bed is too small for all the things I would like to do to you and you're going to need your stamina when it happens."

Holy hotness, this man was incredible and his flirting only proved why dating older men was her jam. "If, you're sure." She managed to say but it came out more like a breathy whisper which made his eyes dilate.

Patrick pressed his strong lips to hers but when Nalani inhaled, he took a moment to explore her with his mouth.

When he slowly stopped, he was only a breath away. But he'd left Nalani panting. He'd barely touched her. What was happening to her?

"Eat your dinner, beautiful. You'll need your strength." Still, he was teasing her with his words and it really did something for her. The thought of him showing her how well he could love a woman was almost overwhelming and she was certain it had nothing to do with her present condition.

"Yes, sir, Patrick," she said and gave him a saucy smile which made him laugh.

He sat back down in his chair that was still pulled up next to her bed and they both ate their dinners and talked briefly about the hospital staff and facility. The small talk didn't distract her from how much she liked this man. Simply being near him was comforting.

Once Nalani finished most of her food, the nurse came in and applauded her and promptly had her take her medication.

Patrick helped her to the restroom again and waited while she washed her face and brushed her teeth.

"Ready for bed?" he asked, and she didn't miss his double meaning. He was so serious most of the time and this flirtatious side was surprising and fun.

"Only if you are," she said making him laugh.

He helped her climb under the covers and then tucked her gently into place before he kissed her sweetly on her forehead, nose, and then lips. He was slowly killing her with foreplay, and she wasn't sure if he knew it. She hadn't wanted anyone in such a long time, not really, and now that she was in a place she couldn't stay, with a man she'd probably never see again, Nalani needed him.

Her sudden longing didn't make sense.

She thought about how quickly they got to know each other. Hadn't she read somewhere that people sometimes form incredible bonds when they go through a tragedy together?

Of course, Patrick didn't go through the kidnapping, but he'd climbed down that steep hill and carried her up when no one else had attempted it. He insisted a helicopter take her to the New Orleans trauma center so she would get the urgent care she needed. Knowing she was alone, he soothed her with his words and comforted her with his warmth by holding her hands, kissing her forehead, and generally reassuring her at every turn. But she wasn't naive.

"What are you thinking so hard about, Nalani?"

She looked over to see him studying her. Could she tell him? "I'm just wondering if you usually watch over the people, you save like me?"

Patrick wiped his hand over the razor stubble on his face. "Never."

They were locked onto each other when the night nurse

walked in to introduce herself and to take Nalani's vitals. It was awkward as the pretty nurse kept staring over at Patrick and then finally asked, "Aren't you Police Chief Morales?"

"Yes," he answered.

"Oh, my God, you look so handsome, I mean younger in person," the nurse said laughing and flirting until she realized Nalani was laying there. "I'm sorry. Is he your boyfriend?"

Nalani shook her head, no, but really disliked how the pretty nurse took that as an invitation to flirt even more. She finished taking Nalani's temperature and then walked around the bed to shake Patrick's hand. "It's so nice to meet you. You've done such an incredible job in the city. When I was in high school, up town, my girlfriends and I were mugged for our jewelry. It was right after school in broad daylight but there is almost no crime like that anymore. You're my hero."

"That is very nice of you to say, Nurse Britney. But honestly, it has been a team effort with our amazing police force working with our prosecutor's office to get criminals off the streets of the city."

"Oh, you are so humble. I like that." She laughed again, practically giggled, and then headed for the door. "If you need anything I'll be on all night," she said staring into his eyes and ignoring Nalani.

When she left the room, he looked back over at Nalani who tried to act like the flirting hadn't bothered her. But she couldn't help herself. "O.M.G. you are so handsome and my hero," she then faked a giggle like the nurse and Patrick was on his feet and closing in on her in her bed.

"You are so cute when you're jealous," he said staring into her eyes. The shocked look on Nalani's face made him laugh harder.

"You wish." Nalani rolled her eyes and then closed them

scrunching up her face because it still hurt. "I think if you play your cards right, she might be willing to do you in a janitorial closet or something. She is on all night, after all."

"You know I'm not interested in that nurse."

"It's none of my business," she said letting her jealousy get the better of her. This medication was like a truth serum or something and she had no filter. She kept willing her mouth to shut but words kept spilling out.

Patrick was super close to her face now and staring into her eyes. "I have never personally gotten involved with someone that I helped in my line of work. Ever. Until you. I don't know why I feel so protective of you, but I do. I can't seem to leave and I'm being unprofessional. I have no idea how to tell you that I want you to come home with me and let me take care of you. You know when they spring you from this joint. So does that clear things up, sunshine?"

Nalani leaned up and kissed him on the lips. She'd always doubted the instant connection people claimed to have with friends or significant others. But she and Tenille Sims had become instant friends back in Hawaii. Then out on a highway somewhere she'd never been, this beautiful man showed up and there was an unmistakable bond between them. It defied logic as she knew it. Her brothers sure didn't seem to like it, but she was used to not getting their approval.

She ran her right hand over his hair and then the fine stubble across his cheek. He was a handsome man with strong features. Nalani was physically attracted to him but his generous nature and the gentle way that he'd cared for her when she was all alone was telling of his heart.

There was no way to describe it without sounding ridiculous and she had no words to respond to him, so she just nodded in understanding.

Everything about this man drew her in.

He held her hand as he sat back down beside her and they remained close, talking about his job and hers for hours. It was the equivalent of staying up all night and chatting on the phone with a crush in school. *What's your favorite music? What was the first concert you ever went to?*

Nalani drifted off to sleep with his words still on her mind, *I want you to go home with me.*

Chapter Seven

When Nalani opened her eyes early the next morning, Patrick Morales was sound asleep on the fake leather sofa in her hospital room. Barely covered in the thin cotton blanket provided by the hospital, he must have been exhausted.

Watching the beautiful man sleep almost made her forget about the pain but this morning it was not going to be ignored. She used her right arm to try and pull her body up so she could turn over but then she hit her injured foot and the pain shot through her leg all the way to her hip.

She inhaled sharply and Patrick was on his feet. "What do you need?" he said, and she tried not to sound as helpless as she felt.

"I'm okay. Just trying to sit up."

Patrick gently scooped his arms underneath her body and lifted her into a seated position so she could use the remote to move the bed.

"Thanks," she whispered, and he kissed her forehead before studying her.

"You haven't had any medicine since last night, have you?"

Nalani shook her head.

Where the hell was Nurse Brittany?

Patrick told Nalani he would be right back and in just a few minutes he returned with the nurse carrying some pain medicine. She looked irritated but Nalani accepted that she could be projecting her own feelings since she was in so much pain.

Patrick's cell phone rang, and he stepped out of the room to take the call. Nurse Brittany watched him go and close the door behind him before she spoke. "Chief Morales must not have gotten enough sleep last night. He certainly got up on the wrong side of the sofa."

Nalani looked at the grumbling nurse and shrugged. Dang that hurt. She had to stop doing that.

"He spoke to my supervisor instead of telling me directly that you needed your medication. I came in here a few hours ago, but you were sleeping. Next time you can press the call button and I'll take care of it. No need to get me into trouble."

"He was simply trying to help me," Nalani said, explaining what should have been obvious to the nurse.

Patrick walked back into the room and the nurse quit complaining to Nalani and gave him a sugary sweet smile. It was fake, just like her bedside manner. Still, she watched him walk around the room to the other side of Nalani's bed and hold her hand. "You should feel better in a few minutes." He reassured her and looked dismissively at the nurse who spun around and left.

"Your brother, Noa, called. He wanted to see if the doctor had come in yet and I told him that we would call him as soon as we heard anything."

Nalani nodded. Truthfully, she felt helpless lying in the hospital bed and having everyone fuss over her. She wanted to get out of there and she felt terrible that her brothers were in town and couldn't hang out with her.

"Did he say where they ended up last night or how they were doing?" she asked, still feeling antsy.

"Reaper sent me a text early this morning and said the guys were staying at his house. He has some small cottages and put them up for the night. He wasn't sure if they wanted or needed to stay on for a few days but for now they are comfortable.

Of course, Tenille and her boyfriend would make room for the Kahale brothers. The Kahale family loved her like she was one of their own and she loved them right back.

Nalani looked relieved and gave him a half smile. "I was worried about them when they left here last night. They were aggravated and I know they didn't want to leave me here." Nalani took a deep breath and looked up at the ceiling. "The medicine is starting to work. Thank you for getting the nurse." She looked at Patrick and grinned. "I don't think she has a crush on you anymore."

He laughed and shook his head. "She's not the one I'm concerned about."

Nalani wondered if she would ever get tired of hearing him say that to her. Had anyone ever acted that way over her? He pulled her hand to his lips and kissed it before he let her go and checked his email and text messages again.

After a few minutes, Nalani pressed the button to raise her bed higher and Patrick looked over to see if she needed anything. "Patrick, I know you're an important man and I'll understand if you need to go into work today."

He kissed her forehead. "Let's see what the doc has to say when he comes in this morning, okay?" Then he went right back to his phone and answered emails and sent messages.

Nalani smiled thinking about how he'd said he wanted her

to go home with him so he could take care of her. He seemed too busy to take care of himself and he certainly wouldn't have time to worry over her.

It was a half hour before the doctor came in. Nalani waited patiently as he checked her shoulder, hand, foot, ribs, scrapes and bruises. They discussed how well she was getting around, which wasn't that well, and pain management. He told her that he wasn't comfortable letting her leave today but he would allow her more visitors so her brothers could come back to the hospital. Then he said he'd be back tonight.

It wasn't exactly the news she'd wanted but at least she could have her family there, which would make them happy too. She called her parents and talked to them for an hour. Then by noon, both Noa and Jensen were holding court with two nurses and a tech in Nalani's room.

Patrick went home to clean up and stopped in his office to work for a few hours. He promised to bring her dinner and kissed her goodbye in front of her brothers.

They grilled her over the relationship, and she told them both to mind their own business. "You guys have dated every single girl on the island and a few that weren't single. If I like Patrick Morales who is a wonderful human that is my prerogative."

Jensen lowered his eyes at his sister. "I spent this morning looking him up online. Did you know that he's thirty-eight?"

She didn't know how old he was because they hadn't gotten to that yet. But she wasn't going to admit that to her brother. "Yes," she said. "He's the same age as Keanu." That was their oldest brother who had been a professional surfer and the one she had the most in common with.

Noa squinted his eyes at her. "Keanu is almost forty."

Nalani shrugged. This was a non-issue, and she didn't care what her brothers thought about it.

"The man is the chief of police in New Orleans, Louisiana. You don't live here," Jensen added.

"I don't know what you want me to say, Jensen. I am still trying to process what I have been through. It's made me question everything. Do you get that?"

Both brothers looked at each other and then at their little sister. Noa sat on the side of her bed and his eyes softened. "We should've never let you out of our sight while that crazy man was still at large. As your older brothers, it's our job to protect you and we failed you, Nala."

He hadn't called her Nala since they were kids. She knew he felt bad but there was no way they could have predicted what Peter Miller was capable of and they certainly didn't know he was in Maui or planning revenge against their family.

"I'm not a child. I would've never stood for you following me around either, Noa." She gave him that smug grin only the little sister of four brothers could manage. She'd always had an army behind her pushing her to hike to the highest waterfalls or surf the biggest waves. Growing up with them had been wonderful but also misleading.

She'd left her home in Lahaina Hawaii for college in California with all the confidence in the world. It was easy making fast friends with people because she'd always been friendly and gotten along easily with others. But she hadn't been prepared for the wolf in sheep's clothing waiting for her. It changed the direction of her life, and she hadn't admitted that to anyone including herself until she'd been locked away for three weeks by kidnappers that planned to kill her.

Suddenly given a new chance at life had made Nalani face facts. She wasn't truly living. After she'd quit school and moved home for good, she simply did what was expected of her. There was and always would be comfort at home, but the cowardice behavior made her ashamed and she wanted, maybe even needed to face her fear, and live her life on her terms.

But as Jensen and Noa stared at her defiantly, she wasn't so sure she would ever have the strength to leave them all again.

Jensen pretended he didn't see the pain of something flit across his little sister's face. She was dealing with some demons that he wasn't sure she would admit to them, but he had some words of wisdom to give her. "I'm not sure who has put it in your head that you have a choice in whether we protect you or not, but it will be quite some time before any of us are going to let you get very far on your own. Ma has already had Keanu and Oren, their other brother, move your things back home from your apartment."

"What?" Nalani couldn't believe they'd made that decision without her approval. "I paid for that apartment on my own. You guys can't just move me home with mom and dad just because it will make you feel better."

Noa smirked. "I think you know we can."

Her brothers high-fived each other and then Jensen lowered his eyes at her. "And we did move all of your things back into your old bedroom. The things that didn't fit are in the garage."

Nalani slowly and painfully managed to get out of her bed and with her good hand on her hip and her hand in the cast pointed angrily at them, she raised her voice. "I am twenty-seven-years-old, and you guys are not the boss of me. I want my things taken back to my apartment immediately or else."

Noa laughed. "Or else what, shorty? You'll hit us with your cast?"

Nalani stepped toward him and hit him in the chest with

her cast which sent pain screaming up her arm just as Patrick Morales and the male nurse who was back on duty walked into the room together.

"Visiting hours are over, fellas," Patrick said before the nurse had a chance. He moved in front of Nalani and held his arm out to move the brothers back away from her.

They all looked incredibly angry at each other and now at him. But as everyone silently glared at each other, the nurse considered whether he would have to call hospital security to break them up.

Chapter Eight

Noa looked at Patrick. "I was just standing there. She's the one who hit me."

Nalani's face was red, and she was gritting her teeth. She looked like she was ready to explode, and it took all of Patrick's self-control to not egg her on more. She was even cuter when she was mad. But the stress couldn't be good for her body, especially if she had a concussion, and using her broken arm to hit people.

"You shouldn't be out of bed, sunshine." Patrick tried easing her back into the hospital bed, but she was still fighting mad.

"This isn't over, you two. I want my things moved back into my place immediately. And it better look exactly the way it did when I left."

Patrick picked her up and sat her on top of the covers which got her attention. She immediately explained how they'd moved her things back to her parents' house without consulting her.

Before Patrick could say anything, Jensen stepped closer.

"Look Nalani, we can't move you back into that place. They've already rented it to someone else. What do you expect us to do, kick them out and move you in?"

"I expected you to leave my things where they were until you talked to me. I am not living at home with mom and dad for the rest of my life. Or working in the restaurant either."

Everyone got silent because working in the restaurant wasn't even an option because Peter Miller had it burned to the ground. It would take some time for it to be rebuilt and they each knew that it took a piece out of their father to see all his family's hard work destroyed.

Jensen spoke through gritted teeth. "You will do whatever is needed to help our family just like the rest of us, Nalani."

Patrick stood and walked to the hospital room door. "You guys can discuss this later. For now, she needs her rest and to not be upset over things beyond everyone's control."

Jensen leaned over and kissed his sister on the top of her head. "We have to leave by the end of the week. It's all hands-on deck to rebuild the restaurant. If that doctor releases you then we'll all go together. That's the end of it," he said before locking eyes with Patrick as he left with Noa right behind him.

When the chief turned around, the nurse was checking her vitals and shaking his head.

Patrick walked over and held her hand in his. Nalani was still furious and huffed. "Can you believe those two oafs. Do they not have lives of their own? I mean, who do they think they are, moving me out of my apartment? I signed the lease, and I paid the rent and utilities there."

"Sunshine," was all Patrick said but the nurse wasn't so understanding.

"The doctor isn't going to be happy when he hears that you used your injured arm to hit your brother." As he lifted it higher to examine the condition of the cast, she winced. "We may need to take this cast off and do another x-ray."

Nalani was even angrier than before as she argued with the nurse. "Is that really necessary?"

The nurse looked straight at her when he answered. "I guess it depends on how badly it hurts right now. Hitting him may have caused the the break to worsen and you could be looking at surgery to reset your arm."

Nalani's angry expression changed to a look of sadness. She let go of Patrick's hand and then rolled over onto her right side and closed her eyes without another word.

The nurse said he would be back with the doctor soon and Patrick waited until the nurse closed the door before, he stood and leaned over the bed to wrap her in his arms. "It's going to be alright, sunshine.

He felt bad for leaving her to go to work. He should have known that her brothers would cause a ruckus. There was something brewing underneath all Nalani's emotions, and it was only a matter of time before they stirred things up with her.

Turning to look at him, she shook her head. He could see her eyes water and wanted to understand why she was so upset with her family who seemed to just want to take care of her.

Patrick nodded toward her arm in the cast. "Does it hurt?"

"A little," she shrugged not remembering how bad that hurt too. She didn't want to admit that it was ridiculous to hit her brother with her cast. Her arm felt like it had its own heartbeat as it throbbed.

"Do you want to talk about it?"

Nalani shook her head but began talking anyway. "My family can be overbearing. I mean, I love them. I really do, but would it be so wrong if I lead my own life and made my own decisions?"

Patrick had left home at seventeen and had been making his own decisions long before then. He'd never once had to fight someone to let him be an adult and hadn't once felt like he needed to prove he was a grown-up. He'd practically been born one.

"Why do you think they feel that way?" he asked, watching her closely now because there was more to this story.

"They've always treated me like that even when I left to go to college. I would come home to visit during school breaks, and they still gave me curfews and talked to me like I was a kid."

"Your parents?"

"My parents for sure acted that way but also, all four of my older brothers and aunts, uncles, cousins, long time workers at the restaurant. It's like the entire island refuses to see me as an adult. In their eyes I'll always be that teenage girl that went surfing with all the boys and waited tables at the restaurant for spending money."

"So why did you move back there?" It seemed simple to him. "People aren't planted like trees and if you're not happy where you are then you could move."

"You make it sound so simple, but life is complicated."

Patrick stared into her dark eyes and grinned. He had no doubt the gorgeous Hawaiian woman was complicated but she was also holding something back. Would she ever tell him what it was? "I have learned that life is as complicated as you make it, sunshine."

Nalani cut her eyes at him but before she could give him an earful of how she hadn't made her life complicated, the doctor walked in with the male nurse, now known as the tattle-teller by his side.

"Ms Kahale," the doctor said, and she didn't like the condescending tone he was using either. She for one was an expert at picking it up and she was ready to give them all hell for being so rude to her. But when he lifted her arm to examine it, she couldn't stop the audible gasp that escaped.

The doctor looked at the nurse and nodded before he turned back to Nalani. "I'm afraid you'll need another x-ray, my dear."

Nalani wanted to complain. She had every right to be angry at her brothers, the doctor, the nurse, maybe the whole universe, but at that moment, she was in too much pain to refuse him.

Patrick walked with her as they took her by wheelchair to remove her cast and x-ray her arm. He stood out in the hallway smiling because her behavior toward her brother said a lot about who she was and he liked her fiery disposition. Who would use their injured arm to whack a sibling?

He didn't have any siblings or much family to speak of, yet he could see how much they cared for each other. Sure, there was a thin line between love and hate but it was clear that she was a little sister sticking up for herself with her big brothers. It didn't matter if they were adults or not. He would have to play referee until she was better though because she clearly wasn't putting her health ahead of her emotions.

As he waited for Nalani to be x-rayed again, his phone rang. It was his good friend, Mayor Alexavier Regalia. "What is this I hear about you taking a week off from work, Patrick?"

He knew his friend would call him as soon as he got the email. "I am entitled to take a few days of vacation, Alexavier. I haven't taken a single day since I started and have quite a bit saved up."

"My friend, I agree. It is way overdue. I'm just curious as to what got you to do it. Are you sick?"

Patrick Morales laughed. Alexavier's sources clearly told him that the chief was spending time at the hospital with a woman. *Sources* being the operative word for his extended Italian family that seemed to be everywhere in the city of New Orleans.

"I'm perfectly fine. Just helping out a friend."

"A cute little Hawaiian female friend, right?"

"Have a good day, mayor. I'll have my cell phone as usual if something comes up. Otherwise, I'll be back in the office next Monday."

Alexavier laughed because he didn't think Patrick Morales would admit that he was smitten with Nalani Kahale. But according to his cousin, Maurice, who was her day nurse, the Chief of Police had it bad for the natural beauty and had hardly left her side since he rescued her. Alexavier was happy to hear the news because the chief had never been serious about anyone for all the years that Mayor Regalia had known him.

Who indeed was Nalani Kahale, and could she get Patrick Morales finally interested in something other than work?

Chapter Nine

From the time Nalani got back to her hospital room, had dinner, and settled in to sleep, she'd known something was going on with Patrick Morales.

He hadn't said very much to her since the doctor said she would be released from the hospital in the morning.

She still had to make appointments with him or his partner that week. They also set up physical therapy for her shoulder but at least she wouldn't have to stay in the uncomfortable hospital.

Was he angry at her for fussing with her brothers? Or disappointed in her for using her injured arm as a battering ram? She was just as surprised as anyone when she hauled off and hit Noa with her cast. Violence wasn't her usual response when one of her brothers made her angry but for some reason, she'd lost her temper and couldn't help it. Could she make things right with him before she fell asleep?

"I apologize if I upset you this afternoon, Patrick. I don't normally argue--that's not true. I do argue but I don't usually get physical when I'm angry."

"You caused the break to worsen." He studied her.

Nalani nodded. "I know it was irresponsible, but you just don't understand how furious he made me. He was gloating that they'd moved all of my stuff back home with my parents."

"That new cast is no joke. You're lucky they didn't have to do surgery."

It was embarrassing enough that Patrick walked in as she swung at her brother. Knowing that she'd made the break bigger and had to get an even longer cast, made it worse.

She tried to find a way to make him understand why that was such a big deal to her. "I felt defeated when I moved home. I had failed an important class and quit the doctorate program. I'd always dreamed of teaching and becoming a professor. But instead, I went home and had to work in the family business as my parents always wanted. I moped around for a while and my whole family freaked out that I might be depressed. So, they started setting me up on dates with appropriate men," she used her hands to make air quotation marks around the word appropriate. It took me forever to move out of there. It took meeting Tenille. Seeing how quick life could turn on a dime, you know she lost her last relative before she met Peter. She didn't know he was capable of those unspeakable things until he drugged her and brought her to Hawaii. He was an illegal arms dealer and told her about his illegal businesses because he planned to never let her go. He'd hurt her in the restaurant parking lot. I saw him and knew I had to help her. I didn't know how bad it really was until that night. She and I sat in my bedroom, and she told me everything he'd done. Said if she went missing, he probably killed her, and she wanted someone to know the details. It forged a bond between us that's unbreakable, you know. Once she felt strong enough, we decided to get an apartment together. It took months to find an affordable place and to make my family understand that we couldn't live with my parents forever. Now that this has happened," Nalani motioned to all of her injuries, "It feels like I'm back at square one."

Patrick moved in closer as she turned to lie on her right side and stared up at him. He kissed her forehead and she closed her eyes so she could remember the moment. "I've just been going through the motions of life instead of doing what I wanted. My mother and father are getting older and for the first time in a long time, they seemed really happy with me."

"It's your life, sunshine. You don't have to do it their way to show them that you love them."

"But what if I'm wrong? It seems like every time I go against what they want me to do, something bad happens."

Patrick locked onto her eyes. Had more than just this bad thing happened to Nalani?

"Why did you really move home instead of finishing your doctorate program?"

Nalani stared into his eyes and he would have sworn in that moment that she had a secret. One she hadn't told anyone else. But Patrick saw the moment she decided to keep it hidden.

There was something in her eyes. But she grinned showing both of those cute dimples on her cheeks. It was a smile that probably got her into and out of a lot of trouble. "I told you that I failed an important class. It was required and I didn't think I could pass it even if I took it again."

Hadn't Detective Ghee who'd known her family and her really well, who also searched for her when she'd been kidnapped told Patrick that she was one of the smarted girls he'd ever known. Nalani had been valedictorian of her high school and a straight A student in college. There was more to the story. Patrick didn't become the Chief of Police because he was just a good guy. He was intuitive about things, and it was clear to him that Nalani was leaving some serious details out of her story. But her eyelids were heavy as her pain medicine worked its way through her system.

She yawned and then took a deep breath like she was trying to stay awake. "I need to text my brothers and let them know I'm going to be set free tomorrow. No doubt they'll try and drag me with them to Tenille's house in the French Quarter where they're staying."

Patrick had waited to tell her that he'd made other plans. He wanted to see what the doctor said before he brought it up again. "I took off the week so I could help you. My next-door neighbor is a retired nurse. She's seventy and bossy as hell but happy to have you come home with me so she can look after you."

"Tenille and Reaper's guest cottages where your brothers are staying, and the main house have tons of stairs. But I understand if you want to go with them. Tenille is there and I'm certain they would all help you maneuver around the place."

Nalani had worried her brothers would still try to force her to go home before she was physically ready. Hearing that they were staying nearby, and that Tenille was there too, made her relax. But she didn't want to stay with her brothers. They honestly didn't have a single nurturing bone between the two of them. Tenille was still recovering from her own injuries and Nalani wanted her sweet friend to take all the time she needed to heal.

"Are you certain you want me to come home with you? I feel like I'll be intruding." She kept watching his face and he knew she was measuring his words as well as his expressions.

Patrick wanted to make it completely clear to her. "I want you to come home with me. You won't be intruding. I have already made the arrangements and honestly, will worry over you whether you come with me or stay with your brothers."

Nalani reached her hand out to hold his and she smiled. "Thank you, Patrick. I would love to go to your house to recuperate."

The smile he gave her would melt the hardest of hearts and it certainly softened hers.

"Sunshine, I can see that you're fighting sleep. You need the rest." He kissed the back of her hand and said, "Close your eyes. I'll be here when you wake up."

As Nalani nodded off to sleep, she smiled and whispered, "Okay, but you have to tell my brothers that I'm going with you."

Patrick laughed and then frowned. That news was not going to go over well with the Kahale brothers but nothing worth having came easy. He would text Noa and Jensen the news and wait for the brothers to freak out.

He might not sleep as he waited for the fall out.

Chapter Ten

Patrick Morales lived in a hundred-year-old shotgun style home in an area of New Orleans called Mid-city. The house had been remodeled when he bought it a few years ago and there were ten steps that led up to the front porch, but the rest of the house was one story.

The eight foot iron fence surrounded the whole property and was simple except for the fleur de lis at the top of each spindle. It was quintessential New Orleans style and Nalani had never seen anything like it. She loved how old world the whole neighborhood looked and smiled when he pressed a button on his SUV and the iron gate opened. Once Patrick parked in the driveway, he helped Nalani out of the SUV. Her brothers had parked their rental car on the street and were walking toward them.

Noa and Jensen weren't very happy with the arrangement of their little sister staying with the police chief. It was hard for them to disagree since there wasn't a lot of room where they were staying and the guest cottages had a ton of stairs that would be difficult for Nalani to navigate.

A white-haired lady came out of the duplex next door and smiled at Patrick. "So, this is our patient?" she asked.

"Yes, ma'am, Miss Newsome. This is Nalani Kahale. Nalani this is Miss Alba Newsome, your day nurse."

"Hi," Nalani said, smiling at the pleasant looking woman walking her way.

"How do you do, Nalani."

"To be honest, I usually do a lot better than this," Nalani replied over Patrick's shoulder since he was still carrying her. "Those are two of my brothers, Jensen and Noa."

"I didn't realize you had an entire army of young men."

"Lucky me," Nalani said in a smart aleck tone she saved for her big brothers. That was when Noa walked over and smiled at the older woman. He also had dimples like his younger sister and large biceps that Miss Newsome admired. He held out his arm for her and helped the older woman up the stairs even though she didn't look like she needed help.

Miss Newsome was a slim woman but strong for her size. She practically hopped up the front porch steps with Noa. She had an old-fashioned doctor's bag with her and seemed eager to help.

She quickly noticed Nalani go pale, including her lips, when Patrick set her on her feet inside. She was woozy and reached for his arm to help steady her.

"Here, my baby," Miss Newsome said as she pulled a side chair toward Nalani. "Have a seat."

All the men looked worried, and the retired nurse tried to calm them down as she pulled a few items out of her bag. "It might be all the medication they have her taking, but she still needs a lot of rest."

The sweet older woman gently patted Nalani's hand. "Don't you worry, little lady. The chief and I will keep a close eye on you and have you back on your feet before you know it."

Miss Newsome looked ten years younger than her seventy years, but she wasn't one to be trifled with as she asked a few standard questions and took notes regarding Nalani's medication. She thoroughly read through the discharge instructions given to them and then repeated to Nalani and Patrick that the most important item was that the young woman needed lots of rest.

She then turned on the brothers. "I used to have two older cousins and they gave me the business whenever we were younger. You fellas go easy on her until she can hold her own."

Jensen and Noa agreed, especially as they watched Miss Newsome check their sister out so seriously. Nalani was a lot worse than they had acknowledged when they first saw her at the hospital. She had been through something horrible and deserved some space to work things out. Neither liked the intense bond Nalani and the chief seemed to have with each other and when the rest of their family found out about it, there would be some serious decisions to be made. But until then, they would let her choose because it had been an awful long time since she'd asked for what she needed. If they were honest, the woman that came back from college in California didn't have the same fire in her eyes as the girl who had left home.

Patrick watched everything Miss Newsome did for Nalani and then took notes when she gave him instructions. It was a half hour later when Miss Newsome finished up and she reminded them that she would be back in four to six hours to give Nalani her medication and to check her vitals again. She was particularly concerned about the bump on Nalani's head and her arm that had been reset in a new cast.

"Keeping that foot propped up will also help with the throbbing pain you probably have, my baby," Miss Newsome said and then she looked at the chief expectantly. He quickly grabbed two large pillows and gently placed them under Nalani foot.

By the time Nalani was comfortable on the couch, both Noa and Jensen were complaining over how hungry they both were. Now that they'd checked out where Patrick lived and whether he was telling the truth about his neighbor the nurse coming over to help, they felt comfortable leaving Nalani to rest. "We'll be back in a few hours," Jensen said dryly and Nalani rolled her eyes.

It still hurt her head, but she needed to respond in a way that they would understand and wouldn't get her fighting mad.

Once Miss Newsome, Noa, and Jensen left, Patrick offered to help Nalani change into more comfortable clothes. "Tenille sent this bag over for you," he said and held up a pink leather duffel bag that looked brand new.

When Nalani tried to stand, he shook his head. "It's okay to ask for help, sunshine."

"You won't be here all the time and I have to try and do some things on my own," she grumbled. Patrick still helped her across the house to his bedroom and then bathroom. "I'm willing to compromise. I will help you until you feel a little stronger. But I'll leave you alone to go through the bag and find whatever it is that you want to wear."

For the first time in a while, Nalani gave him a really happy smile. It comforted him in a way it shouldn't. "I'm going to make us something to eat. Let me know when you need my help."

She agreed and then watched him close the door as he gave her some privacy. She dug through the duffel bag that Tenille had sent to her. It had everything Nalani would need from toiletries to sleepwear. She pulled out a silky red pajama set and smiled that Tenille remembered Nalani's favorite color was red. It was beautiful and just feeling the luxurious fabric made her tear up.

She hadn't thought about the kidnappers since she spoke to the FBI agents. But suddenly, she remembered not feeling like she'd ever get away from them. She was even more certain that Tenille wouldn't make it, and now here Nalani was about to wash up with the expensive soap and lotions that Tenille purchased for her.

Nalani slipped on the silk and shivered at how beautiful it felt against her skin. Even the skinned areas felt cool with the material against it. She stared at her reflection wishing she could brush out her hair and as she gave up trying, she saw Patrick's reflection in the mirror as he smiled sweetly at her.

"You look like you feel a little better," he said as he kissed the top of her head. Then he picked up her new hairbrush and gently began working it through her long dark hair. It wasn't sexual but she couldn't help but feel it was an intimate moment between them and she longed to be able to show him how she felt. Just thinking about him that way made her skin flush and she was ready to blame it on the medication. But when she looked up to see the way he was looking at her, she couldn't say a word.

Patrick sat the brush down and then reached an arm around her to pull her back against his front. Nalani tried to control her breathing as he leaned down and whispered warmly into her ear. "You are so beautiful."

She felt beautiful for the first time in a very long time. She wanted to kiss him so badly and turned to try and pull him close but when she did, the brace on her foot didn't turn with the rest of her body. As she twisted, a sharp pain flew up her leg. Trying to stop herself from falling, Nalani reached out to quickly grab the counter but used her injured arm which sounded with a thud as her cast slammed into the marble countertop and then sent lightening streaks of pain up her arm and across her shoulder and clavicle bone.

She no longer felt beautiful and certainly not sexy. As she let out a whimper and squeezed her eyes shut in anticipation of falling on her face. Instead, Patrick scooped her up and held her against his chest.

It made her feel dainty and feminine and no one had ever made her feel that way. She was the tom boy who went diving over waterfalls and surfing with her older brothers and cousins to prove she was tough even though she loved her books and would rather study history than anything else.

Everyone she dated at home treated her like one of the boys and admitted to being too afraid of her brothers to fool around with her. She'd waited until college to have sex, but it took her dating older guys to realize what she really needed. Physical attraction pulled her in, but an intellectual connection and core beliefs could sustain a relationship indefinitely. At least that's what she decided before she ran home and sought refuge from what had happened to her in college.

As Patrick held her close and carried her back to his giant sofa so she could prop her foot up, she considered how different they really were. He had a career and was revered in this city. She didn't know what she was going to do with her life. Nalani couldn't even tell her family whom she loved what she wanted.

Maybe she was getting carried away with the physical attraction. Using her good arm, she pushed herself up on the sofa. Sinking her teeth into her bottom lip as she tried to endure the throbbing pain in her arm again.

At the moment, she felt like she would never heal from all these physical injuries. There was no way he found her as attractive as she did him. Would they even be able to fool around with her giant arm cast, foot brace, and broken ribs. Sometimes she couldn't catch her breath because it felt like her ribs were pushing down on her lungs.

This was a mistake. She didn't want Patrick to see her this way. Broken. What had she been thinking coming here?

Chapter Eleven

Patrick watched Nalani as she warred with her feelings. They'd had a moment in the bathroom, and he felt the need to have her close. He'd thought she felt the same and had been distracted by those thoughts when she tumbled over her foot brace. He almost hadn't reacted quick enough.

She was small and he hadn't thought twice about picking her up and carrying her. It was hard for him to watch her struggle, but she looked angry instead of hurt.

"What's going on, Nalani? Is your foot okay? Arm?" he asked, looking at her but she avoided his eyes.

"I'm okay," she replied but nothing about her response or body language seemed to back it up.

Patrick pulled a side chair over next to her, like he did at the hospital, and sat close so he could hold her hand. When he intertwined his fingers with Nalani's, she looked at their hands and then over at him.

"You can ask or tell me anything, sunshine."

How did he always look so sincere? Nalani sat there

looking at him for what felt like forever. "Why do you call me sunshine?"

Patrick grinned sheepishly. Then he gave her the best excuse he could think of. "As soon as I heard you were from Hawaii all I could think of was how the sun shined brighter there."

"Yup, it's just sunny paradise, every single day."

He didn't miss how she smirked as she spoke. "I picked up on it before. You're not a fan of island life? Doesn't your whole family live there?"

Now she stared at him.

Patrick Morales had been great at picking up on clues and reading people his entire life, but he had absolutely zero idea what was going on in that beautiful head of hers.

"My whole family is there. And, of course, I like living near the ocean. I mean, what's not to love? Our family business is a favorite of locals and tourists. I will always have a job and won't have to worry about money." She shrugged. "It's not like I'll ever be rich, but I can live a modest life with the riches of nature and all the fun activities that my family enjoys like cliff diving and surfing. By the time I'm thirty I should be married and have at least the first two of my four, five, or six kids. According to my mother, my biological clock is ticking, and I need to get right on that." Nalani glanced at him and then looked past him as she added, "As soon as I get back home."

"So, you do have someone waiting to marry you at home?" Patrick suddenly realized that he'd been so attracted, protective, and overwhelmed by her that he hadn't picked up on that fact.

"No, but that's just semantics, Patrick. My parents have already decided who is good for me, so that I can get on with it.

Don't you worry, they'll have me wedded and bedded by the end of summer."

Why did that make him so angry? He could see how disappointed Nalani was over the prospect of marriage and kids, but he physically wanted to punch someone. Instead, he took a deep breath and held her hand with both of his.

"So where did you see your life going if you weren't in Maui, married with kids by thirty?"

Nalani slowly licked her lips and looked uncomfortable. Patrick realized he hadn't offered her anything to eat or drink.

He jumped up and she noticed he was flustered. "What can I get you to drink? Water? Iced Tea? I might have some Dr. Pepper in there."

"Water is good."

He nodded and she saw how he ran his hands over his unshaven jaw line and then his hair as he walked toward the kitchen. It was several minutes before he came back but when he did, he had a platter with a ham sandwich, a cup of chicken noodle soup, and some crackers.

"Are you hungry?" he asked but before he gave her a chance to respond, he added, "You need to eat. If Miss Newsome comes back to give you your medicine and you haven't eaten, then she will scold both of us."

Nalani smiled. He wasn't very comfortable taking care of someone and she wondered if he'd ever had to do it before. She slowly pushed herself up on the sofa and carefully turned so she could hold the food in her lap. That was when Patrick realized she couldn't balance it all and he told her to hold on.

He walked out of the room again and this time when he came back, he had a large oak t.v. tray that looked like it weighed a ton. It was old but well-worn and Nalani was certain he ate dinner on it whenever he was home.

"Thank you," she said. "Aren't you going to eat something too?"

Patrick nodded and then left the room to make himself a sandwich.

It was another fifteen to twenty minutes before they were both settled and eating but he hadn't forgotten where they'd left off. "Alright, sunshine. I want you to eat but I also want you to tell me what it is that you want if marriage and kids are off the table."

Nalani was sipping the broth from her soup as she nodded. "It's not so strange to not want the same life as your parents. I'm not saying that I won't ever get married or have kids, it's just not on my radar yet."

Patrick ate half his sandwich in three bites. "What are you interested in then?"

He'd never met a woman that didn't want those traditional things and he was even more curious about her answer now that it had taken so long to get back to it.

"I love school and learning. I always thought I would be a teacher but not elementary or high school. I wanted to teach at a college--live on or near a college campus and be a professor."

A life in academia would have been dreadful for Patrick but he smiled as he saw the stars in her eyes. It had been her dream. "You were in graduate school when you quit and moved back home."

It wasn't a question and Nalani could see that he was still confused about what she'd told him before about college.

She had to stick to her story and tell him the same things that she'd told her family and friends back home. "I always wanted to do that but I wasn't good enough. At least at the time. I failed a class and my advising professor had told me that it really wasn't for me."

"What the hell does he know? It was one class. Why did you really quit, sunshine?"

Nalani had told that same story to at least seventeen members of her family, her mother and father, all four brothers, plus a few aunts, uncles, and cousins. Not even one had responded that way. It took her a minute to think about what she needed to say.

She nodded like she was going to answer him, but he could see by her expression that she didn't want to explain, not really. "Dr. Lemay knew a lot. He was the head of the program, and everyone respected him."

Patrick's intuition finally kicked in and he suddenly knew that Dr. Lemay was the problem in whatever had happened to make Nalani quit school. "Sounds to me like he took a lot of liberty with his opinions. You already had your undergraduate degree, with honors, and your master's degree plus were two years into the program. Sunshine, you were only two years away from your dream career."

Nalani's face looked dark when he pointed out the obvious. Didn't she know he was on her side? "It was a long time ago and I don't feel like talking about it anymore."

She gently pushed the tray away and slowly lifted her foot to rest it back on the pillows. He was certain she was starting to feel the pain again in her foot and possibly her ribs. She was holding her side and grimaced as she tried to pull the blanket over her.

Patrick jumped up to help her and warmly wrapped her in the blanket before he kissed her forehead. He wanted to point out that it hadn't been two years since she quit and that she could easily pick it back up. However, she truly looked like she was hurting, and he didn't want to upset her on top of the physical pain.

"Is there anything I can get you?" he asked but before she could answer him, Miss Newsome rang the doorbell and then stuck her head inside the front door. "Everyone still decent?" she said loudly and then stepped into the house laughing at her own joke.

She could see Nalani laying there partially curled up on the sofa. Pain was written all over her face. The sweet, retired nurse jumped into action, grabbing Nalani's medication, more water and after she medicated Nalani and checked her blood pressure and temperature, Miss Newsome pulled out a heating pad. It looked like it had been around since the seventies with a super long cord and extra-thick but worn blue padding.

Smiling at Nalani, she patted her hip. "I know it's old school and most doctors don't even consider these small things when they prescribe pain medications but trust me, my baby, this will give you the comfort you've been missing.

Nalani reached up and held Miss Newsome's hand to thank her. She was a thoughtful woman and she wanted her to know how much she appreciated her. But after the conversation with Patrick tonight, Nalani was certain the comfort she needed wasn't going to come from the heating pad.

Chapter Twelve

Nalani woke up disoriented before sunrise. She sat up too quickly and her ribs protested. Her foot throbbed and her arm ached. Sometime during the night she'd moved to a giant king size bed. This was Patrick's bedroom.

She gasped from the pain and held her side which sent Patrick into alert as he jumped up off the leather recliner in the corner of his bedroom. "Are you okay?" he asked and stopped to look at the beautiful woman in his bed.

Her hair was mussed up just so, falling around her face and below her shoulders. The red silk pajamas made her skin and hair glow and he wanted to climb under the covers with her.

"I'm okay. Just moved too quickly," she replied looking back at the handsome man who gave up his own bed for her. Why was he sleeping in that uncomfortable-looking chair?

"You know I would have been fine in the living room or in your spare bedroom." Nalani's voice was strained, and she couldn't hide her physical pain this morning.

Patrick sat on the bed next to her. "The spare room only

has workout equipment, and you didn't look very comfortable in the living room."

She managed to smile for him. He was the most considerate man she'd ever met. "Thank you, Patrick," she said and then squeezed his hand. When he locked onto her eyes, she forced herself to ask the question she'd needed to ask him all along. "Are you certain having me here isn't an imposition? I mean, you've already done so much for me and I don't expect you to keep--well, to keep doing it. I'm not your responsibility."

He stared into her eyes for a long time, and she'd give anything to know what he was thinking. Looking around Patrick's home, it was clear he'd lived alone for a long time. His place looked efficient like a bachelor pad with all the essentials, a big sofa and television, but zero throw pillows, art, books, or flowers. The man enjoyed his quiet single life, and she understood that on a deeper level.

When he didn't let go of her hand, Nalani figured that was a good sign but if she had to guess, this was where he had an out, and he would take it.

"Do you want to go somewhere else, Nalani?"

"You can't answer my question with another question."

Patrick grinned and she could see the sparkle in his light blue-green eyes. "Actually, Ms. Kahale, I can, and I did."

"Fine," she said with challenge in her eyes. "Do you, Patrick, want me to go somewhere else?"

He laughed at her answering his question with a question now and shook his head. It wasn't an answer, but it seemed to be all she was going to get from him at the moment. So, they would keep pretending like she belonged there and as if this was a normal thing for her to stay with him as she recovered from her injuries. At least until one of them made a change.

"Are you hungry?" he asked.

"I don't usually eat breakfast, but I could use some coffee if it isn't too much trouble."

"Coffee, I have," he said and then he was off to make some for her.

Nalani managed to scoot out of bed and slowly made her way toward the kitchen. It was tough and she held on to the door frame as she tried to stand there and watch the police chief nonchalantly as if the pain wasn't running through her body.

As soon as Patrick turned the coffee pot on, he turned toward her. "Sunshine, you can't hide the way you feel. It's written all over your tight expression. Let me help you into the living room."

"I got it," she said and turned slowly shuffling her way toward the front of the house. Patrick was on her in three big steps.

He gently scooped her up into his arms and carried her the rest of the way. When he set her down on the sofa, he saw her wince as she tried to adjust the pillows behind her. Patrick helped her and then turned her face toward him. "Sunshine, I have never broken my ribs but I did bruise them once. It was unbearable. Breathing hurt. Just because the docs let you out of the hospital, no one expects you to be able to do things on your own yet. Take it easy. And let me wait on you for a while. Okay? I want to. I want you here." He leaned forward and kissed her sweetly on the lips.

It wasn't like her to second guess herself so much. She wasn't insecure but his affection didn't mean the same thing to him as it did her. She had to stop swooning over his kindness.

When he left the room again to go pour up their coffee, she mentally scolded herself. Patrick Morales was a thoughtful man. He knew she was miles away from home and that her brothers were bossy and couldn't take care of her properly. That was all. He already got the retired nurse next door to step in and help. It was just his way of being kind. He helped people for a living. She needed to get over herself. Her emotions were all over the board and it had to be because of the trauma she'd endured. Having a near death experience would make anyone want a life reset and that was all that was happening to her.

Patrick came back with a tray of coffee, creamer, sugar, and cinnamon rolls. "I don't have much in the way of groceries, but I did have these on hand." His smile was disarming and hard to refuse.

What woman wouldn't enjoy his attention?

"Thank you, Patrick. I don't usually eat in the morning, but I can make an exception."

He set the tray down on the coffee table and asked her how she liked her coffee so he could make it for her. Again, he was just being sweet.

Her father spoiled her a bit like that, but her family was mostly overprotective. Her mother didn't quite know what to do with a girl after being a boy for so long. Once she had Nalani, she tried to treat her like one of the boys.

The only difference was the overprotective behavior that ensured Nalani was never left alone. Both of her parents had that in common for their daughter and had even indoctrinated her brothers into constantly following her around. The boys ran around like pack animals so it was odd for everyone when she wanted to play alone.

Nalani surfed and went cliff diving with the boys but she craved private time to read or study. It wasn't until she got to college that she indulged in alone time.

It had been almost two years since she had that and she'd

almost given up on the comfort that lifestyle provided. Being here with Patrick sort of felt like that refuge and Nalani liked it more than she thought she should. There was a time limit on this little get away and depending on how fast she healed, there wasn't much else she could do but enjoy it for the limited time they had together.

Nalani sipped her coffee and watched Patrick eat two cinnamon rolls. It was peaceful here in his home and she could understand with his stressful job how important this space had to be for him.

"How did you bruise your ribs?" she asked.

He smiled at her but seemed surprised by her question. "It was an accident."

Nalani handed him her empty coffee cup then slowly leaned back on the sofa to look at him. "Car? Motorcycle?" she asked, prompting him again.

"I was hit by a parade float."

He wasn't going to offer up any details and Nalani squinted her eyes at him. Whenever the answer to a question is parade float, an explanation is in order. "You know where I'm from, where I went to school, even how long I went to college and have met two of my brothers. You can tell me this story, *chief*, or I'm not offering up anything else about myself."

Patrick grinned at the way she called him chief. "It was my first year in New Orleans and I was working undercover on one of the Mardi Gras night parades, undercover. It had been a busy day with people drinking too much and getting out of hand but finally slowed down to a low roar. One of the floats got a flat tire so they stalled on the route for a while and the one nearest me had thrown a ton of beads and toys to the crowd. But just as they began to move, these kids ran in between two floats to pick up beads off the street. The bigger kids moved out of the way but these two younger boys were still down there and weren't going to make it out in time. I ran and pushed them out of the way but got clipped by the bumper."

He lifted his shirt and showed her a long-curved scar that ran from his ribs around to his back. "I had to have a hundred or so stitches and my ribs were bruised on this side too."

Nalani gently ran her hand across the scar. "That must have really hurt," she said and when she looked up at him, his eyes were dilated.

"Being on desk duty for six weeks hurt worse," he said as he picked up her hand and kissed the back of it before standing up to take their dishes back into the kitchen.

It was getting harder trying to keep his hands off her and he knew she was not in any condition for more than a little flirting. Besides, her brothers were ready to rush her home as soon as possible. If Noa or Jensen thought things were getting serious between them then she would be gone the next day. He couldn't understand why she didn't stand up to her family and while he didn't understand it, there would be consequences to them getting romantically involved.

He heard Miss Newsome at the front door and ran to let her inside. While she tended to Nalani, Patrick explained that he needed to pick up a few groceries and asked his neighbor to stay a while.

He avoided looking at Nalani because he needed some separation and he wouldn't be able to do that if he looked into her deep brown eyes or if she turned those dimples on him.

Did she know that?

Chapter Thirteen

Miss Newsome was no nonsense when it came to caring for a patient but her older years had softened her. She checked Nalani for fever and her blood pressure before she handed her the next dose of her medication.

She also made Nalani eat a little more food to keep her from getting nauseous from the pain medication. After plugging in the heating pad for her and fluffing a few more pillows around the little Hawaiian woman, she made herself a cup of coffee and sat in a chair facing Nalani.

"You and Chief Morales are cute together."

Nalani could feel a warm sensation spreading throughout her body as the medication eased the pain. It made her smile and the comment from Miss Newsome only intensified that feeling.

"I don't know how together we are, but he's been really sweet to me."

Miss Newsome eyed the young woman in front of her. She vaguely remembered being in her twenties and not being so sure of herself when it came to relationships. If she'd had any idea how easy men were to read she could have saved herself a lot of heartache. "Sweet girl, do you see the way he looks at you?"

It was hard to know whether it was the medication or not but Nalani felt really emotional discussing Patrick with the older woman. Her eyes watered as she spoke. "He's a great man but I think it's his nature to look after people. I mean, he's the chief of police and he's spent his adulthood as a soldier or working in the police department. It makes sense that he puts everyone before his own needs, don't you think?"

She could see Miss Newsome weighing her words. "Six months after he bought this house, I was still working and had just come off a twelve-hour shift. I pulled up next door to my house around eight and as I climbed the steps to my porch, I had a heart attack. The chief came home to grab a quick bite to eat and found me on the ground. He performed CPR until the firemen got here and rode in the ambulance with me. I'm sure he saved my life. He is a great young man."

Nalani nodded. Miss Newsome confirmed what she'd known all along in the depths of her heart. Patrick couldn't help himself. He was a hero and had to help others.

Clearing her throat, Miss Newsome smiled knowingly at Nalani. "He does go out of his way. My nephew is a police officer and has been on the NOPD since before Chief Morales took over the reigns. He'll tell you that everyone loves and respects him more than any other police chief or superior they've ever known. Patrick Morales is also friends with the district attorney and the mayor. The way they all work together is the reason our city is great again."

Nalani pulled her covers up over her lap. She was feeling sleepy and trying to stave off the emotions right below the surface. Hearing how wonderful everyone found Patrick

Morales was comforting. But it hurt to be right about his intentions for helping her.

The kind retired nurse stood and stretched before she picked up Nalani's drinking glass and her own coffee cup. "You know Nalani, in the three years that he's lived here, I've never seen him bring a woman home. Not once."

Miss Newsome winked at her and then walked back to the kitchen. Nalani could tell the older woman was a straight shooter, but she didn't trust her own judgment. Was she telling her what she thought she was telling her?

When Miss Newsome returned, she had a fresh glass of water for Nalani and encouraged her to drink some of it. "I can see you doubting yourself or the situation, little lady. And you don't seem like the kind of woman who's usually insecure about things. We don't have control over who we are meant to be with and sometimes only get one chance. Don't be like me and let it pass you by. I would give anything to go back now."

Nalani could see the loneliness on the sweet older woman's face, and it made her sad. What had happened to Miss Newsome?

Before the conversation got more personal, Patrick returned carrying several grocery bags and a new sense of purpose.

"Here let me help you with those," Miss Newsome jumped up and went toward Patrick but he wouldn't let her carry anything.

He looked over at Nalani and smiled before he turned toward his helpful neighbor again. "If you don't mind unpacking some of this, I'll go back and grab the last two bags."

Miss Newsome followed him into the kitchen and got straight to work. Nalani could hear them talking in the kitchen, but their voices seemed to be getting further and further away.

It was several hours later before she woke up to find Miss Newsome gone and Patrick napping in the recliner across the room from her. An old black and white movie was playing on the giant television, and it was almost dark outside.

She watched the handsome man sleeping and wondered why he wasn't married and why he didn't seem to date anyone seriously. If what Miss Newsome said was true, then why did he bring Nalani to his home and insist she stay with him when her brothers so easily would have taken her with them?

It did seem in his character to protect others, but this was beyond his normal behavior, at least according to his lovely, observant neighbor. That sweet woman nailed the situation when she said that Nalani wasn't the type of person to struggle with self-doubt. The one time she'd allowed that to rule her actions, she'd regretted it and would give anything to go back and change things.

But this situation was difficult too. What if she only felt this way because she'd almost died, and he'd been the one to help her? Wasn't that a thing? And what if he also felt close to her because he'd seen her at her worst and saved her?

They both could be suffering from that syndrome. Nalani rubbed her forehead trying to remember what it was called and when she looked up, Patrick was watching her.

"Everything alright?" he asked, and she nodded.

"What's it called when a victim falls for their caregiver?"

Patrick shook his head. "I think you mean, when a victim falls for their kidnapper. It's called Stockholm Syndrome."

Nalani lowered her eyes at him. "No, I remember now. It's called transference."

Patrick walked over to Nalani and sat on the edge of the sofa next to her. He intertwined their fingers and smiled at her.

"There is Rescuer Complex and The Nightingale Syndrome. Don't forget The Savior Complex."

Nalani shook her head and he looked into her eyes. "Are you worried that is what we're doing here, sunshine?"

"I'm not worried but it doesn't make sense, does it?"

"Which part? The fact that we didn't know each other until a few days ago and now we're here at my house. Or the way that we feel so familiar with one another?"

"The feelings that I have for you don't make sense. I don't believe in love at first sight. I mean, how can we have a deep connection when we hardly know each other?"

Patrick leaned forward and tucked her blanket around her body, leaving his arms around her. "Is there a reason why you need to dissect this so completely right now? Are you uncomfortable with me or staying here?"

Nalani shrugged. "Miss Newsome said you saved her life."

"I was just in the right place at the right time."

"She also said since you've lived here that you've never brought a woman home."

"My job is demanding, and I don't date much."

"She said we're cute together and then asked me if I saw the way you look at me. Then she added that we can't control who we are supposed to be with and to not be like her and let it pass me by."

Patrick leaned forward and kissed Nalani. She was working herself up and he could almost feel her nervous energy. His kiss was sweet and warm, but she was needy and hot.

He moved closer and she pressed her chest against him, holding onto his arms to steady her as the kiss became desperate. They wanted to be closer but were mindful of her injuries.

Patrick wound one hand into the back of her hair and held it at the nape of her neck. Nalani held on to him tighter. The kiss was new yet familiar, disbelieving but trusting, and passion with extra heat as they tangled together.

They may have only known each other for a few days but when they touched it felt familiar like where they belonged. Slowly, they parted but their breathing was in step and fast paced. It felt like they'd been fused together in the most delicious way and neither understood it but it felt right.

Neither of them could speak as they stared at each other. There were times in life when words weren't enough. This was one of them. She leaned forward and rested her head on his chest.

The kiss had been better than most of the sex Nalani had in the past. She did need to dissect this situation because it felt familiar and comfortable and nothing else in her life made sense anymore.

She was not a flighty person who ran on emotion and dreams. For most of her life she'd been grounded by the familiar family life and responsibility. Quitting school had almost broken her but she rebounded at home. Her safe place.

But now, her safe place felt like him and if she'd ever been unsure of herself, it was in this moment because she didn't have the power. This man she'd just met did.

Chapter Fourteen

Patrick held the woman that had shaken up his world. He'd wanted to be close to her for days. It wasn't like him to be touchy-feely and the way he'd acted since he met her, randomly kissing her forehead or holding her hand was against his normal nature.

He'd lived his life with so much self-control it was almost scary. Yet, she drew him in like a siren and he constantly had to check himself to make sure he wasn't acting inappropriately. He'd never wanted anyone or anything as much as Nalani Kahale.

Never taking time off from work or wanting more than a little sex from women, she had so much control over him, and he could suddenly tell that she didn't know it.

"Are you alright, sunshine? I didn't mean to hold you too tightly. I was trying to be gentle." He leaned back to look at her face.

He looked for signs that she was in pain, but she simply stared back at him. Patrick wiped his face with his hands and then ran them over his day-old whiskers. He needed to shave.

He needed to take a cold shower. Perhaps he should go back to work?

Nalani nodded. "I'm okay. You didn't hurt me. You'd never hurt me on purpose."

He leaned in close again. "I wouldn't hurt you on purpose--ever," he whispered, and she leaned up to kiss him sweetly.

The tenderness made them admit their feelings. "This isn't something that has happened to me before. I need to be near you and make sure you're okay. I can't explain it, but this just feels right." Patrick leaned forward and kissed her forehead. "I can't imagine being anywhere but here with you right now. But I'll do whatever you want, Nalani."

"I want you to tell me about yourself and I don't want to have any secrets between us," she said.

He agreed. "I want to shut the entire world out and safeguard our time alone."

"I want you to share your bed with me," she said and then she leaned into him again as if the truth took all her energy.

Patrick moved up beside Nalani on the large sofa and held her next to him. He knew her medication would wear off soon and then Miss Newsome would be back over. They had more time alone than in the hospital but still there would be interruptions.

"I'm afraid I invited your brothers over for dinner."

"I wondered why they hadn't come over yet."

"They spent part of the day helping Tenille. She needed them to move some furniture at the boarding house where she used to live in Maisonville. It seems, she's still going to waitress part time at Main Street Grocery but also manage the boarding house for the elderly woman who owns it."

"My brothers told you that?"

"Yes."

"So, she's going to stay here and not move back to Texas?"

"I think so, sunshine."

He couldn't see her face, but he could feel her smile. Tenille was her closest friend and the time they'd spent together in Maui had sealed their friendship. Being close to Tenille would be comforting for his girl.

"When you feel up to it, we could drive across the lake. I have a small cabin there. We could eat at the restaurant where Tenille works so you can meet her new friends here too."

Nalani didn't know how long it would be until she felt better but the idea of seeing Tenille more often lifted her spirits. "What time will the boys be here?"

"I told them seven."

Nalani looked at the clock. They had an hour until then and she hoped to make the most of it. She leaned into Patrick, and he held her close. He'd gone to the grocery store but if he ordered pizza for dinner then he could have more time like this with Nalani.

"What do you think about pizza?" he asked.

"Great idea," she replied, and they stayed snuggled up together for another half hour.

Oddly enough, when her brothers arrived, it felt normal for them to be visiting her at Patrick's house. They laughed and joked around with Patrick as they filled their plates with pizza. Noa brought her a large slice of pepperoni and Jensen carried drinks for everyone as they set up dinner on the coffee table so she could continue resting on the living room sofa.

Noa shook his head as he folded a large slice and ate it in three bites. "Bruh, I can't believe you didn't get pineapple on any of these. You know we're from Hawaii."

"Pineapple on pizza is an abomination, Noa. You'll have to eat that somewhere else," Patrick replied.

Nalani and Jensen laughed at the look on Noa's face. Noa had never met a pizza that he didn't like, and it was a tell that he felt comfortable enough to joke around with Patrick.

The boys told them all about the boarding house and helping Tenille. She was still recuperating from her injuries and Reaper had a hard time letting her go to Mrs. Bower's boarding house until Noa and Jensen explained they would do all the heavy and not so heavy lifting.

They explained that The Main Street Grocery was actually called Miss Lynn's diner by the locals, but no one knew why it was named the other. Overall, dinner was fun and exhausting.

Nalani laid back on the sofa and only sat up when Miss Newsome dropped in to give her the nightly dose of her medication. Miss Newsome declined to eat pizza. Then she told the guys that they needed to eat healthier tomorrow to make up for the nutrition deficit from the poor dinner choice.

All three, Noa, Jensen, and Patrick flexed their muscles to show Miss Newsome that they were healthy. In the end, she offered to cook dinner for all of them the next night.

It had been a wonderful evening, and Nalani felt at ease as she visited with her brothers, talked to her parents on Jensen's phone, and thanked Miss Newsome for taking such good care of her.

By the time they all left, the medication was flowing through her body, and she'd settled in on the sofa. It was almost eleven and Patrick gave her a sweet smile when he sat next to her.

"I know you're exhausted, sunshine. You can't hide it. That beautiful face tells me exactly what I want to know."

She smiled and carefully moved her legs to the side of the sofa to stand. Patrick watched her but before she could take her first step, he eased in next to her and offered her his arm to hold onto.

He could have easily picked her up but he knew it was important for her to feel independent. It was going to take some time for her body to heal but every day she would make little strides.

It took a few minutes for her to get settled but once she was tucked into bed, he began to remove his shirt. "I can leave this on if it will make you more comfortable."

She shook her head but never broke eye contact. Patrick removed his shirt and then his pants, revealing Calvin Klein black underwear that clung to him like shorts.

When he slid under the covers, he moved into the middle of the bed closer to her but waited for Nalani to decide whether to snuggle in or not. It didn't take but a few seconds for her to slide into place next him.

As she curled into place, he couldn't help but smile at how perfectly they fit together. She was built like a surfer girl but small and feminine too. There wasn't anything about her that he would change and he fell asleep knowing that he would move mountains if she needed him to do it.

The next evening, Miss Newsome brought over a seafood casserole with a large green salad for the group. The casserole wasn't very good but the guys marveled over the salad and her homemade salad dressing. They all laughed and talked for two hours over the meal and finished every morsel of food the older woman made, including the bread pudding for dessert.

Nalani didn't point out that this meal with a loaf of French bread and dessert wasn't any healthier for them than the pizza. The sweet older woman had tried and that was what mattered. The guys did the dishes and Noa and Jensen walked Miss Newsome home before they left.

They fell into this routine over the next week where they all did their own thing during the day and then ate dinner together each evening. Nalani was beginning to get around a little easier and the doctor's office called to set up her physical therapy. She would start the next week for her shoulder and then pick up additional therapy on her foot once the break healed.

She was a bit nervous, not knowing what to expect, but Miss Newsome reassured her that it would be basic in the beginning as they determined her mobility and waited for her cast to be removed from her broken arm.

Noa and Jensen watched their little sister more closely because they could see the subtle changes in her. As Miss Newsome helped her into the living room, Patrick began putting food away as the brothers loaded the dishwasher.

"How would you say she's doing?" Jensen asked Patrick.

Patrick had wondered how long it would take for them to bring her recovery up with him and he'd been ready for it. "I think every single day brings its triumphs and challenges. But therapy should help as well as time."

Nalani had always been fearless growing up and neither of her brothers were used to seeing her nervous over anything. The fact that physical therapy had her rattled was upsetting. Of course, they'd known she put on a lot of her bravado when she was younger and trying to keep up with her brothers who began cliff diving as teenagers. But all that confidence had seemed to stick as she went off to college and became a young adult.

Watching her depend on Miss Newsome and Patrick made them worry for her. "You think she's still too unsteady to go home with us?" Jensen asked.

Patrick stopped what he was doing to look at Jensen and

Noa who both looked worried. "You'll have to ask her that, but I could see the doctor's giving her their approval in a few weeks."

When Noa and Jensen looked at each other again, Patrick knew something was going on and he was going to have to press them to admit it. "Just tell me," he said and to his surprise, they did.

Chapter Fifteen

"We thought we could extend our trip here until our sister was well enough to travel. But construction on the restaurant has already begun and it's going faster than expected. Supplies are showing up and we both feel like we need to be there. Our dad is supposed to rest and be recuperating at home, but he goes to the site every day. And we aren't making a difference here. We could make a big difference there." Noa said.

"Of course, everyone expects Nalani to go back with us," Jensen added.

Patrick had to go back to work next week, and he figured The Kahale Family would get pushy about Nalani going home soon. "It's a difficult situation, guys, but I think you can both see that she isn't ready. Emotionally she's handling things better than most, but physically she is having a hard time just moving across the room. The doctors aren't going to agree that she can fly with those cracked ribs. You know she already reinjured her arm."

Patrick never pressed Nalani to talk about what had happened to her with Peter Miller. He'd heard firsthand when she spoke to the FBI agents but the emotional trauma she had to endure never seemed to bubble up to the surface. Instead, as they laid in bed each night, she entertained him with stories of growing up on a tropical island. Patrick had never thought much about not having a family but as she laughed and told him of all the Kahale family adventures the differences between their lives was vast.

This woman was eleven years younger than him, but she had lived more in her 27 years in Maui than most did in a lifetime. He wasn't sure if New Orleans, as great as the city was, could keep her interests.

Noa and Jensen finished loading the dishwasher and didn't discuss taking Nalani home any further with Patrick. They'd spent the week watching the man with their little sister and it was clear the bond they had was growing stronger by the day.

When they finished cleaning the kitchen, Miss Newsome was ready to go home a little earlier than usual and Noa offered to walk with her. It gave Jensen time to speak with Nalani directly about leaving.

"How is Dad doing? Honestly?" Nalani spoke to her parents every day but she worried they were holding back so she wouldn't worry.

"He's great, Nalani. He is getting around a lot better than you. Keanu and Oren are having a hard time keeping him away from the restaurant and Ma is just running behind him. You know how he is and something like this only pushes him harder."

"If you promise he's okay, then I-I'll admit that I really need more time here," she said and reached out to hold her brother's hands. She hadn't left Patrick's house since she got there a week ago and something that had been so simple to her before, like walking up a set of stairs felt insurmountable. "You know I don't like to ask for help and here, well, you can see that I don't have to. Miss Newsome is over every few hours to make sure I take my medication or to verify that I'm not doing too much. And Patrick is worse than her. It's really overwhelming."

Jensen understood what she was saying. The Kahale Family was loving but also pushed you to your utmost edge sometimes. They were all competitive and it made them hard workers. It was the way their father was wired and when their oldest brother Keanu was born, he set the bar high because he won everything. Cracked ribs and a few broken bones wouldn't get any of them out of work, even Nalani especially since most of her scrapes and bruises were healing quickly on the outside.

Then there was the matter of how his little sister felt about the chief. She dated several guys back home but not once had she acted the way she does around Patrick Morales. Jensen and Noa both could see how much she cared about the man already and Patrick felt the same about her. It was going to be a problem.

Before Jensen could reassure Nalani, his cell phone rang right on time. Their parents had planned to call and talk to all of them together tonight. They decided all three of them should return home together and were going to call and tell Nalani to buck-up and get on the plane with him and Noa.

For once, it was Jensen's turn to run interference for her. Like when she wanted to go away to college and their oldest brother Keanu sat down with their parents and talked them into letting her go away to school.

Instead of letting them talk to Nalani again, he shushed her and stood up to take the call a few feet away. She could only partially hear the conversation but heard Jensen say she'd over done it that day and had to go to bed early. He then said that the doctors were concerned about her, and she had three appointments the next week, instead of explaining they were all with physical therapy.

He flat out lied about Tenille coming over although she did call daily to see how Nalani was feeling. He said that she had her own private nurse but didn't admit she lived next door or say a word about Patrick Morales. Did they even know she was staying at his house? She hadn't told them but she'd figured her brothers had.

Nalani grew madder that she was a twenty-seven-year-old woman who couldn't stand up to her parents and tell them that she wasn't ready to come home. Then made herself feel better that her brother was in his early thirties and couldn't tell the truth. Or at least he didn't want to deal with the aftermath of telling them the truth since they wouldn't agree with Nalani staying.

Noa walked back inside just as Jensen got off the phone with their parents. Jensen told them that everything was set. He and Noa would fly home the next day. Nalani could stay a few more weeks until she was stronger.

Patrick stood there watching the brothers look at their little sister and it was clear they were communicating something to each other without words. He guessed it was a sibling thing but he also felt that way with Nalani.

Jensen and Noa stayed thirty minutes longer and then kissed Nalani goodbye before they left, promising to text her when they landed in Hawaii the next day.

That night in bed, Nalani seemed extra tired and instead of talking about what had happened earlier that evening, she curled up next to Patrick and closed her eyes.

Was she avoiding conversation with him on purpose?

Patrick wrapped his arms around her protectively and let

her sleep. If she needed a night to process everything, then he would give it to her.

At five in the morning, Patrick woke up before his alarm. It wasn't anything new to him as he'd been an early riser since his military days. He quietly got up, showered, and then headed to the kitchen to make coffee.

He went through his emails lamenting over the large amount of work waiting for when he returned to the office. As he finished sending his last response, he heard something crashing in the bathroom and hurried to see if Nalani was okay.

When he knocked on the door, she sounded frustrated but told him he could come in. He wasn't prepared as he stepped inside and found her wrapped in a towel, the bathtub filled with water, and something that looked and smelled like lavender sea salt all over the bathroom floor.

"I'm sorry for the mess. Tenille packed this in my bag with all the toiletries and the idea of a bath sounded nice. At least until I slipped trying to pour some of it into the tub."

Miss Newsome had helped Nalani wash her hair and take a shower all week but it was too early to disturb the older woman next door.

Patrick smiled at her and then told her he would help her. "Let me grab the broom. I'll be right back," he said before turning around and leaving the room.

The sight of Nalani standing there in a towel looking so helpless got to him and he laughed at himself, maybe he truly did have the Savior Complex when it came to her.

When he returned to the bathroom he had a broom, a dustpan, and what looked like a plastic bag off a loaf of bread. "Give me your arm, sunshine," he said and then she realized that he planned to cover up her cast.

It only took him a couple of minutes to get her cast covered and to sweep up the large salt crystals into a pile. He held her good hand and eased her into the tub, trying to give her as much privacy by looking the other way as possible. But there was no way to miss her beautiful body as she slid into the warm fragrant water.

The modern claw foot tub was a proud feature of the home according to the seller, but Patrick had never used it the entire time he'd lived there. Suddenly, he was very happy to have it.

He went back to work, cleaning up the lavender salt off the floor before he turned back to look at her. "Would you like me to wash your hair?" he offered.

Nalani licked her lips and he could see her face flush. But she nodded and thanked him for helping her. It was an intimate moment for them but they both tried to act as if it were a normal occurrence. At least until he began to massage shampoo into her long dark hair.

Patrick massaged her scalp and admittedly took an extra-long time with her tresses. Nalani quietly moaned as she leaned back in the tub and closed her eyes. When she opened them, he could feel the way she looked at him.

"Ready for me to rinse?" he asked but he barely recognized his own deep voice.

Nalani sat up straighter in the tub and her breasts were barely visible above the water, but it was enough to make Patrick breath heavier. He gripped the water wand tighter as he began to rinse the shampoo out of her hair, he could see her gripping the side of the tub with her good hand too.

Moments later, he grabbed a towel and reached his hand out to help her get out of the tub. Again, he kept his head turned out of respect.

Once he had a towel around her body, he used another to

dry her hair. He was gentle as he combed it out and then used her hair dryer.

It may have been the most sensual thing anyone had ever done with her, and it wasn't even sex. She felt closer to him and longed for even more.

He looked at her in the mirror and gave her a wicked grin. Patrick Morales was slowly making her come undone.

"Hungry?" he asked, and she didn't miss the double meaning to his question.

"I think I could eat all day," she replied, and he laughed at her response as he wrapped both of his arms around her.

When he leaned forward to whisper into her ear, her entire body got goosebumps. "I can't think of anything I'd rather do than spend an entire day in bed with you, sunshine. But your body needs more time to heal."

She couldn't hide her disappointment. Shouldn't she be the one to decide if she was healed enough? As he carefully removed the plastic bag over her arm, slipped back on her foot brace, and helped her get dressed, she figured she probably did need a little more time. But it didn't make things any less frustrating.

Patrick offered to make them something to eat, and Nalani managed to make the toast while he did everything else.

Both were quiet and more comfortable being together. She figured the weight of her family's expectations were removed and it naturally made her relax. Patrick seemed happy to still have her there.

At the dining room table, they sat next to each other as they ate and drank coffee. They discussed their schedules, his for work and her doctor's appointments, for the upcoming week. Neither admitting how much they regretted returning to the real world. They only had the rest of the day and tomorrow to spend together before life interrupted everything.

"I go in really early Monday but Miss Newsome will come over early. I hope to come home for lunch but I usually don't get in until after seven at night."

Nalani smiled. He was worried about leaving her. "I'll be fine."

"I want you to be more than fine."

Chapter Sixteen

After clearing their breakfast plates, Patrick looked at her and she couldn't read his expression. Was he sizing her up?

"What do you think about getting out of the house today?"

Nalani wanted to cheer.

"It may be too much, but I told you that I have a cabin on the water across the lake. It'll take about forty-five minutes with traffic, but we could go spend the night there."

Growing up as a kid who played outside had always made Nalani appreciate nature more than most. She was up and headed to the bedroom to get her shoes and a light jacket.

Patrick packed them some provisions since he hadn't been to the cabin in over a month and didn't have a lot there.

He loaded their overnight bags and the extra items, and they were on their way in less than half an hour. It was the first glimpse Nalani really had of the city in daylight.

On the way home from the hospital she had to lay back in the seat because of the pain in her side. But just one week later, she could sit up and enjoy the incredible city.

Patrick pointed out an historic cemetery on the way to the

interstate which fascinated Nalani. She'd never seen monuments like that before and told him that she would love to take a historical tour around the city one day.

He smiled as her eyes lit up and then continued telling her everything, he knew about the areas they passed through while on the way to the longest continuous bridge over water. It would take them to Maisonville and his quiet place.

As they traveled over the bridge, Nalani marveled at all the water, and he could tell she missed home. When three pelicans flew beside the bridge ahead of them, she laughed. "They look prehistoric," she said, and he realized she'd never seen a pelican in real life.

"I guess they probably do, sunshine," he agreed.

As they took the winding road into Maisonville, Nalani smiled even more. It was winter in South Louisiana and a bit cold, but today the sun was shining and the water glistened through the trees, showing her their best side.

"It's beautiful here," she said more to herself than to him. When they pulled into his private driveway and up to what he called his rustic cabin, Nalani laughed.

It was a raised Acadian style home with a large porch and cedar wood beams. The place was stunning. "This is it?" she asked and leaned back in her seat as if to take it all in.

Patrick smiled as he hurried around the SUV to help her get out. They had been in the car a little longer than he'd expected and the ground was uneven. He didn't want her to hurt herself.

"I'll unload our things in a minute. Let me show you around," he said, pride all over his face.

The house was raised a lot higher than his home in New Orleans and her eyes got big when she thought about having to climb the double staircase. Before her injuries she would have raced Patrick up those stairs. And possibly beat him to the top.

He turned and picked her up as if she weighed nothing. "What are you doing?" she asked, half laughing. "That's way too many stairs. You can't carry me up all of them."

He climbed each one and counted on his way up. "Eighteen stairs, hmpf," he said when they reached the top as if it was nothing.

"Put me down," she insisted but he could see the way her eyes gleamed.

He had pulled all his furniture inside, so the porch was bare for the cold months. He explained that he usually didn't come here in January and February because he was too busy with carnival season.

By mid-March or early April, everything would be in bloom and he spent a lot of weekends here. He liked to fish and just relax on the back porch which was bigger than the front one.

His house was on the water and certainly not what Nalani would call a cabin. It wasn't a mansion, but it was bigger than his home in the city. It was hard to imagine Patrick alone here. And Nalani would have questioned him more but again this place didn't have any frills like throw pillows, art, or plants. But he had a few nice pieces of comfortable furniture and a large television like most guys needed in a weekend spot.

Nalani's body felt like it was vibrating a bit after sitting in the car for so long and she walked even slower than usual as she made her way to the double French doors that led out back.

There was a clear view of the lake and a short pier. Again, exactly what a single guy would need. Patrick walked up and wrapped his arms around her from behind.

"It's a beautiful house, chief," she said leaning into him. "How long have you had this place?"

"I bought it years before my house in New Orleans. It's actually how I met Alexavier. Before he was mayor, he was a successful attorney and began investing in real estate. He'd planned to flip this house. Maisonville is a quiet little town and people acted like this was a million miles away instead of the easy forty-five-minute drive from the city. He couldn't get anyone interested in it as a fishing camp, so he began putting money into it. The kitchen is new, and all the hard wood floors were refinished. Alexavier thought if he made the porches grander and the bathroom more spa-like then someone's wife might fall in love with it. It didn't happen and sat on the market. I heard him grumbling about it at a bar one night and told him that I would be interested in a fishing camp. He laughed and told me that I could get it for a steal.

"I did, too." He smiled and she understood this place really meant something to him. "I'd never lived in a house before. I grew up in a trailer, moved all over the place with the marines. Rented apartments most of the time as an adult, so I was really proud of buying this house.

Nalani turned around in his arms and hugged him. It was a big deal to buy a home but for someone that had never lived in a house before, she imagined it was paramount.

"What was the first thing you did after you bought it?"

He laughed and she thought he looked a little embarrassed. "I brought a sleeping bag and some fast food. Sat on the end of the pier and ate my burger and fries until dark and then slept that first night in the living room on the floor.

Nalani kissed him sweetly. "Exactly what I would have done too," she said.

The kiss he gave her after that comment showed how much

he appreciated her. She held on to him tighter and the kiss deepened.

Realizing how hard he was pulling her body into his, he loosened his grip and took a step back. It was getting harder to keep his hands off her. And he didn't want to anymore.

Patrick lifted her chin and warmly kissed her lips again. "How are you feeling, sunshine? Do you need to rest?"

"I feel great," she said ignoring the way her ribs were singing at that moment. He must not have believed her with the way he lowered his eyes.

"I have a big outdoor settee thing. I don't know what you call it but it's round and has like this thick cushion. Sometimes in the summer I'll sleep outside on the back porch."

He held out his hands, "Stay here. It'll take me just a few minutes to set it up."

Nalani wanted to tell him not to go to any trouble, but he was bounding out the door excited like a kid to show her this couch thing. She couldn't help but laugh as she watched him pull out two giant wicker pieces that each looked like half-moons. Together they would make a perfect circle.

She quickly opened the French doors and then ran to open the front door for him. He winked at her with his arms full and set down the half he'd carried along with a massive cushion.

He kissed her on his way back out again to get the rest of it. Within a few minutes he had it hooked together and the cushions in place. "What do you think?" he asked, and she put her hand over her mouth to keep from smiling to big.

It was the first time she'd ever seen him so carefree and happy. "I love it," she said as she laid across the cushion and wiggled to test it out. "It's perfect." It truly was incredible and reminded her of a fancy resort lounge set. The wind blew across her and she shivered but still didn't move.

"Hold on," he said and dashed back inside for a minute. When he returned, he was carrying some pillows, a big comforter, and snacks.

"Thought we might hang out here for a while?"

Nalani smiled as he sat the snacks on a side table and then spread the comforter across her and the rest of the settee. He placed a pillow under her head and then two in his spot. When he climbed on top and laid beside her, she realized just how big this thing really was. She leaned in close to his side where she fit perfectly. It was hard not to think of all the great uses they could get out of this piece of furniture.

He must have thought the same thing as he turned toward her. "We can come back here when you're better, sunshine. But today, you need to rest."

His chivalry was getting to be really annoying, and she was ready to tell him so, but he intertwined their fingers and kissed each one of hers. It took her breath away.

Patrick stared down at how small and delicate her hand looked in his. He'd never been so comfortable around a woman or wanted anyone around like he did Nalani. It felt strangely natural to have her in his private space.

"I would like to see you surf one day," he announced.

Nalani held up her foot and then her hand with the cast. "It might be a while."

"I have only been to Hawaii once. I visited O'ahu. Some of my marine buddies and I tried surfing. I was able to stand up on the board my first try."

"That's impressive, chief. My oldest brother was a professional surfer and I've been on boards since I was three."

Patrick thought she was extra cute when she got competitive. "I thought you were a book worm, loved school, and everything about academia?"

"Growing up in Hawaii with four older brothers, I had to keep up with the pack."

"I bet you did, sunshine." Patrick kissed the top of her head. "I noticed how your brothers looked at you after they discussed going home without you. What was all that silence about?"

Nalani slowly sat up and turned around so she could look at Patrick. "They both understood that I have too many injuries to fly back yet. They'll make my parents understand. But when our family needs something then all of us do everything, we can to help them. It's the way my parents have always been and the way they raised us."

When her expression changed, he knew she was going to get serious. "My parents don't know I'm staying with you. I didn't tell them, but I'd thought Jensen or Noa would. They didn't. I'm afraid if my folks found out now, I think they would flip out. Maybe I'm not injured as badly as they were told and would want to know why I'm not there.

"They are good as gold, and I love my family. If you met them, you would understand why. My dad is larger than life and has never met a stranger. Mama would take care of every single person that ever needed her. I swear they would pull you in from the start. Loving others is what they're about but with that love comes some serious expectations. I mean, they wouldn't expect something from me that they wouldn't expect to give themselves, but they don't pull any punches when it comes to individual wants or needs. It's all about the greater family good or it's really not that important."

"But you went away to college?"

Nalani nodded. "My whole family knows I'm a book worm and when I told them I wanted to teach, they loved that idea. Until I told them that I wanted to get my doctorate degree, become a professor, and teach at a university."

Patrick smoothed her hair away from her face and kissed her forehead. "I'm guessing there isn't a university there where you could do that?"

Shaking her head, Nalani pulled the comforter up higher. "It took my oldest brother Keanu sitting down with my parents, aunts, and uncles to explain to them that I was smarter than all the rest of them." She looked up at Patrick. "But that's not true. I just enjoy studying and learning things. Anyway, he told them that anyone in our family that worked as hard as I did academically deserve to go away to college. He also told them if they wouldn't support that decision then he would do it, he would pay my tuition."

"I already like this man," Patrick replied.

"He's the best. And that was all it took because my dad wasn't about to let anyone else take care of me. He said he would pay for my education and that was final. I swear when I graduated undergrad, I had fifteen people in the stadium. When I finished my master's degree and got accepted into the doctorate program, Keanu took me and our other brothers to Las Vegas for three days."

If Patrick hadn't known already, hearing about the support her family gave to her and many others proved how completely different Nalani's life was from his.

"When things didn't work out those next two years, I was so homesick. It costs a fortune to get your doctorate and my father wouldn't hear of me getting student loans." Nalani paused and had a far off look in her eyes.

After the awkward pause, she looked up and smiled at Patrick. "My parents make a decent living with the restaurant, but my family is far from rich. Well, except for Keanu."

Patrick nodded, "The surfer."

"Yes. Anyway, I owe my mom and dad everything for supporting me while I lived in California. That's why, this whole thing--" she motioned between them, "This whole thing between us, can't last because I can't stay here. I have to go home in a few weeks whether I want to or not."

Nalani pushed away from Patrick and hurried into the house.

Chapter Seventeen

Patrick hadn't wanted to think about the expiration date on this thing between them but before Nalani said it, he'd known she couldn't stay. He'd figured the age difference would be enough but there were so many other things that would keep them from being compatible long term.

Still, he'd been drawn to her. Nalani Kahale was gorgeous but also brilliant, determined, confident, independent. All the qualities he could ever want and never thought he'd find in one woman.

It had been his life's story that when something good happened, it didn't last. His own mother told him that he'd been born this amazing healthy baby boy and his father took one look at him and left.

He'd lost count of all the apartments and trailers that his mother rented for them, to later be kicked out because she didn't pay the rent. Hell, if he made a friend in school, they moved away.

It wasn't until he joined the Marines that things began to turn around for him. But he'd learned to mostly live his life alone. He'd protected his privacy and even as the chief of police wasn't in the news like so many of his predecessors. Patrick found that if he ran a clean department and kept the citizens safe and happy then they didn't need to see or talk to him as much.

But this little Hawaiian woman had turned him upside down. He'd never taken off from work since he became the chief, but he'd done it for her. Even though her brothers came to help her, Patrick insisted on taking her to his house to recuperate and then after a week of being together, he showed her his Fishing Camp of Solitude. Sure, it wasn't an official name, but he'd never brought another woman to see it.

Seeing her upset and having her run away from him was painful and he'd been considerably worse. There had to be a reason the universe put them together if only for a moment of happiness.

He walked back inside his lake house, thinking she'd gone to the restroom. It was empty. He quickly checked the whole house, and she was gone.

Patrick's stomach dropped when he thought of her being out in the cold night air alone. He snatched his keys from the counter and ran out the front door. But there she was sitting on the top step, crying.

Without saying a word, he sat down and put an arm around her waist. She laid her head on his shoulder and they stayed like that for a long time.

Once the wind began whipping around the outside of his house, he knew he had to get her inside. Sometimes, it got bad enough that his porch sounded like a wind tunnel, and he was sure it would pick up tonight.

Patrick stood and reached out to help Nalani to her feet.

He held her hand as they went back inside. He still didn't know what to say to her to make her feel better.

She would be going home to Maui in a few weeks, and he had to go back to work in New Orleans. But they had time together now and he would try and cheer her up the best he knew how.

The open concept lake house felt dark tonight and he knew it was because Nalani was upset. He set her up on the sofa with the pillows and comforter they'd used outside.

Once she was settled, he brought her some water and her medicine. "Miss Newsome would never let me forget it if I didn't make sure you took those pills." He winked at her and then went back to the kitchen to make them something to eat.

He brought her a tray with chicken noodle soup and a turkey sandwich with toasted bread. He had the same except when he sat down, he added half a bottle of hot sauce to his soup.

They looked through a movie guide and he was surprised to find that she really did like action movies too, thanks to her brothers. Between the two of them they'd seen almost everything. So they chose one they'd seen before but was one of their favorites.

They took a brief intermission while Patrick took her dishes to the kitchen and then made popcorn. After she ate a little of her favorite snack, she snuggled up next to him. She may have liked the movie but she was still in her head from earlier and seemed sad to him.

The thought that he might have contributed to her unhappiness had him rattled. He didn't want her to fall asleep feeling that way. He threw a piece of popcorn at her, but she didn't notice. So, he threw another and that time she cut her eyes at him.

"Need some attention, chief?"

He laughed. "I don't know what you're talking about, sunshine."

She looked back at the television, and he threw another piece of popcorn at her, this time she caught it. Patrick leaned down and ate it out of her hand which cracked her up.

"What are you doing?" she asked and when he threw the popcorn, again it landed inside her shirt.

He leaned over and picked it up with his mouth, slowly licking her skin along the way. When he looked up at her, she was sinking her teeth into her bottom lip, and he needed his mouth there.

Their lips collided and she grabbed at his shirt with her good hand and the one in a cast. It took some doing but she managed to unbutton it and he kissed her harder as she pressed her body against his.

When he slowed down, she looked into his eyes. "You can't tease me like this and then stop," she said, and he saw that bottom lip pout and he wanted her more than ever.

He carefully maneuvered her, so she straddled his lap. "I have no intention of stopping," he said, and he kept his word for the next hour making love to her.

When Nalani woke up the next morning, her body hurt in the most delicious of way and then some not so great ways too. Still, she chose to think of the good and made her way to the restroom and the beautiful tub in there.

She was super careful when she pulled out the body wash to use for bubble bath, so she didn't spill it like the bath salts.

Miss Newsome had given Nalani a wad of plastic bags that would fit over her cast perfectly. It took her a few minutes, but she managed to get it covered just so and carefully slipped into the warm water up to her neck.

The clip she'd tried to put into her hair came undone and she gave up trying to keep her hair dry. The warm water felt so good on her body and the vanilla brown sugar scented bath was just what she needed.

She closed her eyes thinking about Patrick and then felt his warm lips on hers.

"I think there's enough room in here for both of us," she said, and her eyes looked like shiny black diamonds.

He was out of his clothes in seconds and when he slid into the tub slowly, her eyes never left his body.

He faced her but kept his hands on each side of the tub showing her that she had control here. That was when he watched her slowly sit up on her knees and ever so carefully moved to straddle his lap.

When she leaned in to kiss him, he wrapped one hand in her hair and the other gripped her hip. Careful at first, they loved each other until the water in the tub became cold.

Patrick got out first so he could help her. As she stood on the tile floor, Nalani tried not to laugh at the enormous amount of water they splashed out of the tub.

He laughed too and then threw four large towels down to soak up the mess. There wasn't time to clean up because two times with her was not enough.

They needed all morning in bed to quiet their desire to a low roar. It had been burning for a solid week and neither one of them tried to deny it any longer.

&

It was midafternoon when Nalani woke up. She could feel her shoulder throbbing and realized she'd slept on that side for the first time since she'd injured it. Slowly sitting up on the side of the bed, she swung her legs around and took a deep breath.

She had exercised parts of her body that she hadn't used in years. Making love with Patrick was even more incredible than she had imagined.

That was saying something because she'd thought about him that way several times. He was strong and a man who liked control. But he'd tempered his own desires allowing her to go at her own pace. It was incredible and thoughtful. She didn't know what to do with herself because she couldn't stop smiling. There was definitely a connection between them, and it was hard to explain.

Slowly heading to the restroom, Nalani got a quick glance at herself in the mirror. She was a rumpled mess. Naked with all those bruises and scrapes on display. How had she not scared Patrick off.

Getting straight to work on her tangled mess of hair, she brushed her teeth and washed her face too. Rummaging through the clothes that Tenille had sent for her, there was a floral dress with long billowy sleeves. It was beautiful and she could slip it on easily, which mattered most lately.

When she pulled it over her head, Patrick startled her by whistling from the doorway. "You look beautiful," he said and then he took three large steps to stand in front of her.

It was hard to look at him and not want him again. She tried to smooth down her long hair. "Want me to brush your hair for you, sunshine?"

The way he was looking at her only made her want him more. She didn't trust her words, so she nodded instead. He held her hand and led her into the bathroom in front of the large mirror over his sink. When he stood behind her and gently ran the brush through her hair, she stared at his handsome face.

He was thorough as he began at the ends and made his way to the top of her head. Finally, tangle free, he made large sweeps of the brush from the top of her head to the ends of her hair. Why was that so sexy?

He caught her staring at him and winked her way. Then he stepped closer so his hard body touched hers and leaned down to whisper into her ear. "Everything okay, sunshine?"

"Just some aches and pain," she replied and tried not to look at him and give her longing away.

Patrick was adept at reading her mind or her body. She wasn't sure which but when he offered to kiss it and make it better, she was so relieved she almost climbed on top of the bathroom counter.

Instead, Patrick leaned down to kiss her. It was deep and sensual, and Nalani was certain she'd never been kissed like that before. He hoisted her up and she wrapped her legs around his body as he slowly walked them into the bedroom and his large bed.

He seemed to think better of it as he laid her down and then hovered above her. "I don't want to hurt you," he said, and she saw that deep control he always had slipping.

"The doctor said that activities that made me breathe deeper were good for me."

Patrick spent the next hour being really good for her, over and over again.

༶

"Where are we going?" Nalani asked with a huge smile on her face.

"This is called a Sunday drive and you will just have to wait and see, sunshine."

"A Sunday drive?"

Patrick grinned as he remembered visiting with Mayor Regalia's Italian family. They had lived in the city for generations and Patrick loved to listen to the stories they told. One in particular was about how Alexavier's dad courted his mother. He would take her out on long Sunday drives.

When he woke up that morning the idea popped into his head as if it was something he had done all the time but there was no stopping the plan from happening. After making love with Nalani for most of the day, doing something romantic was important to him.

"This is an old romantic way of courting a young woman in New Orleans," he said. "Going on a Sunday afternoon drive."

The idea of being courted in an old-fashioned way by Patrick Morales got her attention and Nalani wasn't sure she'd ever forget this.

Once they got across the bridge back into the city, he stopped and bought her a bottle of coke a cola. The drink came in a glass bottle, and so did his Dr. Pepper. Then they were off.

He pulled into a beautiful park area filled with giant oak trees covered in moss. Then regaled her with the history of City Park. "Some of the Oak Trees here are over 800 years old," he said. "And it's one of the largest urban parks in the country."

Nalani reached out and held Patrick's hand. The park was stunning and gave her a different view of the city. She hadn't realized there was such a large green space in this city.

Next, he drove her past a few of the large cemeteries and promised to take her on a tour as soon as her foot healed completely.

Lastly, he drove her down St. Charles Ave and some of the side streets to show her the old homes there. She'd never seen that type of architecture except in history books and she was absolutely taken with the incredible city.

It was dark by the time they made it home and Miss Newsome had left a note on the door. She wrote to tell them that she knew they were out for the weekend but stopped by in case they got back early so she could check on their patient.

Nalani grinned that Miss Newsome was such a sweet hearted woman and couldn't believe she'd ended up here simply by chance. The universe had a way of realigning your life and you had no control over it.

She and Patrick ate breakfast food for dinner and then he went through the mail and got things ready for work the next day. While he was busy, Nalani talked to Tenille on the phone for over an hour.

When they climbed into bed, Nalani was tired in the most delicious way, and she snuggled up next to Patrick who might just be the love of her life.

Chapter Eighteen

It wasn't ideal to wake up alone at Patrick's house the next morning, Nalani thought. She instantly missed him and the quiet was unsettling. There was always someone around her at home in Hawaii. Often she'd craved alone time when she was there, but this was different.

She scolded herself that she was being silly and that she needed to pull on her big girl panties and start her day. First, she would make some coffee, then she would clean up and get dressed.

Miss Newsome would be there by nine and after they spent the morning together at physical therapy, Tenille was supposed to come over and visit.

She dragged herself to the kitchen where she found a pot of coffee already made for her and a sweet note that said, *Have a great day, sunshine,* from Patrick. It made her miss him even more.

Carrying her coffee cup into the bedroom, she got dressed, and then tried to brush out her hair. How could she manage all the things with Patrick but still not use a brush without it hurting?

She gave up and instead twisted her hair into a giant messy bun on top of her head. It took her twenty minutes to make up the bed, but she didn't give up. It was only fair that she pulled her weight around the house since Patrick had gone back to work. She wanted him to come home to a clean space.

Thinking back to her life before, she couldn't believe how much she took it for granted. Bending over to put things in the front load washer now was difficult and vacuuming impossible. Still, she tried her best and the look on Miss Newsome's face told her that she had made the place look better.

"Little lady, I am going to call Patrick and tattle on you if you don't stop cleaning."

Nalani laughed until she saw Miss Newsome's serious face. "I just wanted to make it look a little nicer for him, that's all," Nalani explained.

"Those bones need rest to heal and although you have to move around for your lungs and ribs, this is too much. Too much, I tell you," Miss Newsome pulled out her medical bag and took Nalani's temperature and then blood pressure.

"See. You even have an elevated blood pressure."

Nalani looked at the numbers Miss Newsome wrote down and then shrugged. It didn't hurt quite as much as it did last week. She smiled at Miss Newsome. "I'm not even sure I know what blood pressure does. I mean, how serious is that anyway."

Miss Newsome didn't admit that Nalani's medication could cause her blood pressure to go up. She needed her patient to rest and this was the way she would convince her. She explained that it was a measure of how well the blood flowed through the body to organs and tissue and it was serious. It was enough to make Nalani sit on the sofa and then prop up her feet.

They talked about Hawaii while Nalani put another ice pack on her ribs and then she confided in her new older friend how sweet Patrick Morales was to her and how he'd planned an afternoon showing her the historic City Park and old homes in the city. "He called it a Sunday drive."

Miss Newsome approved of Patrick Morales and then got a far off look in her eyes. Nalani gave her a few minutes because she didn't want to intrude on something that appeared to be important to the caring woman. When she looked over at her young patient, Nalani couldn't help but ask, "Where did you go?"

"I was just thinking about when I was your age," Miss Newsome said. "And in love."

Was it obvious that she was falling in love with Patrick? She felt it in her bones but she also knew there were serious barriers for it to go much further.

She smiled at Miss Newsome. "I could use a good love story, if you feel like telling it?"

"I'm afraid it doesn't have a happy ending like your generation always expects. But it has a wonderful beginning and middle," Miss Newsome replied. "Do you still want to hear it?"

Nalani had a huge grin on her face as she nodded and pulled more pillows around her body so she could get comfortable.

Miss Newsome got that look in her eyes again. The one that said she was back in time. "I was a young nursing student after the Vietnam War. Many of our guys came back and were pretty beaten up, not just physically but also emotionally. The country wasn't so nice to them, even the doctors and nurses had to deal with a lot of attitude. There seemed to be two camps of thought. One side that believed service was a duty and honor and the other side, the hippy-type that was against war and the military. The country was divided. Working in the hospital environment was strict and you either followed the rules or were fired. Plain and simple. There was zero fraternization between the doctors which were mostly male and the nurses who were female."

Nalani locked eyes with Miss Newsome. "What was his name?"

The older woman seemed to blush as she thought about the man she'd loved. "Dr. Hirsch Bixby."

"Now that's a name," Nalani teased and they both laughed.

"He was quite the man." Miss Newsome smoothed down her sweater. It was obvious to Nalani that the older woman still cared about him. She waited until Miss Newsome found her words again.

"Dr. Bixby was five years older than me but already an accomplished surgeon. He took his job seriously but unlike many of the other doctors in the hospital, he was thoughtful. He didn't just bark orders out to the nurses but instead asked respectfully and always thanked us politely.

"I was still new but attending another surgeon who was about to perform surgery on a man with a broken leg. Dr. Bixby was in the room too but he was just observing. Before the surgery began, I set up the room and a tray of surgical instruments for the procedure. The surgeon was too busy talking when he came into the room and he bumped into the tray, knocking everything off it and onto the floor. It delayed the surgery by twenty minutes, and he blamed it all on me by saying I wasn't ready. He was quite nasty about it and yelled at me. The head nurse, who I was already frightened of, heard the commotion, and came running to help. She also scolded me in front of everyone, told me I wasn't going to get paid for that morning, and then sent me out of the room."

"They could do that?"

"It was a lot different for women back then. Even women in more powerful positions didn't have a strong enough footing to stand up to a surgeon." Miss Newsome's eyes got bigger. "But another doctor, a surgeon, could do it and that is exactly what Hirsch did for me that day. I was crying in the nurses' locker room, and he came in there and told me to dry my tears. He walked me back into the aftercare room where the surgeon apologized to me and the head nurse. I was afraid that I would get fired after that incident but instead, I was treated with more respect and things got a little better for all of us young nurses in the hospital because Dr. Bixby started a campaign that we were all on the same team and needed to treat each other that way. Forget about the divide plaguing the rest of the country, we worked together in order to give the patients the best care."

"He sounds wonderful," Nalani said.

"It gets better," Miss Newsome laughed. But before she continued, she offered to make them some more coffee. She came back from the kitchen with a lighter step and Nalani hoped the story had more happy times than bad.

"Doctor Bixby got more popular which meant he was busier than ever and he liked having the same team with him during surgery. He requested a specific anesthesiologist and me as his nurse. It was a joy to work with him, but we put in some really long hours. That went on for months and then on a rainy Friday in November of 1975, I'd worked a fourteen-hour shift and got off at seven. It was already dark, and I was exhausted. I didn't see any wood in the road and ran over it with my pinto which was a popular small car back then." Miss Newsome sipped her coffee and Nalani could tell she was right back in the fall of 1975 for a moment.

When she looked up, she was smiling bigger than Nalani had ever seen her. "There I was, in the pouring rain, trying to figure out how to change a tire when Hirsch stopped to help me. He pulled out a large flashlight and told me to wave it so cars could see us out there and then he changed my tire in less than ten minutes. We were both soaking wet and he looked at me with these dark smoldering eyes and asked me to have a drink with him." Miss Newsome leaned in and whispered, "At his house."

Both women laughed but it was no laughing matter. Nalani could tell there must have been some serious chemistry between them. "His home was beautiful, and he had a full bar off to the side of the kitchen. He made us hot buttered rum, which I'd never had before. It was such a grownup drink, and I wasn't much of a drinker. I sipped the drink as he got me a towel. Then he went and changed his clothes. When he came back, he brought me one of his shirts and I changed out of my wet clothes. I was a small thing back then and his shirt swallowed me. I could tell he liked the way I looked in it and I certainly was taken with him." She waggled her eyebrows.

"He had this sunken living room and a U-shaped sofa built in gold velvet. It was very stylish for the time. We curled up on that sofa, drinking rum, and talked for three hours. I still lived at home and almost forgot to call my mother. She was a worrier and I had never lied to her before. I lied that night. I told her that I was needed at the hospital and wouldn't be home until the morning. It was the first night I spent with him."

Nalani understood what it was like to have overprotective parents, but Miss Newsome grew up in the sixties and seventies. This was the twenty-first century and things should have changed by now.

"Were your parents suspicious?" Nalani worried over what happened between Miss Newsome and her first love.

"My father died when I was in high school from a crazy accident. He was walking down the road and a brick fell off a building downtown and hit him in the head."

Nalani's mouth opened but no sound came out. That was as tragic a story as she'd ever heard.

"I know. My mother never got over it or him. That incident made her into the champion worrier that she was and I couldn't leave her alone."

Nalani reached over and held the sweet woman's hand. "I'm sorry. Tell me more about you and Hirsch."

She wanted to see the happiness on Miss Newsome's face again. "Well, he was a glorious lover and I had never been happier. Of course, we had to keep our relationship quiet because it was strictly forbidden at the hospital. But we managed to keep it hidden from everyone only seeing each other at his home or the occasional weekend trip to Mississippi. The Gulf Coast was happening then, and we could go out without running into anyone we knew."

Miss Newsome finished her coffee and took her cup to the kitchen. When she returned, she took the melted icepack and put it back into the freezer. Nalani watched her and couldn't believe that was the end of the story.

When Miss Newsome came back into the room, Nalani gave her a hard stare. "You can't leave me hanging like that Miss Newsome. How long did you see each other? Did you marry him? Have kids? Where is he today?"

Miss Newsome looked at the clock and told Nalani that

she needed to eat something. You haven't had anything today and your medication is going to wear off before lunch.

While Miss Newsome worked on sandwiches in the kitchen, Nalani grew impatient. She slowly made her way into the kitchen and watched her caregiver whose expression didn't give anything away.

"I don't think I can eat anything right now, Miss Newsome. At least not until you tell me what happened."

The older woman cut her eyes at Nalani. "I'll tell you the rest as you eat. Deal?"

"Deal."

"But I have warned you already and I want to emphasize it again--you are not going to like it."

Chapter Nineteen

Miss Newsome had done an amazing job of distracting Nalani from missing Patrick. History was her thing and hearing about Miss Newsome's love affair in the seventies had pulled Nalani in from the beginning. It was easy to forget how events shaped society and Nalani was intrigued with how men and women were products of their environment almost as much as they were created with their family's genetics.

The struggles a young Miss Newsome faced in the seventies made Nalani feel like she was being thrust back in time. She knew that the country was divided over the Vietnam War and that women had a harder time getting respect in the workplace.

However, studying the time period was completely different than listening to a firsthand story from someone that lived it. In fact, she'd thought she was prepared for the details but as she noted all the differences from that time, she couldn't help but also find the similarities in her own life.

Hearing Miss Newsome explain how her mother was a worrier and she lived at home in her twenties, had immediately gotten Nalani's attention. She understood that life was made up from your choices but what happened when you felt like you didn't have a choice? Had Miss Newsome felt that way too?

Her love affair didn't have a happy ending. Was that because of the hospital rules, her mother, or had life or rather death intervened? Perhaps Nalani and Patrick's love affair was doomed too, but she had to hear how her doppelganger had made it through the heart ache.

When Miss Newsome warned her again that there wasn't a happy ending, Nalani needed to hear it even more. "Go ahead. I can handle it if you can."

"Life isn't always pretty," my mother used to say. And I learned the hard way that we're responsible for our decisions, the good ones and the bad ones. Sometimes we never find out which side our decisions fall on and then again, other times--" Miss Newsome didn't finish that sentence. She didn't have to because Nalani was living a life based on her decision to leave the doctorate program and hide away at home. Now she was stuck there like someone had glued her feet to the ground and not even a violent kidnapping was going to set her free for long. She couldn't disappoint her parents, brothers, or extended family.

But this wasn't about her, this was Miss Newsome's story, and it didn't necessarily align with Nalani's life. "Hirsch and I were together for ten years and we went through a lot. Of course, the beginning was amazing. We would sneak to his house for dates and like I said before, go to the Gulf Coast to bars and dance or go out to eat because we didn't know anyone there. That went on for several years until one of the hospital administrators saw us together one night. He was cheating on his wife with a young nurse and threatened Hirsch when he saw us. But Dr. Bixby was not one to back down and he told that man in no uncertain terms that he would tell his wife and also have his job if he breathed a word of it."

"He sounds great," Nalani said thinking of how strong of a man Patrick was too.

Miss Newsome nodded but her face grew serious. "Of course, neither of us were doing anything wrong except keeping our affair secret from my mother and the hospital. We had every right to be together otherwise. Still, that young nurse and the administrator didn't last long and when he tired of her, she went to the hospital and told on him as well as us. They fired her. But they also called Dr. Bixby and me into the office. Hirsch was upset about it and wanted to tell the hospital that our private lives were none of their business. I begged him not to tell. I needed my job. It was the only way I could afford to take care of my mother. It was our first real disagreement.

"Everyone forgot about it and things finally went back to normal. We kept seeing each other privately at his house but stopped going to the Gulf Coast. After a year or so, he really wanted to go on a vacation, and I agreed to go away with him but for only a few days. My mother had started having health issues and it was getting harder to leave her home alone at night. I asked a neighbor to look in on her and we went to the Florida Keys."

Nalani almost teared up when she saw how happy that vacation had made Miss Newsome. "I had never been away on a vacation like that before and oh, Nalani, it was beautiful. Soft sandy beaches with crystal clear water." Miss Newsome laughed at herself and then patted Nalani's hand. "What am I saying? You grew up in Sunny Paradise, Maui, Hawaii." She laughed again.

"Hirsch had grown up with money and his family apparently traveled when he was a child. He'd been everywhere and knew that I would love it. We sunned on the beaches and ate boiled shrimp. It was amazing. Then he asked me to marry him."

"Oh my goodness. He did?" Nalani tried to stand up. She'd thought she'd figured out how the story ended but had zero idea that he'd proposed.

"He did and he had this gorgeous ring and everything." Alba Newsome could remember everything like it had just happened. They'd swam in the ocean and laid on the beach for most of the day, but he had made reservations for dinner. They showered, got dress, then made love, showered again, and redressed for the evening. When he escorted her to the lobby, she saw the flower petals that led out to the beach where a table had been set up just for them. Hirsch Bixby had worked as a doctor on the front lines of the war but after four years, he returned home a new man with a love and respect for life. He wanted to share the rest of his life with her and promised her the world.

They made plans for the rest of the week. She would tell her mother first and then they would go to the courthouse and make it official. They would tell the hospital once everything was on paper. They would no longer be on the same team, but they could work at the hospital since they were married.

"The day before we returned home, my mother had a stroke and was rushed to the hospital. She kept telling them that I was there because I had lied to her and told her I was working all weekend. She was so belligerent that they ended up calling the police because she had them convinced that something had happened to me.

"We landed at the airport and were greeted by law enforcement who drove me straight to the hospital. Everyone found out that Dr. Bixby and I were out of town together. Mother flipped out. The stroke was mild but back then we didn't have the medications or therapies like we do today. After a week in the hospital, they released her. She needed constant care in the beginning which worked out because the hospital fired me."

Alba wiped her eyes. It was still a difficult memory for her and she'd kept it packed away for years. "Don't mind me. It was so long ago."

"Life isn't fair," Nalani whispered and held Miss Newsome's hand.

"Hirsch tried to help us and tend to my mother but she blamed him for me not being home when it happened. No matter how much I apologized for lying to her, she couldn't forgive me until he and I broke off the engagement."

"You broke up with him?"

"I tried to make it work but as long as she was angry, I couldn't marry him. How could I leave her like that? He was understanding for a long time. It took her six months before she could walk steady again and I went back to work for a small hospital for half the pay I used to make. Being the new hire, they gave me the worst hours and between caring for mother and work, I just didn't have anything left.

"It was exactly a year from when he proposed and he told me that he loved me but if I wouldn't marry him that he wanted children and wasn't getting any younger. I gave him back his ring and I heard three years later that he got married."

The painful smile on Miss Newsome's face told Nalani everything she wasn't saying. Letting Hirsch Bixby go may have been the best thing for him but the worst thing she'd ever done to herself.

"He was the love of your life?" Nalani asked.

Patrick walked in the front door and immediately saw the seriousness on both women's faces.

Miss Newsome stood up and grinned. "You never know, there may be someone out there for me, still."

Patrick looked confused and Miss Newsome kissed his cheek and told them she would check in later, but they could call if they needed her. She couldn't have run out the door any faster if she'd tried and Patrick looked at Nalani's sad face.

"Everything okay, sunshine?"

"You know that saying, if you love someone set them free?"

"Yes, I think so--" he watched the anger in her eyes grow.

"Well, it's garbage," she said and then slowly walked out of the room and firmly shut his bedroom door.

He'd simply come home for lunch and check on her before she had to go to physical therapy. Having Miss Newsome watch over her had seemed like a good idea but now he wasn't so sure. She was upset and he had no idea what that was all about.

Suddenly, there was a knock on the front door, and it pulled him out of his worry. When he opened it, Tenille was standing there with a huge grin on her face. She had a black eye the last time he saw her, but it had healed. The inside corner of her eye was still bloodshot but otherwise she looked well.

"Where's our patient?" she said with a grin.

Before he could respond, Nalani came out of the back bedroom and hugged her friend. She'd been crying and even when she'd been thrown out of a moving vehicle she hadn't cried.

Clearly Tenille had never seen her upset like that before either as she turned and gave Patrick a stern look.

He was in trouble.

Chapter Twenty

"I can take a hint. I'll go out for lunch," he said but before he walked away, Nalani reached for his hand.

He turned toward her, and she kissed him hard on the mouth. Then she hugged him like she'd never let go. "Is there anything I can do for you, Nalani? Do you need me to stay and take you to your appointment?" he offered as he held her tightly.

She leaned up and kissed him again. The way she looked at him made him feel ten feet tall. He would do anything for her.

"Tenille is here. I'm okay. Honest," she said and the vulnerability in her voice made him feel even more like a caveman.

"I can take off the rest of the day, hell, the rest of the month if you need me. I have plenty of vacation time built up." He said not taking his eyes off her.

She shook her head, no, and leaned up to kiss him sweetly. "I'm good. We're going to have some girl time."

He looked over at Tenille who was smiling at him now. He grinned back and kissed Nalani on her forehead. "Call me when you get back from the doctor, okay, sunshine?"

She nodded and then he left so they could talk.

"I think I misread the situation when I first saw you. I thought he'd done something to upset you but then I thought maybe you two needed to be alone," Tenille said staring at her friend. "If your brothers saw you look at the chief that way, I am pretty sure they wouldn't have left you here."

Nalani laughed and then her eyes watered. She was a ball of emotions and couldn't control it.

"Hey now, are you okay?" Tenille asked. Things were clearly moving fast for her friend and the chief but something else was going on too.

"I don't know what's wrong with me. I'm never emotional. You know me."

Tenille reached out to hold Nalani's hand. "I think falling in love can do that to you."

Instantly thinking about Miss Newsome and the responsibility she chose over love, Nalani shook her head. Life wasn't fair. "You know I can't stay here. Noa and Jensen said the restaurant is coming along faster than expected and my dad isn't well enough to help. They need all hands on deck, literally, to get it up and running."

Verifying they had enough time before Nalani's appointment to talk, Tenille gently pulled her friend over to the large sofa so they could sit down. It was the first time in their friendship that Nalani needed advice and Tenille was happy to repay the love and kindness she'd been given. "You aren't in any condition to help them right now. Besides, I heard that half of Lahaina is helping with the restaurant, so I don't see why you can't stay."

Nalani looked past her as if she could see something Tenille couldn't. "Patrick is a wonderful man. A hero around here. He couldn't leave his career and community. And whether or not my family has a lot of help, they expect me to be there. You know my father paid tons of money for my education and living expenses in California. It's the least I can do to pay him back."

Tenille had never pressed Nalani about the reasons she left the doctorate program. Noa told her privately that Nalani was the smartest person he knew, and he'd never expected her to move back home permanently.

It was clear to see that Nalani was an overachiever and hard on herself. Tenille watched Nalani in Maui and always wondered if she was fulfilled. Of course, she was successful in the family business and besides waitressing, she'd helped with the books and streamlining some of their ordering processes. But she always seemed too big for that place.

"I love your family. You know I do. And I get wanting to do right by them. I'm not sure I can ever pay them back for everything they did for me and I was only there for ten months. But you deserve to be happy and fulfilled too. I'm certain they want that for you."

The Kahale family gave all they had to each other including friends and the community. Her grandfather started that restaurant, and her father grew it to what it was today. The money they made there had sent cousins to trade schools and helped take care of their family as well as many others. It mattered to the community.

Her father was injured in the fire that destroyed it. The fire was started by the psychopath who was after Tenille. Nalani was the one who helped Tenille escape him in the beginning, which pulled her entire family into the drama.

She felt responsible. It was her duty to go home and help, especially if her father was still unable to work. It was difficult to explain this to Tenille without making her feel guilty too.

"I can be happy there helping my family," she said putting as much sincerity into the lie as she could muster. "What I can't do is be selfish. You feel that way after being there for less than a year. Imagine growing up around them and their selfless behavior. I'm not sure I'll ever measure up."

It was hard hearing her friend doubt her worth. Nalani absolutely saved Tenille's life. But she understood the compelling need to do right by her family because they were wonderful people. She only hoped they would see how much Nalani needed Patrick too and encourage her to embrace her happiness even if it led her to New Orleans.

After all, late at night Nalani's mother would talk to them about finding true love. She would say it was one of the most important things in life. Then she would talk about how her family moved to Maui from Mexico when she was a young girl, and it was fate so she could meet her prince.

Nalani's parents met in high school and were inseparable from the age of fifteen. They built a friendship and love that has lasted over forty years. Late at night, Tenille and Nalani would talk about finding that kind of relationship.

Tenille smiled at her friend. "You are one of the best people I know, and I feel lucky every day that you were at the restaurant that night and today are my friend. You do more than just measure up, Nalani. Don't forget it."

Those words were what got Nalani through as they went to physical therapy, and she was put through torture to get her shoulder mobile. According to her physical therapist, it was a mild session and all they could do until her ribs healed and she got her arm cast and foot brace off.

After physical therapy was done, Tenille told Nalani more about the boarding house in Maisonville, that Tenille was helping run and Miss Lynn's Diner where she still worked part time. Hearing about the community that Tenille found after all she'd been through, warmed Nalani's heart and gave her hope. It was her family's unspoken motto, to help others, and she'd absolutely done the right thing by helping Tenille.

When they got to the house, Tenille made them some hot tea and they didn't run out of things to talk about for the rest of the afternoon, which was usual for them. Nalani had physical therapy again in two days and agreed to go with Tenille to Maisonville then.

When Patrick got home, he found Nalani asleep on the sofa and watched her sleep peacefully for a few minutes before kissing her and waking her up. He was getting used to having her in his life.

He shook his head. This is temporary.

"What time is it?" she asked groggily, and he smiled at her dimples. He'd told her he wouldn't be home until late but then couldn't wait to get home to her. He even picked dinner before getting there at six.

"I thought you said you had to work late?" she challenged him.

He kissed her again because he couldn't resist her. "You didn't call me after your appointment today and I wanted to make sure that it went okay."

She hadn't had a cell phone in weeks and marveled over how she didn't miss it until Tenille left and she didn't have a way to call him. She told him that she'd gotten carried away talking with Tenille.

"And you didn't have a phone once she left," he smiled and pulled out a bag with an iPhone in it. "I picked this up for you."

That was no small gift and Nalani felt guilty he spent so

much money on her. "You didn't have to do that, Patrick. I'm sure my phone is still in my car at home."

"Call me selfish but you aren't there, and I want you to have this now."

"It's too expensive."

"It's a gift. You're supposed to just say thank you."

Nalani sat up on her knees and leaned over to kiss him. Alba Newsome and Hirsch Bixby's love story had a sweet beginning too. It was too soon for her to think about the middle or the end of this love affair with Patrick Morales.

So, she began unbuttoning his shirt and kissing her way down his body. "Physical therapy was awful," she whispered. "I think I need some sexual therapy to make me forget about it."

He watched her take her time exploring his body and he knew even more than before that he would change his future plans for her.

But would she ever follow her heart for him?

Chapter Twenty-One

It took two full days for Nalani to recuperate from her first physical therapy session. PT was terrible but the way Patrick made her forget about it Monday night, made her smile through the pain at Wednesday's appointment.

Tenille teased her friend for blushing as the handsome physical therapist flirted through the entire session.

He had worn gray athletic pants and a white long sleeve shirt with the hospital's insignia, but the material accentuated how turned on he was from working with her.

It was hard to overlook and when they finished, his female coworker scheduled Nalani's next appointment and apologized for not seeing what was going on sooner. She explained that he was new and certainly unaware of the situation, but she would tell the poor guy after they left that he needed to wear different pants.

The moment Nalani and Tenille climbed into her little red sports car, they both laughed until they cried. It was embarrassing and hilarious at the same time. They were still laughing about the innocent incident when they got to the diner in Maisonville.

Tenille introduced Nalani to the owner of The Main Street Grocery, Miss Lynn. She was an older woman with white hair and the sweetest disposition. Everyone loved her and referred to the restaurant as Miss Lynn's place instead of by its name.

It was lunch time, and the restaurant was busy so it took a few minutes for her friend Olivia to come over and introduce herself. She'd been teasing the Mayor of New Orleans, who was her boyfriend, before she walked over to chat.

"I could see the way you two were laughing when you walked in here. Fess up and tell us your private joke," Olivia said.

Nalani looked at Tenille who couldn't stop laughing. Olivia had a sharp wit and a confidence that made her irresistible. Tenille loved her like a big sister, and she told her every detail of what had happened at physical therapy, including when the male therapist stood closely behind Nalani to help her lift her arm and began to sweat profusely.

"You better hope Chief Morales doesn't take you to physical therapy," Olivia said and that was when they all saw that Alexavier was standing there listening too.

He shook his head and leaned in to speak quietly. "I'm quite sure he will want to take you to your next appointment."

Nalani, Tenille, Olivia, and Miss Lynn all stood there with their mouths opened. Alexavier kissed his girlfriend, and she trailed after him as he headed out to the parking lot.

"He's going to tell Patrick, isn't he?" Nalani asked looking at the other three women to agree or disagree with her. They all looked nervous but didn't confirm or deny it.

A couple of minutes later, Olivia walked back inside. They all heard her say, *Sugar Honey Iced Tea.*

Why did that sound like a swear word, Nalani thought.

"I apologize for all of that, Nalani. I tried to talk some sense into him, but he says it's guy code and he has to tell Patrick. Just prepare yourself to answer some bullheaded questions when you get home, okay?" Olivia said.

Nalani told her that it was okay. Honestly, she couldn't imagine what the big deal was, and she didn't think that Patrick would think it was either. When another friend of theirs, Sydney Bell Gentry came into the diner, they ran the situation past her too. She laughed and told Nalani that her husband Ryan was cut from the same cloth as the mayor and the chief, so she better get ready to prove to him that he has nothing to worry about because she wasn't interested in anyone but him. "They can't help but get a little jealous. At least until they put a ring on your finger."

Olivia laughed. "That's not completely true. I saw Ryan giving the O'Malley's Moving truck guy, Chuck, what for when he hugged you here at the diner a few weeks ago."

"I told him that I'm seven months pregnant and no one is looking at me like that, but he disagreed," Sydney was a beautiful redhead and pregnant she was one of the most stunning women Nalani had ever seen.

Nalani thought all the women from Maisonville were great but she still wasn't sure that all the fuss they were making over her flirty physical therapist was really that big of a deal. They went on to discuss tons of other things like how Miss Lynn made the best pies in the state and then they ate a piece of her amazing strawberry pie.

Ryan, Sydney's very hot looking husband came into the diner to see what was taking so long and to also get a piece of pie. Apparently, his sister and her fiancé were getting married in a few months and everyone discussed whether her soon-to-be husband would ever talk her into moving out of the city.

Tenille reminded them all that it was a straight shot across the bridge to New Orleans and that it was quite possible to enjoy both Maisonville and the city of New Orleans. There was no reason to have to choose one over the other.

Spending the afternoon chatting with the smart women in Tenille's circle had been one of the single best days Nalani had in a long time. They were all so different and yet had a lot in common. It was exactly what she needed in her life. A little diversity.

After hugging everyone and leaving the diner, Tenille showed Nalani around the small town of Maisonville since Patrick had only taken her straight to his house there. She reached over and patted Nalani's hand and told her how happy she'd been since Nalani got there.

"I know it's a small town but everyone here is fantastic. The lake we drove over surrounds the town on two sides and there's a river on another side. There are a lot of people who retire here but with Ryan Gentry and Sydney renovating half of the houses in town it feels like a sort of revival."

Nalani laughed at her friend's word choice. She'd always thought of a revival as a religious experience.

"Seriously, Nalani. It's awesome to watch and be a part of something so wonderful." Tenille showed her the most stunning house in town, a large white home that belonged to the Gentry family.

"Doesn't that place remind you of something?" Nalani asked but she couldn't recall where she'd seen it before.

Next, they stopped in at Mrs. Bower's boarding house so Tenille could introduce her to Mrs. Bower and although it was getting a bit late, they sat on the porch and drank iced tea with her.

Mrs. Bower was in her eighties and hilarious. She had Nalani and Tenille laughing until they almost cried. She had stories about who was dating who and who cheated at cards. She had a stronger dating life than either of them. She bragged that she was a hot ticket because she owned her home.

She taunted Tenille about Reaper and told her to tell him her cane was warmed up if he stepped out of line with her. Then she offered to have a chat with Chief Morales if Nalani needed her help.

Tenille assured Nalani that she didn't need Mrs. Bower to help her and then told the sweet lady she needed to retire her cane.

"Oh, I can't retire my stick," she said. Then she explained how one of the men in her social club rode a motorcycle and tried to date all the senior ladies. "He's eighty-two and wears a black leather jacket. Slicks back his hair too. He came over here the other night and strutted up the steps tripping over his own feet because he wears combat boots instead of orthopedic shoes like he's supposed to. I told him that he needed to get back on the horse he rode in on." The funny older woman smirked. "He doesn't even ride a Harley. The nerve. He's already jumped the shark and needs to stop pretending he's The Fonz."

Nalani only knew who The Fonz was because her oldest brothers watched reruns of the show Happy Days when they were younger. Her father would always reference, jumping the shark and they thought it was so cool. He'd agreed and said it was the highlight of that show to him when he was a kid but turns out, it means you've hit your peak and are on the down slide.

Tenille didn't get it but Nalani promised to show it to her on her phone later.

As they left Maisonville, Tenille confided in Nalani that the town was nicknamed Renaissance Lake because people who moved there got a second chance at love or life. She'd never been superstitious but she told Nalani that she certainly believed in the magic of the little town.

It was the sweetest thing Nalani had ever heard and she hugged and kissed her friend for introducing her to her lovely friends and giving her such a wonderful afternoon.

Patrick was already home when they drove up, so they said their goodbyes and she walked into the house to share her amazing day with him. But when she walked in the door, he was pacing the floor and had an upset look on his face.

"What's wrong, Patrick?"

Chapter Twenty-Two

"What's wrong?" Patrick replied with the same words as he held up Nalani's cell phone.

He had spent an hour helping her get it set up last night. Then Nalani left it at the house on the bathroom counter when she left to go to physical therapy.

"I didn't mean to leave that here. Honestly, I'm just not used to carrying it with me anymore. Isn't that strange. I mean, I've had a phone since I was twelve." She laughed at herself, but he didn't seem to calm down.

"Did you go to physical therapy today?"

"I think you know that I did," she responded with a challenge.

"Is it too much to call me afterward and tell me how you are doing? Or that you are going across the lake to Maisonville? And won't be home until late?" He was getting more worked up and she remembered the ladies discussing their boyfriends and husbands that were also a bit overprotective.

"I should have called."

"You should have called," he repeated.

"But the last time I checked, you aren't the boss of me. And the physical therapist was just being a flirt. He didn't mean anything by it, and you don't have to go all caveman over something so insignificant. Newsflash, men flirt with me sometimes."

She stood in front of him staring into his eyes and thought for a minute he might explode. Suddenly, his expression cooled as if he absorbed the words she'd just said. This side of him was scarier, chilly, and no nonsense.

"What did you just say? The physical therapist was inappropriate with you today?" Patrick's voice was steady.

Nalani was certain that Mayor Regalia had told Patrick what he'd heard. Wasn't that why he was acting all overprotective? "Did you talk to the mayor?"

"What does he have to do with this?" Patrick asked without an ounce of inflection in his voice. He was cold as ice.

"Nothing. How did you know I was in Maisonville?"

"Because Reaper called and asked if you and Tenille were back yet because he hadn't heard from her."

"Oh."

There was a long pause as he stared at her and she stared back at him.

Finally, he spoke. "That's all you have to say to me?"

Nalani had grown up mostly around boys and the one thing they didn't do was over apologize for things. Her mother would say she was more wolf than girl and sometimes she thought that was true. She'd shrug if she did something wrong and never apologized excessively like most girls. She'd learned that from her strong mother. "Actually, I don't have anything else to say to you. You're being unreasonable and behaving like a bullheaded shark."

She turned and went into his bedroom, slamming the door.

It was a bad habit she'd developed as a teenager and her father reinforced the door jamb to her bedroom years ago so she could get it out of her system. But this wasn't her house, and she shouldn't have lost her temper. She didn't like that unfeeling side of him. And how dare he ruin her lovely day by acting like a jerk.

It was thirty minutes later when she heard a knock on the bedroom door. She was lying in the bed with only her bra and panties, too tired to change clothes she'd just removed the ones she had on earlier.

Patrick knocked again, "May I come in, please?"

"Yes," Nalani said and then realized she'd whispered. Louder this time, she said, "Yes."

Patrick only paused for a second when he saw her there without any clothes. She pretended like it didn't matter to her. He sat on the end of the bed for a minute before he began to apologize. "I'm sorry for losing my temper. You didn't deserve it. When I realized you didn't call, I tried to call you and it went to voicemail. Then when I got home and you weren't here, I got worried."

"I shouldn't have forgotten the phone. I really did mean to call you, but I got distracted. Tenille and I talk constantly when we're together. Then we got to Maisonville, and she introduced me to all of her friends there. Before I knew it, there were five of us laughing and talking. The mayor stopped by for a second and then we went to the boarding house, and I met Mrs. Bower. It was a lot."

He agreed. "That was a lot for you. Are you okay?" She seemed to push through physical that most men he knew couldn't.

Nalani nodded but she wasn't okay. She didn't like the

distance between them. He was still studying her when she shook her head no.

"What's wrong, sunshine?"

"I've never been very good at apologizing. It's not that I don't make mistakes, but I try to be mindful of what I say and do." She looked remorseful and he reached out his hand to hold hers.

"I was worried. I have a problem when it comes to you, sunshine." He paused and stared into her eyes. "This thing between us has grown into something I've never had with anyone else."

Nalani sat up and wrapped her arms around his neck. "What are we going to do about that, chief?"

Patrick carefully lifted her into his lap as he kissed her warmly on the mouth. Coming home and not finding her had upset him. He overreacted when she walked in the door and now with her barely clothed in his lap, he planned to apologize to her properly but as he wrapped one hand around her waist and the other in her thick dark hair, there was a knock on their front door and then the doorbell rang.

Leaning back, Nalani smiled at him. "You better go." She looked down at her half naked body and then back up at him. Perhaps she needed to get dressed.

Growling in the back of his throat, he stood with her still in his arms and warmly kissed her below her ear. It sent shivers down her body. "Don't you dare get dressed," he said before carefully laying her down on top of his bed.

Then he headed out the bedroom door to see who could possibly want to visit this late. When he turned on the front porch lights, he could see Miss Newsome standing there but something was wrong with her. As he opened the door, she fell into his arms.

"I got you. Easy now," Patrick said as he carefully lifted the elderly woman and carried her inside. He yelled for Nalani who wrapped up in one of his dress shirts and came hurrying into the outer room as fast as her injuries let her.

She gasped as she saw how pale Miss Newsome was and then grabbed Patrick's phone from the kitchen counter to dial 911. "Is it your heart?" Nalani asked so she could give the operator some of her information.

Patrick nodded to Nalani but kept talking to Miss Newsome. "Alba, you should've called me instead of walking over here."

"It wasn't that bad until I stepped up onto your porch. I think the steps got to me."

Patrick shook his head. The elderly woman was as hard-headed as she was wonderful. "Don't worry. They'll be here in just a few minutes. I'll go with you to the hospital. Okay?"

Nalani walked over to hold Miss Newsome's hand while Patrick went out to the street to make sure the ambulance stopped at the right location.

It took ten minutes for the firetrucks to arrive and then another five before the ambulance got there. But they had the sweet older woman loaded up quickly and Patrick grabbed his phone and gave Nalani a quick kiss before he took off toward the hospital.

The moment she was alone, Nalani shivered from the quiet. Life could turn on a dime and she'd grown up in such a grounded atmosphere that it always took her a moment to deal with emergencies. In stressful situations, she'd freeze and take in everything around her but it usually took a while to process what actually happened.

It was why she handled the kidnapping so slowly. Even though they'd kept her drugged for part of it, she assessed what was happening and even through the torture, it felt like an out of the body experience.

Thinking back to her time in college, she had been shocked over her professor's behavior but she didn't freak out or act impulsively. She took her time to weigh what happened as well as her options. Then she packed up and went home. It was her refuge away from the rest of the chaotic world and she wondered if she'd ever really be able to live anywhere else.

She went into the bedroom to look through Patrick's clothes until she found some black sweatpants and a long-sleeved shirt. She needed something comfy to put on and his clothes would be perfect. Although they had been laundered, they still smelled like him and she snuggled up with a blanket and her phone on the sofa, hoping that Miss Newsome would be alright, and that Patrick would be home soon.

Five hours later, Nalani woke up when Patrick walked through the front door. "Hey," she said, still half asleep.

He grinned at her as he walked over to the counter to put his keys, wallet, and phone down. When he turned around, she could see the exhaustion in his eyes. Slowly, she managed to stand and walk over to him.

When she wrapped her arms around his waist, he kissed the top of her head. "She's going to be just fine. It was a problem with her pacemaker, and they had to recalibrate it or something. Apparently, she was distracted with all of our needs and didn't call her doctor this week when she felt off."

"What?" Nalani was disappointed that Alba didn't mention it as they'd gotten so close over the past week.

"They are keeping her for twenty-four hours to monitor her heart but expect she'll be able to resume her regular activities when she comes home." Patrick rubbed his face and looked at his watch. "I need to grab some sleep and go into the office in a couple of hours."

Nalani followed him into the bedroom but as she climbed into bed, he was already asleep. She'd never seen anyone fall asleep before their head hit the pillow. She usually had to calm her thoughts and sometimes laid there for a couple of hours before she finally drifted off.

She cared about Miss Newsome and certainly had feelings for Patrick. New Orleans was interesting and the history of the city more than intrigued her. Plus, Tenille lived here now and she felt a sense of community around them while visiting Maisonville.

A place where you could begin again sounded wonderful.

It was hard not to fall for New Orleans or Maisonville and the idea of finishing her doctorate degree and the possibilities of a new relationship was exciting.

But didn't things always feel that way in the beginning? Patrick was caring and thoughtful, but he also needed his own space. She understood that even more when he took her to his house on the lake. He'd lived alone for a long time, and she wasn't sure if there was room in his life for her or anything new.

Nalani turned over as the thoughts of staying ran through her head. What was she going to do?

Chapter Twenty-Three

Waking up in bed shouldn't be that difficult since Nalani had done it for most of her life. But it didn't feel right anymore. She grumbled as she sat up in bed and it took her a few minutes to stop focusing on the pain.

She'd always led an active life and didn't want to slow down. Her body protested this morning in a way that let her know she'd overdone it the day before. Her arm ached and her ribs throbbed as she tried to move.

As she put weight on her foot, she smiled that at least something on her body felt like it was healing. She lifted it up and moved it around. "Finally!" she said and headed to the kitchen.

Patrick was gone, of course, but he'd left her some coffee and a mug beside the coffee maker. But this time he hadn't left a note and it bothered her.

By all accounts, it was considerate that he'd made her coffee, but she had a weird feeling. She doubted her place there. After spending hours trying to fall asleep last night, she'd thought about life in New Orleans with Patrick, a career, Tenille, and new friends.

She'd already told Patrick that she couldn't stay, and they hadn't discussed being together outside of this time. He was certainly used to his own schedule. She wasn't even sure he wanted more.

Looking at her reflection in the microwave before she heated her coffee, self-doubt threatened to swallow her as she tried to smooth her tangled long hair.

It was something she'd never experienced until the assault in graduate school. She'd gone back to her apartment and curled up under the covers in her bed unable to stop shaking.

In fact, it wasn't until she quit school and moved home that the internal shaking finally eased. Being around her family had calmed her in a way she didn't think anything or anyone else could.

The saying, hindsight is 20-20 meant more to her now than ever before. It was just so clear what Dr. Robert Lemay's intentions were from the moment she entered his classroom and advisee study group. He'd handpicked the group, handpicked her. It made her angrier now.

It was her first assignment for his class. He'd handed the papers back making sure others saw that she'd failed the assignment and her paper was covered in red ink. He stared at her as he said, "Sometimes attractive people are given a better grade than they deserve, but that is not how I handle my class or students."

Then he told the small group that just because they had made it that far with their education didn't guarantee they would make it to the end of the doctorate program.

No one said a word as he ranted for twenty minutes, and she left the classroom stunned. Once she got back to her apartment, she reread her paper trying to see what she could have done differently.

She spent hours rewriting it and emailed it to him at three in the morning. He never acknowledged her effort and certainly didn't respond. It took her a month before she found the nerve to ask him if he saw it.

That was just the beginning of his degrading behavior toward her. Things never got better.

She quit at the end of the semester and moved home where she finally felt like she belonged. Her family threw a big dinner party like she'd graduated from the program instead of quitting.

They were honestly thrilled she was back home for good, and no one questioned her why. Not really. Things just felt like they were the way they were supposed to be, according to her parents.

Nalani lived at home, worked for her dad at the family restaurant and never looked back until she saw Peter hit Tenille that night in the parking lot. Suddenly, she was compelled to help another woman escape abuse. They became instant friends and lived together for ten months before Tenille had to leave. It wasn't until her friend was gone that she could accept that she'd also been a victim.

But it was too late, and she couldn't admit what had happened to her to anyone. She was ashamed. It wasn't because of how things escalated, she could reason with her own emotions because that wasn't her fault. No, the shame was over the way she handled it. She'd always been so strong. Her own mother called her a wolf.

There was no way to confess that when it counted, she didn't fight back. She wasn't the wolf anymore but instead a scared rabbit. When they threw her the welcome home party, she went to her bedroom and cried. No one knew she longed for her fierce heart.

Then she packed it all away until Tenille came into her life. Once Tenille left town, Nalani suddenly faced all those hidden feelings. Her father noticed first when she refused to go out with any boys her family tried to set up with her. She stopped dating all together and stayed in her apartment whenever she wasn't working.

Her mother had just noticed something was wrong when Tenille's stalker, Peter and his men swept in, burned their family business to the ground, and kidnapped Nalani. Had she been grateful for the change? Had she handled the kidnapping well because she welcomed death as opposed to living a life she hadn't wanted?

Nalani went into the bedroom to change into her clothes, forgetting her coffee in the microwave as she pushed thoughts of her life in California away. Robert Lemay was the head of the History Doctorate Program and beyond reproach. He had all the power. She hadn't any other choice but to leave like she did and that was that. No reason to beat herself up over the past. She refused to look back because she wasn't going in that direction. She was a Kahale and they dusted themselves off and kept moving forward.

As she finished brushing her hair, a task that was still taking much longer than it used to, she heard the doorbell ring and knew it was Tenille. She was there to pick Nalani up for physical therapy. She'd sent Tenille a text late last night telling her that Miss Newsome had fallen ill and wouldn't be able to take her as they originally had planned.

Tenille would have been in bed but without a doubt as soon as she saw that Nalani needed her, she was there. Their friendship was true, and they had a connection that defied time.

As she opened the front door and saw Tenille it lifted her spirits. But when Tenille saw her face, she reached out and held her hand. "What's wrong. Don't tell me that it's nothing because you and I both know better. I'm early and need some coffee. I'll go make us both a cup so you can fess up."

Nalani still wasn't ready to talk about her past. She could talk about Patrick though and Tenille would be the perfect sounding board for her current boyfriend woes.

As they settled onto the sofa, Nalani sipped her hot beverage avoiding Tenille's stare. It wasn't like her holding back. "Tell me what's going on."

Nalani looked at her sweet friend and shrugged. It was her thing, and she couldn't stop doing it. "I've just put myself in an impossible situation here and I don't know what to do."

"You mean with the chief?"

"You've seen him. He's wonderful. I really like him, but--"

"He doesn't live in Hawaii and your family won't understand if you want to stay here?"

Nalani stared at Tenille. When had she gotten so observant? "Something like that."

The time they had spent together in Hawaii had been stressful for Tenille. Always looking over her shoulder and worried that she would bring danger to the precious Kahale Family that had helped save her. Nalani had always been like a big sister to Tenille, strong and independent. This was a different side to her. "Sweet friend, what's the rush? You're still not in any position to travel home and the restaurant isn't finished yet. Have you even talked to the chief about it? I mean you are living with him here and from the looks of it, things seem comfortable."

"Do they? I'm not so sure. He's so busy and I am getting better. It's been interesting but how could I possibly fit in around here?"

"It's been my experience that everyone fits in here. You haven't gotten out much but New Orleans has a little something for everyone. And you already know how I feel about Maisonville. It's the perfect little place to go and recharge your energy, creatively or romantically. You just need a little more time."

Nalani drank the rest of her coffee as Tenille talked more about the little town that had become her home. "I love our place in the French Quarter, but Michael has become really good friends with Ryan Gentry. He's Sydney's husband. He remodels homes and she is the designer. Anyway, Michael is interested in a new project and Ryan has a couple of houses that he wants to show us."

Nalani had only heard about the amazing home Michael, who everyone else called Reaper, had spent years remodeling. Jensen and Noa both stayed in his guest houses and couldn't stop talking about how incredible the main house was and historic. She already liked the New Orleans architecture and looked forward to hearing the history of their property.

"You two are going to move to Maisonville permanently?" That would mean that Tenille would be a solid forty-five minutes away, if Nalani stayed, and they wouldn't see each other as often.

Tenille smiled. "I still try to help out at Miss Lynn's restaurant, but my hours have fallen way below part time and I also help Mrs. Goings with the boarding house. But Michael works mostly in the city. I think we both envision living in both places. Plus, it's easy going back and forth once you get used to it. It's sort of like going from Lahaina to Wailea."

It didn't feel that close when they traveled across the twenty-four-mile bridge to Maisonville but Nalani didn't know her way around yet. Would it ever really matter? What would she do if she moved here permanently? She had responsibilities at home.

The half grin on her lips was telling. Nalani was making every excuse to leave when in her heart she didn't want to go back to living with her parents or working as a waitress at her family's restaurant.

"I think it's time to go," Tenille said.

Nalani nodded and then realized Tenille was talking about for her physical therapy appointment. She wasn't looking forward to that either. But at least when they returned, Miss Newsome should be home and she always kept Nalani entertained.

But first, she needed to meet up with the sadist, which is what she and Tenille called the physical therapist who'd flirted with her behind his back.

The parking lot was packed when they arrived, and it took fifteen minutes to find a parking spot. Tenille had insisted on dropping Nalani off at the front door, but she refused. That was the friend she'd grown to love in Hawaii. Determined and bold.

They sat in the outer room after signing in and the physical therapist came running over to apologize for making them wait but he had a new patient that day and her doctor wanted to go over some of her needs.

Tenille teased her friend. "He has no idea that he is flirting with the chief of police's girl and that if he keeps it up then he is headed for a lifetime of parking tickets and constant surveillance."

Nalani laughed and then wondered if Patrick thought of

her as his girl? That was when she heard someone thank Dr. Bixby and Nalani almost gave herself whiplash as her head swiveled around to get a look at the doctor.

Dr. Bixby was tall and gray haired. He certainly was older, but he looked more like he was in his sixties instead of his seventies. If Miss Newsome was seventy, then he had to be seventy-five.

As another physical therapist walked Dr. Bixby out, Nalani impulsively stood and called his name, "Hirsch?"

Chapter Twenty-Four

Everyone in the outer waiting room watched as Nalani called the doctor by his first name. He turned and smiled warmly at her as she quickly looked down at his ring finger which was bare.

Perhaps he didn't wear a wedding ring at work?

"I'm sorry, do I know you?" Hirsch Bixby replied. He had a strong voice.

Nalani gave him her best smile, knowing her dimples usually disarmed people. She couldn't help it, but she had to interfere. "No, sir, but I think my neighbor used to be a close friend of yours. In fact, she was just talking about you the other day."

He nodded as if he understood and everyone in the room seemed interested in their conversation, waiting to hear more.

"Do you remember Miss Alba Newsome?"

The genteel doctor's eyes watered. "Alba? She's your neighbor?"

"Nalani? You ready?" The physical therapist seemed overwhelmed with his schedule and rudely interrupted her conversation which clearly was important. She held up her finger telling him to wait a minute.

"She sure is and she looks fantastic. Well, except she had a little thing with her pacemaker, and we had to call an ambulance last night but she'll be home this afternoon."

Hirsch Bixby held a large worn hand to his heart. He hated to hear that Alba wasn't well. She'd broken his heart so many years ago and then he'd married a sweet woman and had two sons. The marriage was convenient, but it wasn't really love. She'd left him for someone else, but they'd remained friends and raised the boys together. He'd spent the rest of his life living for them and his patients. Hearing Alba's name did something for him though.

The physical therapist was getting antsy, and Nalani had to think quick which was still hard for her, post-concussion. "What are you doing for dinner, Dr. Bixby? Want to come over and have it with us? I can promise you, she'll be there."

She asked Tenille to give him her address and phone number and then went back for her torture session.

It was after four when Tenille dropped Nalani and her groceries off at the house. She asked her repeatedly if she needed any help especially since she clearly had been put through the ringer by her physical therapist lover boy. But Nalani told her that she would be fine. Once she hugged her friend good-bye, she prayed that she could pull the dinner party off.

She slowly washed all the vegetables for the salad and then marinated the chicken in pineapple and teriyaki sauce. She put off making the rice until she got ready to cook the chicken but decided to go ahead and slice the fresh pineapple. It was still too early for fresh pineapple stateside, so she wondered where it had been grown. It didn't smell or taste as good as the ones at home but it would have to do with the instant dinner party she was throwing.

Nalani was getting excited and a little nervous.

Patrick didn't answer his phone so she sent him a message regarding their dinner plans and hoped he would be home in time to start at seven. Next, she needed to check on Miss Newsome and make sure she came over for dinner.

At six-thirty, Nalani slipped into the long casual red dress that Tenille had picked out for her. It was one of the only nice things she had that would fit over her arm cast and allow her to move freely with the brace on her leg.

She was aching even more than earlier and needed to finish everything before Miss Newsome or Dr. Bixby showed up. There still wasn't any word from Patrick and it upset her to think that he would miss the first meal she cooked and the sweet reunion.

Setting the table had taken her three times longer than it should have but she thankfully had everything ready with the food in the oven to keep it warm ten minutes before seven.

Just as she sat down on the sofa, the doorbell rang and she slowly managed to stand to answer it. Hirsch stood there in slacks and a sweater. In his hand were a bouquet of flowers he handed to Nalani and another of roses that he had for Miss Newsome.

"I'm afraid you are the first one here, Dr. Bixby. Can I get you a drink?"

They settled on iced tea and sat down on the sofa together. Nalani made small talk which wasn't hard with the sweet older man, but she kept glancing at the clock on the wall and hoping that the two of them wouldn't have to eat alone.

Finally, about ten minutes after seven, Miss Newsome knocked on the door. When she stepped inside and saw Hirsch

Bixby for the first time in twenty plus years, she thought her heart had stopped.

Nalani reached for her, but Miss Newsome stepped toward Dr. Bixby. Neither of them spoke but went to each other and hugged for the longest time. Nalani teared up seeing them both so happy and then wished she only had dessert. The two of them clearly needed some time alone and having them wait because she prepared dinner seemed wrong.

They went through the motions as Nalani led them into the dining room and poured drinks. She heard them whispering to one another and laughing quietly as Nalani went back into the kitchen. She quickly checked her phone and still there was no word from Patrick.

She could see Hirsch and Alba from the kitchen. They held hands as they sat close to one another. When they leaned in and shared a kiss, it was the single sweetest moment Nalani had witnessed in a long time.

It was clear Patrick wasn't going to make it for dinner or even call her back. She was happy and overwhelmed with the outcome of her matchmaking. As the sweet couple whispered more and seemed to not notice that Nalani was still out of the room, she paced back and forth in the kitchen. What could she do? Miss Newsome and Dr. Bixby would stay for dinner to be kind, but Patrick wasn't going to show. It would feel off if she made them stay and honestly, she was ready to drop from exhaustion.

The physical therapy alone was too much but she'd gone to the grocery store, cleaned up the house a bit and cooked a big dinner. The thought of serving it and then having to clean up would possibly make her cry.

She walked back into the dining room but it took a minute for the older couple to look up at her. It was easy to see what she needed to do. "I'm afraid that Patrick can't make it tonight and I overestimated my ability to host a dinner party with my injuries. Would you two mind taking a raincheck and this dinner over to Miss Newsome's house so I can go soak in the bathtub?"

Holding two plates full of food already wrapped in tinfoil along with half the cake she'd baked covered in a homemade whipped topping and fresh pineapple, Nalani knew they'd agree.

"Sure, my baby. I'm sorry you aren't feeling well. Do you need me to stay and help you?" Miss Newsome was always taking care of others.

"Don't be silly. You two take this food. I hope you enjoy it."

Miss Newsome hugged her and then Dr. Bixby hugged her too before they made there way to the front door. Nalani moved slower but she managed to get to the door before they closed it, wished them a goodnight, and then locked up.

The kitchen would have to wait as she peeled off her clothes and climbed into a steaming hot bath. She didn't take time to wrap her arm cast so she would just have to be careful not to get it wet.

She swiped at the stray tears that fell down her cheeks and wasn't sure if she was upset over her aching body, the fact that she hadn't heard from Patrick, or over the simple fact that she couldn't cook a simple dinner and have guests over without falling apart.

Closing her eyes, she took a deep breath and then heard her phone ringing in the other room. She couldn't get out of the tub fast enough to reach it before it stopped ringing and honestly, if that made Patrick mad then so be it. She wouldn't get out of that tub until the water turned cold.

Thirty minutes later she climbed into bed with a towel

wrapped around her body and her hair still up in a clip. She would just lay there a few minutes and then go clean the kitchen.

Six hours later, she woke up naked under the covers. Had she turned the lights off? She got out of bed and saw all of her dirty clothes in a pile beside the dresser. It was two in the morning. Had Patrick come home?

She made her way into the living room and saw him asleep on the sofa with the television still playing in the background. He'd eaten dinner because his empty plate was still on the coffee table.

When she walked into the kitchen, it was spotless. She peered into the dining room, and it also had been cleared. He'd worked more than sixteen hours and still came in and cleaned up her giant mess.

Things felt off between them, but she missed being close to him. She carefully slid in beside him and wrapped her arms around his middle. It was incredible how warm his body always felt even though it was winter.

It didn't take long, and she drifted back to sleep. Being next to him felt right but they would have to talk in the morning. Unfortunately, as the sun peered through the living room and right into her face, Nalani woke up alone in the house again.

Was he trying to give her a hint?

Chapter Twenty-Five

Patrick didn't want to leave before Nalani woke up again, but he couldn't help his crazy work schedule. Carnival season was early this year, and he had no control over the way the calendar fell.

He knew that Maui was a destination all year long but for most of the country, January and February were the slowest months for tourism. That wasn't the case for New Orleans. Especially when carnival season arrived on January 6th. It was mostly locals that participated in the weeklong celebrations of twelfth night but this year Fat Tuesday was on February 13th which meant the heavier crowds, a million plus people, would come into town by the last week of January.

There were plans that had to be organized, reorganized, and then finalized so that the events could happen. Most people had no idea that the local police department worked around the clock during carnival and joined forces with additional law enforcement to keep things peaceful.

He should have talked to Nalani about it sooner, but she

had a lot to deal with regarding her health and he didn't want to stress her out even more.

This morning when he got into the office there were more shifts that needed to be rearranged and expenses he needed to sign off on and he didn't have time to worry about his love life.

By eight, the office was alive, but he'd kept his head down and focused on the tasks at hand until he heard Mayor Regalia clear his throat.

Alexavier Regalia was in his last term as mayor, but he refused to slow down. He would end his eight-year reign as the beloved city mayor by working just as hard on those last days as he did the first.

He was carrying two cups of coffee and Patrick laughed when he saw Alexavier standing in his doorway. "You better watch out, the paparazzi could be anywhere."

Mayor Regalia laughed. During his first campaign for mayor someone set up an Instagram page called Regalia and His Coffee. He became famous for it and there were thousands of pictures of him drinking coffee in various places around New Orleans. There were also thousands of followers, and the pictures sometimes made the evening news. A "Where's Mayor Regalia" tagline was added at some point and had become locally popular as a New Orleans-esque *Where's Waldo.*

Patrick taunted him about it regularly especially since he was in many of those pictures too.

Alexavier handed his friend, the chief, a hot cup of Joe and then had a seat. "Things look good for carnival this year?" he asked but Patrick had a suspicion that was not why the mayor stopped in to see him.

"As usual. We have it running like a well-oiled machine these days. Hard work plus determination equals success," Patrick said as he set down his papers and picked up the coffee.

"I heard you still have company."

Patrick drank more coffee and looked at his friend the mayor, but he didn't respond.

"A beautiful woman from Hawaii, I hear?"

There was no getting out of this conversation, but Patrick was not looking forward to it. He should have realized that Alexavier would be around to pry because the man lived to know everything that was going on with everyone.

"Yes. Nalani Kahale is from Maui. You remember, friends with Reaper's girl. The one who was dumped out of the SUV. You sent a helicopter to help me get her to the hospital here."

Patrick knew good and well that Alexavier knew exactly who was at his house, but the man was going to sit there and pretend like he didn't remember just so Patrick would have to talk about it.

Smiling slyly, Alexavier drank his coffee before finally nodding that he understood. "Refresh my memory. Have you ever gotten personally involved with a victim of a crime here or anywhere?"

"You know good and well that I haven't."

"In fact, you don't date women exclusively or what-- more than two or three times before you move on. It's sort of your rule, right?"

"I have a ton of work to do Regalia. Is there a question in there?"

Alexavier laughed at his friend. He could tell he was getting hot over the questions, and he didn't really want to make him angry. He just wanted to see him happy. Happy like he was with Olivia Dufrene.

"Not really a question but more a bit of advice, old friend. Neither of us are getting any younger. This city and carnival season does run on a dime, thanks to you and all your hard work. You've got the right people in all the right places but what you don't have is someone in your life. Being alone is no way to live and when you leave this earth, my friend, you are not going to say *I wish I had one more day at my job.*"

"How the hell do you know what I'm going to say on my deathbed?"

Alexavier threw his empty cup into the garbage can by Patrick's desk and walked to the door before he answered. The man was the king of suspenseful pauses. "Because I've lost enough people in my life to know that everyone, and I do mean everyone, asked for more time with their family. And it's not too late for you to get one of those for yourself."

The mayor turned to walk out of Patrick's office but then turned around and added, "My kids are going to need some good kids to play with and I'm counting on you to make sure that happens."

Patrick shrugged. Alexavier and Olivia weren't married or expecting children yet. And Patrick had zero intentions of having any. His childhood had been a nightmare and he wouldn't help bring any rugrats into the world. He'd sworn off dating, marriage, kids and the whole thing.

He watched Regalia walk down the hallway and shake a few hands before he was out of sight. The man was a natural born politician. Always kissing babies and shaking hands. What the hell did Alexavier know about Patrick's real life or Nalani Kahale?

They'd had a connection from the start but that didn't mean anything. It couldn't undo what Patrick had lived through as a kid or young man. He wasn't the marrying or family type. He never had been because he'd never had one.

Nalani admitted she didn't like living in Maui and had worked toward a different life, but it didn't work out. She felt responsible for the time she'd spent trying something else and now owed it to her family to fall in line and work at the restaurant. She would live there just like everyone else in her family. Her own brothers made it clear that she would be going home and planned to come and fetch her again once she was well enough to travel.

No, his friend the mayor had no idea what Patrick and Nalani were up against and there wouldn't be a love story between them. Just a few nice memories and a few weeks of getting to know one another. It would have to be enough.

Patrick threw the rest of his coffee into the garbage. He couldn't concentrate on his paperwork now and closed his office door so he could have peace and think. Nalani was probably awake now and getting her own coffee. She looked completely exhausted lying in his bed with the towel partially wrapped around her. Her hair was still wet, and she was curled up in a ball when he covered her up with the comforter on his bed last night.

He couldn't believe how great the food was that she'd cooked, and it didn't look like she'd even eaten any of it. Of course, he had all those messages from her last night that he'd missed because he'd turned his phone off while in a meeting and forgot to turn it back on.

So, his girl had found Miss Newsome's long lost love and then sent them off to eat the amazing chicken dinner she'd prepared. He ate two helpings of chicken and a large piece of the cake with Pineapple. He didn't even know she could cook.

He smiled. She was full of surprises and deserved more than him hiding out at the office pretending to work when things were truly organized for the upcoming events. If he were honest with himself, he was starting to get too close to her and having her at his house and in his bed was making him nervous.

He was already getting used to it. He was getting used to her and that only had one type of ending. Heart ache for them both.

But she'd been so sweet curled up next to him on the sofa that morning and again he wondered how exhausted she must have been since she didn't wake up after he kissed her forehead. She simply snuggled in closer to him and he wanted to hold her tight. Maybe hold her forever.

Patrick scrubbed his hand down his face and then over his shaved jaw. This was complicated and all because he'd inserted himself where he didn't belong. But now he was involved, and would it be wrong for him to spend a little extra time with her?

Didn't she deserve to know how wonderful the dinner was last night and have him take her to physical therapy for once? He would do better by her even if they only had a limited amount of time left together.

They could have a great love affair and then end things amicably. She felt like she was needed at home in Hawaii, and he lived and worked here in NOLA. One more week and she'd probably be gone.

He didn't second guess himself again, he simply grabbed his wallet, keys, and phone and headed out the door. "Call me if anyone needs me," he said to anyone who was listening and then headed home as fast as he could get there.

Chapter Twenty-Six

Patrick walked in the front door and straight to Nalani who was walking slowly into the living room with a cup of hot coffee. It hit him in the gut that he'd left her alone so much. She was surprised to see him, and he understood it because he'd clearly set an expectation not to count on him.

He took her coffee cup so he could set it down on a side table. Then he wrapped his arms around her and kissed her like he meant it. His hands were wrapped in her hair, and he held her so close they felt like they were breathing the same air.

When they parted, she smiled at him and whispered, "Good morning."

He scooped her up and carried her over to the sofa and she reminded him that she could walk and that her physical therapist wanted her to do a lot more of it so she would get back her mobility.

"Is this the same PT that flirts with you regularly?"

Nalani rolled her eyes while Patrick grabbed her coffee cup and handed it over to her. Then he kissed her forehead and asked her, "Is it?"

"I am not going to answer that."

Patrick smirked as he sat down next to her. She looked at him strangely and then shook her head. "What are you doing home?"

"I live here."

She shook her head again. "Okay but that still doesn't explain what you are doing here when I know you have to work."

"I don't have to work. Work is handled."

"But I didn't even see you last night. I have hardly seen you in days."

"About last night--"

She reached out and held his hand. "I need to apologize for blowing up your phone. I knew you were busy, and I had a bit of an attitude when you didn't answer. It wasn't your fault that I came up with a scheme to reunite Miss Newsome with her lost love for dinner at our house. It was impulsive and I'm never impulsive. Then you got in after a very long day at work and had to clean up that huge mess. I'm sorry."

"Look at you apologize."

She bumped her shoulder into his. "I told you that I was going to try and be better."

"You are perfect the way you are, and you have no reason to apologize to me for last night or anything. I was upset when you didn't answer your phone the other day and then I went and turned the sound off of mine during a meeting and didn't hear any of your messages in time for dinner. When I got home, you'd already fallen asleep. I ate most of the dinner you made. It was amazing. You're a great cook, sunshine."

He hadn't called her sunshine in days, and she wasn't sure why it made her emotional but it did. What was this man doing to her? She laid her head on his shoulder and sighed. It was comforting to just have him near.

Patrick wrapped his arm around her. "I didn't know Miss Newsome was missing an old boyfriend."

"She confided in me a few days ago and when I went to physical therapy yesterday, Dr. Bixby was there. It was strange because he told us last night that he was semi-retired. It had to be fate since we both ended up at the same place at the exact same time and I had to act fast."

Nalani couldn't forget how Alba and Hirsch looked at each other last night or how they held hands.

"I guess they were happy to see each other then?"

"They couldn't get out of here fast enough."

Patrick knew Miss Newsome didn't have a family, but he had never asked her why. He didn't have anyone either and she'd made him feel normal for wanting to remain single. They'd become good friends and although he usually worked holidays so those with spouses and kids could take off, he would eat holiday meals with her. She seemed happy. Perhaps he was the only one that didn't have someone.

"You, okay?" Nalani asked when Patrick got that far-off look in his eyes.

"Always," he replied because at that moment he did have someone who wanted to be there with him, and he wanted to make her happy.

Nalani nodded to his response, but she knew he wasn't being honest because no one was always okay. Some people were happier than others but words she would use to describe Patrick would be dutiful, hardworking, considerate not jovial, happy, or even content.

He never talked about himself or opened up to her and they'd had quite a few heart-to-heart discussions about life, her family, their careers, and education. But she couldn't say she really knew him.

Trying to change the subject, even the one inside her head, he kissed her and then asked how she was feeling.

"I'm good," she said, not admitting that she was still sore from physical therapy and understood now why they gave her off every other day.

"I was thinking since you love history that we could go on a little history tour of New Orleans together?"

That sounded amazing to her. "But I'm afraid I can't walk for a long time without breaks."

"I was thinking we could mostly make it a car tour. Buy some snacks and drive around to show you different areas and things. Did you know that New Orleans has more historic districts than any other city in the United States?"

"No, I didn't know that." Was he really going to take off the entire day and drive her around the city? "Are you sure you can take off all day like this?"

"Stop worrying about me, sunshine."

"I would love to hang out with you all day and do a driving tour of historic New Orleans. But you have to answer a question first."

"Okay."

"Does anyone else worry about you?"

Standing up and holding his hand out for Nalani to help her to her feet, Patrick grinned at her as she waited for an answer.

"I've told you that I don't have a big family like yours. I don't really have any family at all. Never had one and probably never will."

That response made Nalani instantly sad, but she didn't unpack those emotions in front of Patrick. He was so matter of fact when he said it. She needed time to process the words. How could he be alone his entire life?

Those words hung between them as they climbed into his SUV to go on their historic tour adventure. "First, you haven't had much coffee and since we are going to start this tour uptown, I want to take you to District Donuts."

"It's historical?"

"No, it actually opened the year I moved here. Everything is fresh, including the sprinkles they put on the donuts. It's just a great place to grab some food and I loved it when I was a beat cop uptown."

Nalani suddenly realized they were going on a Patrick Morales New Orleans tour, and she was even more excited because she might finally get to know more about him.

One maple bacon donut, a brown butter drop, and two coffees later, they were on their way through uptown New Orleans. "There are 21 historic districts, but we are going to start with The Garden District which is number one on my top five list."

"You have a top five list?" Nalani found that funny. It wasn't funny as in humorous but funny interesting since Patrick was so reserved. Admitting that he liked something enough to put it on a top five list made her smile.

"I definitely have a list," he replied and then reached over to hold her hand. "You love history, and I can promise you that these areas will transport you back in time."

Patrick Morales was quiet and a bit stingy with his thoughts, but he certainly paid close attention whenever she spoke. It was one of the sweetest things to Nalani. She pulled his hand up to her lips and kissed it which caught him completely by surprise as he tapped his brakes and then quickly looked up to make sure someone wasn't going to rear-end his SUV.

She watched as he put his conservative face back on and she rested their hands together in her lap. "Which of these is your favorite?" she asked as he drove them slowly around the neighborhood.

"I like a lot of them. I spent my first two years in the police force working in this area. Got invited to a lot of parties too. These folks welcome everyone into their homes. There were times I went to a party with so many people that I never did see the owners."

"You're a party guy?"

Patrick laughed at her comment. "Hardly. That was back almost ten years ago, and I mostly went to parties and events to get to know everyone from the area. It's the best way to earn their trust."

Nalani nodded and then pointed to a great big home that looked to be three stories. It was beautiful. "What's the craziest thing you saw while you worked in this area?"

Patrick's eyes got bigger. "There is a house in this neighborhood that looks like something out of that show Hoarders. Seriously, we had a wellness check and when we got there, we couldn't find the homeowner because there was barely a trail through the inside of the house. Turned out, he also didn't have any hot water. From the outside, it looked great, but we had to take him out of there for health reasons. Someone in his family then came and cleaned things up."

"Wow. Just goes to show that you can't judge a book by its cover."

"Sunshine, you have no idea."

Nalani held his hand a little tighter as they continued to drive around and see as much as possible.

"Where did you go after The Garden District Detail was over? Is that what you call it?"

"I worked with some old school cops, and they called it my beat." He seemed to think that was funny for some reason, but Nalani just waited for him to answer.

"We'll have to backtrack a little because the next historic district is closer to my house in Mid-City. You see, The Garden District is a bit quieter and once my superiors figured I was going to stay and that I wasn't squeamish, they sent me to work in Tremé which is our next stop on the tour."

"Never heard of it," Nalani admitted.

"It is full of history and most of the older residents can recite it to you like they're reading it out of a book."

Nalani couldn't wait to see the area but also to research everything on her computer when she got the chance. Traffic had picked up and it took them twice as long to get there than expected. But Patrick began telling her about the history along the way. "St. Augustine Catholic Church is the oldest African American Church in New Orleans and the oldest African American Catholic Parish is in Tremé."

They drove through old neighborhoods and the homes were smaller than The Garden District, but they had tons of charm. Clearly built during another era, Nalani pulled out her phone and struggled to take a few pictures. Patrick helped her get a few homes that she was sure were hundreds of years old. It was fascinating to her, and Patrick stopped talking so she could take it all in.

"I guess it's too soon to eat lunch?" he asked and then grinned because he wasn't hungry yet either. "The reason I ask is because Dookie Chase's restaurant is amazing and world famous for her fried chicken and creole food."

Agreeing that it was too soon, Nalani still took pictures of the restaurant before he took her off in another direction. It was obvious that he was fond of the Tremé District.

"How long did you work this beat?"

Grinning, Patrick pointed out a convenience store on the corner. "I used to stop in there almost every night for coffee. It wasn't great but the owner usually worked the night shift, and he always had the best cop jokes."

He turned down a neighborhood street and seemed to be reminiscing. "This area still had some gang violence back then. I was here for three years, and it was clear that most of the problems came from outsiders coming in and starting trouble. It was hard to make the rest of the city understand that it wasn't the residents of Tremé but the old police chief grew up here and he understood it. He assigned more police coverage and it helped."

Pointing to a playground with a basketball court, he smiled again like he was remembering something. "Just like in The Garden District, I needed to get to know the people in the area. I would play ball here whenever I got off and you wouldn't believe the people that came out to watch us. At first, it was just a pickup game with about eight of us, four on four. But word got out and more cops joined in, and more men wanted to play. Eventually, we had wives, girlfriends, parents, kids, and some grandparents bringing lawn chairs out to watch us."

"I'm sensing a pattern here." Nalani admired the older homes but also how clean the sidewalks and the park were. "You wanted to earn their trust?"

"To be honest, I felt more comfortable here than in the Garden District. This was more like my neighborhood growing up and keeping everyone safe in Tremé was a personal mission for me because I didn't feel safe as a kid."

Chapter Twenty-Seven

Patrick was absolutely in control of his universe and hearing he didn't feel safe growing up hurt Nalani's heart. She leaned across the arm rest and kissed his cheek. Patrick was tall and athletically built but until he mentioned playing basketball, she hadn't even thought about it. "Playing basketball was a way to bring them all together?"

"I just remembered how I didn't have anything growing up but I could go to a park and find other boys there with a basketball. It was fun. Kept us busy and out of trouble because we would play for hours."

It was difficult to hear how alone Patrick was as a kid, but it made sense that he was comfortable being alone as an adult. "Where were your parents?"

"I don't remember my dad. He left us when I was born. My mother had a string of boyfriends, and she drank or took whatever pills she could get her hands on. It was in my best interest to not be at home."

"Was it hard when you had to leave this area?"

Patrick's jaw tensed as he pulled out onto the main road

and thought about life as a beat cop. "I was furious and at first refused to go. I had kids that I was checking in on and quite a few that were being raised by elderly grandparents, so they needed me."

He looked over at Nalani briefly and then admitted something that he hadn't told anyone else. "My chief was right for moving me. I was getting too personally involved with some of the residents and couldn't be objective anymore. It was a tough lesson. One that changed my career."

This tour was so much more revealing than Nalani could have imagined. Patrick Morales was opening up to her for the first time. It was clear he didn't share his personal life with anyone. Had he ever been close enough to another woman or even friend to discuss his life?

"Backtracking again," he said. He was set on getting them to the next historic district on his list. The list she would discover was all the areas he worked when he was a police officer for eight years in the city.

"I've heard that you can look back on your life when your older and clearly see three maybe four pivotal moments that put you where you are," Nalani said as a statement and not a question. She didn't want to ask questions and throw off his train of thought since he was sharing so freely.

"I can see that. Guess I'm old because I can already see three or four." He winked at her and then showed her a building that said Mardi Gras World.

"This is the Warehouse District and was my third beat when I was a cop."

Nalani noticed as they continued driving that the buildings were built right up to the sidewalks and close to the road. It looked so distinctly different from the other areas they'd toured but also looked older and certainly historic.

"This area was a far cry from what I was used to in Tremé. In fact, it was downright boring. There was a lot of commercial business but also some old warehouses that were turned into residential places. Overpriced apartments or condos if you ask me but still the folks who lived here just had a different vibe. I would get a few calls for domestic disputes or some minor vandalism but mostly I just drove around handing out a ticket here or there."

Nalani watched him drive around not really connected to this area like he had been to the others. "You didn't like it here?"

He laughed. "I was petulant and didn't want to like it. Worked here for a year and it grew on me. Took yoga from that shop over there and on payday would get a great sandwich from St. James Cheese Company. There is another location in the Garden District, and it felt like comfort food. Are you hungry yet?"

Nalani shook her head. "I'm still good. We can stop if you are hungry."

Shaking his head, Patrick told her he had another place in mind for them to eat. On the way out of the warehouse district, he pointed out the World War II Museum and told her that it was his favorite in the city.

They seemed to be going back and forth across town, but she wasn't sure and didn't want to stop his progress by asking. Patrick seemed to avoid the interstate and she smiled at how well he knew the city streets. This was his home. He was the chief of police and he cared about his city.

"I only spent six months in the Marigny and Bywater District, but I really liked it." Patrick drove down some of the most narrow streets Nalani had ever seen and she held her breath whenever there was a large SUV parked on the side and he had to ease by them.

This area was old but had a cool artist vibe with brightly painted houses and buildings with artists' graffiti everywhere. She instantly loved it, but it was hard to imagine Patrick there. He had so many fascinating sides to him, and she wondered how many years it would take to really get to know him.

He parallel parked on one of the busiest narrow streets and gave Nalani a big smile. "If you aren't hungry now then you will be as soon as you smell the pizza in this place."

It was mid-afternoon now and as soon as they got out of the car, the smell of Italian spices made Nalani's stomach growl. Pizza Delicious wasn't the most original name for a pizza joint but if the line of people out the door was any indication of how good this place was then she couldn't wait.

Patrick ordered enough food for an army and when they sat at the table, he leaned in and said that the only thing better than eating here was the leftovers.

The giant pepperoni pizza was mouthwatering good, and Nalani told him it was the best pizza she'd ever eaten. Then she laughed when he offered to buy another one to take home. "We have half of this one and those garlic knots," she told him and then added that he was going to make her fat before she went home.

After that comment, Patrick got strangely quiet. Most guys didn't like to talk about women and their weight, but she strangely suspected it was the comment about going home that got him thinking. She felt the same way too, but they hadn't discussed any of it.

It was time to change the subject. "Where to next?"

"Our final destination is one of our most famous."

"The French Quarter?"

"Absolutely. It was a lot different since most of my duties involved tourists and not locals."

Nalani instantly loved the old architecture in the French Quarter area. She'd read a long time ago, in high school, how the area was designed by the governing body over it at the time.

"The early settlers of Louisiana were French but the architecture here is actually Spanish. Funny, right? Apparently, France had to pay off some war debts and surrendered New Orleans to Spain for something like forty years." Patrick looked proud to tell her that little historical fact. "Do you think you can walk a little bit? I can park closer than most, perks of being the chief, but I thought we could have dessert at Cafe du Monde?"

Nalani wanted to tell him that she would hike a mile in her leg brace to try beignets but instead she just nodded and quickly climbed down out of the SUV when he parked.

"Slow down there, hot rod. They won't run out."

As soon as the piping hot beignets were set in front of her, Nalani stuck her finger into the piles of powdered sugar. Looking around, she couldn't imagine how much they went through in a month because everyone's plates were piled high with the white stuff. Patrick handed her some napkins and then told her that it was impossible to eat them without getting powdered sugar all over your shirt, even with a napkin which made her laugh.

"And these are definitely French," he said as he took a huge bite.

There were three beignets on each of their plates and Nalani shamelessly ate all three of hers.

By the time they climbed back into his SUV, it began to rain and she had never wanted to take a nap so badly. "This has been the best day ever," she said and he agreed.

"It was certainly some of the best food I have ever eaten." She wanted to tell him that learning more about him had also made her day, but she didn't want to point it out in case he continued telling her stuff.

When they pulled into Patrick's driveway, Nalani noticed Miss Newsome and Dr. Bixby sitting on her front porch. They were deep in conversation and Nalani wondered if they had talked like that all night.

Patrick waved first and then they waved back. But it was clear they didn't want to chat. They were too busy catching up.

"I've never seen Miss Newsome look like that."

"She looks like she's happy and in love." Nalani said as she slowly navigated the steps into Patrick's house.

"Love?"

Nalani waited as Patrick stepped up beside her to unlock the front door. "Yes, love. Why not? You think she's too old to find love? Haven't you ever been in love with anyone?"

She knew instantly that she shouldn't have asked him that question. He'd flippantly told her that there wasn't anyone before her but she was pretty certain he'd been a player. He was too good looking for that not to be true.

"I have never been in love. Not sure if I can fall for someone like that." Patrick said as he put his keys and wallet into a bowl in the middle of the dining room table.

It was exactly what she needed to know and completely the opposite of what she wanted to hear.

"Me either," she lied and then went into the bedroom and shut the door a little too hard.

Chapter Twenty-Eight

"He really said that he wasn't sure he could love someone?" Tenille asked as she handed Nalani a cup of hot tea. She took Nalani to her doctor's appointment and then they went back to Tenille and Reaper's house in the French Quarter.

Reaper built them a fire in the courtyard fireplace he'd recently built for Tenille. He also helped carry the tea pot and cookies out there but tried not to listen to their conversation. He wrapped his arms around his girl and kissed her warmly before he left them alone to talk.

The way he looked at Tenille and the way she looked at him was a reminder to Nalani of what she didn't have. She couldn't even say if they were her relationship goals because it was overwhelmingly beautiful to see her best friend loved so completely.

It took all of Nalani's concentration to go back to talking about Patrick. "We had an incredible day together. He showed me his favorite areas of the city, told me the history, and for the first time shared some of his past. He doesn't talk about himself and hasn't let me into his life, not really. I suddenly realized that he'd been trying to send me that message all day with little glimpses into his world. Then when he said that comment I knew this thing between us was temporary." Nalani didn't admit that Patrick also slept on the sofa last night. She looked down at her leg which was itchy and cold since the doctor said she could go without the brace now. She would have to continue physical therapy, but it already felt much better.

"You're going to leave, aren't you?" Tenille sat her tea cup down and reached her hand out to hold Nalani's. "I don't want you to go. Stay here with me. You could get into the doctorate program at Tulane. We would have so much fun."

"We would have fun, but my family expects me to come home. My dad still hasn't been cleared to go back to work and the restaurant opens in a couple of weeks. They need me."

"You're not fooling me. I saw you reading and studying all those history books. You still want to be a professor and teach. You don't want to be a waitress or work at your family's restaurant forever. And you aren't going to find anyone there because all the guys are scared of your brothers."

"I love my family."

"Of course, you do. I love your family. Everyone loves your family. But that doesn't mean that your life is there on the island."

"He doesn't want me, Tenille. And I'm needed at home. I'll come back for your wedding. Now tell me more about the history of this house and property. You said that Reaper used historical salvage to remodel the house?"

Tenille's heart hurt to see her friend upset over Patrick Morales. They seemed perfect together, but it was hard to see the inside of a relationship. If Nalani felt that he wasn't interested in a serious loving relationship, then he hadn't shown her enough affection. Shame on him. So, she did her best to get Nalani's mind on something that she loved, history.

Reaper joined them and gave all the details of the property and the French Quarter from back in the 1700's. He truly loved restoring this place but also learning who the previous owners were. They talked for hours about the rogue blacksmith who was a womanizer. His wife took care of him, and no one ever questioned her when the blacksmith went missing. It was fifty years later when the first house was built on the property, and they found his body.

"No, the house is not haunted," Tenille added before Reaper began teasing her friend about doors closing or opening without anyone around. They laughed and talked about the rich history of the city until dark.

"Make sure this is what you really want before you go, okay?" Tenille said as she dropped Nalani off at Patrick's house.

Miss Newsome and Dr. Bixby were heading out to dinner, and she waved to them as they pulled out of the driveway next door. Patrick surprised her by being home already and she double checked her phone to verify that he hadn't tried to call or send her a text.

He hadn't.

She turned around on the porch to wave to Tenille so she would go ahead and drive off. For some reason she didn't want to enter the house with her watching. Truthfully, she dreaded going inside and facing Patrick. Honestly, they didn't need to talk about anything. He was ready to move on and so she would go home. It was time.

She needed to call her brother to get him to book her ticket home and tonight. Then she would say goodbye. Perhaps he didn't know how to tell her directly that he was done, or he wasn't interested. But his actions were spoken louder than any words. No need to drag things out.

When she unlocked the door, she saw him sitting on the sofa with a beer. It was mostly dark in the room, and he didn't even have the television powered on.

"Good evening," he said, and she could tell that wasn't his first beer.

"Hey," she said. "You didn't call or text me."

"I see you got your brace off today."

"Yup. Feels better. Freer."

Her phone rang and she looked down to see that it was Jensen. How did he know to call her? She excused herself and went into the bedroom so she could talk privately.

Planning to get him to book her flight for tomorrow, Nalani was not prepared to hear the news about her father. "What do you mean he's back in the hospital?"

"Dad kept complaining about shoulder pain and then his left arm went numb. We all have told him he shouldn't be at the restaurant, that we could handle setting everything up but you know him. They have him on heart monitors. The doc says his recovery will be longer than they originally thought and certainly longer than dad wants. He won't slow down unless someone makes him. You know you are the only one he ever listens to around here. Unless you are here to make sure he rests then he's going to try and manage things."

"Okay. Well, I got my leg brace off today. I still need physical therapy, but I can get that at home. Can you get me a ticket?"

Jensen paused before he asked, "Things okay with the chief?"

Her brothers had grown to like Patrick and she should have known he would ask how things were going between them. She had no intention of discussing her love life with any of her older brothers.

"The chief is fine. Just busy with work and I'm needed at home."

"We can handle things here, shorty."

"Uh-huh. That's exactly what I thought when you said dad was at the restaurant telling everyone what to do." Nalani couldn't help but act a little snarky with her older brother. It helped her ease things in her own mind.

"Text me when you make the reservations. See you tomorrow." It was time. Nalani was beginning to feel lonely here with Patrick's indifferent feelings. She was needed at home. Her father would rest if she were there because he would listen to her. If only she could make her heart understand this was the right thing to do.

Jensen cleared his throat over the awkward silence between them. "Before I forget, Nalani, someone from your college called and was looking for you. I can't find where I wrote down the name, but it was an old professor of yours needing to speak to you as soon as possible. I'll send you the information as soon as I locate the post it notes."

Nalani's heart stopped when he said it was an old professor. It couldn't be Dr. Lemay. He wouldn't dare track her down at home. Would he?

She took a deep breath and slowly let it out. "Thanks. Text me everything and Jensen, hug mom and dad for me. I'll see everyone tomorrow."

As soon as she got off the phone she flopped down on the bed and pulled a pillow over her face. This day just kept on giving.

She heard the notification from her phone and picked it up to look at the text. Professor Helene Rolland had been one of her favorite teachers. She'd worked at the college for years. It still didn't make sense that she would want to talk to Nalani after all this time, but she had always been an interesting and fair professor. Nalani decided to call Professor Rolland in the morning.

As she undressed and put on her pajamas, she had thoughts of her last days in California on her mind. She'd slowly packed her apartment but by the time she took her last final for the semester, she had everything done. Dr. Lemay had continued to text her inappropriate messages and she didn't bother to take his final. He was such a horrible human and she wouldn't give him the satisfaction of having her in class again, much less take an exam that he would no doubt give her a failing grade. Everyone acted like he was some kind of God. He was so arrogant, Nalani decided if it ever rained in Southern California, Robert Lemay would drown because his nose was stuck up so high in the air.

She shivered thinking about that horrible man. He deserved to be fired. Perhaps even brought up on charges but she hadn't been strong enough back then to be the one to do it. Nalani had felt strong and confident her whole life. Who wouldn't, coming from a family like hers? Both her parents were hard-working, amazing people and all four of her brothers were great too. Sure, they hovered over her growing up but she'd had a wonderful life and truly felt charmed with how easy things came to her.

When she'd met Dr. Lemay for the first time, she'd had a huge crush on him. He was older but polished and confident. One of the smartest history professors she'd ever met which was saying something because by the time she'd started her doctorate program, she'd studied under some of the best.

He'd blindsided her when he gave her a failing grade for her first paper in his class and as her adviser, he constantly made snide comments to her under his breath but also out loud in front of her advisee group.

She certainly didn't have a crush on him after that and when he cornered her in his office late that night, she was shocked. It was absolutely the last thing Nalani had ever expected and she stood there frozen as he exposed himself and then pushed her up against his desk running his hands up her skirt.

When she finally gained control of her senses, she ran out of there leaving everything behind except her purse and keys. She didn't stop running until she got to her car and then she cried all the way to her apartment. It was one of the most cowardly things she'd ever done and she was unsure what to do afterward. She was ashamed of putting herself in that position. It was an unspoken rule that you shouldn't go to a man's office or hotel room late at night after everyone else was gone. At least, she certainly knew better. Especially with four older brothers who would remind her that she had to look out for herself because they wouldn't be there in California.

Dr. Lemay was a respected professor and the whole time she was certain he'd hated her. It put her in a position to constantly try and earn his approval. It was so underhanded and cruel. She still felt like a fool and had never told anyone. After she'd quit school and moved home she vowed to never think of him or the situation again. She'd done a good job of keeping busy and not allowing herself to have regret. Being home and around her family reminded her how strong she truly was and managed to refuel her confidence.

It was why she was able to so quickly help Tenille. It was also why she had started thinking about going back to school somewhere else. And when she'd been kidnapped, she promised herself that if she made it out of there, she would try again.

Wasn't that what she was doing here with Patrick Morales?

She took a deep breath. She needed to go have the uncomfortable conversation they had both been putting off. As she walked into the outer room, Patrick studied her closely and she got goosebumps over what that used to mean. But tonight, instead of want in his eyes, he looked sad.

"You're leaving, aren't you?"

Chapter Twenty-Nine

Patrick Morales had her totally confused. Hadn't he already left her?

The courageous police chief had rushed down that steep hill and pulled her out of the ravine before anyone else. He held her hand in the helicopter and stayed with her at the hospital every minute to reassure her that everything was going to be alright. Once her family got there, he still watched over her. And when she couldn't find the words to tell them she wasn't well enough to travel, Patrick stepped up and insisted she could stay at his home where he had the retired nurse next door on standby to help.

Now as she looked at him, sitting there as distant as any stranger, her heart felt heavy, and her eyes burned. She was a grown woman but still it felt like losing her first love and she figured that was because it had been the real thing for her.

"My father is in the hospital again. He's stubborn and won't listen to anyone except for me. My mother gets flustered, and I need to make sure she's taken care of too." She managed to speak without getting emotional. The Kahale's were made of strong stock.

Patrick had been locked onto her stare but now looked down at his empty beer bottle on the table. "I'm sorry to hear about your father."

That was all he had to say? This wasn't about her family, and he knew it. Didn't he? Still, she avoided talking about their relationship or the end of it. "My brother is booking my flight and will text me the information."

Still avoiding looking at her, Patrick stood and walked back into the kitchen for another beer. He came back with two and offered her one, but she declined. He opened one of the bottles and took a long drink from it.

"Are you okay?" Nalani thought that maybe something happened at work.

"Great," he said and continued drinking. When he finished the bottle of beer, he opened the next one, drinking it slower.

Great, that was his standard answer. He was all surface and no depth.

"Well, I guess I'm going to bed. I'm tired and need to pack in the morning." Nalani stood with zero pain; she was walking better than before. None of this mattered. Things had changed and she couldn't do anything about it. She just couldn't get out of there fast enough.

Walking into the bedroom, Nalani was hurt, not angry and shut the door quietly. No need to get fired up anymore. He was done. As she laid down, she pulled his pillow over to her and held it tightly.

In the outer room, Patrick sat on the sofa for two more hours finishing the last of his alcohol. He couldn't remember the last time he'd drank five bottles of beer. It barely took the edge off and he grew angrier as the night dragged on. He didn't want Nalani to leave but he knew she couldn't stay. Better to let her go now before it gets harder. He wasn't good for her.

He'd made some hard choices about his life years ago. Now he was pushing forty. She was too young for him. She would eventually want marriage and children and it would hurt her when he told her he wasn't interested in either.

Her family was such a big part of her life and he had no one. He hadn't seen or heard from his mother, Sheila, in ten or more years. He wasn't even sure if she was still alive. It was surprising she'd even made it to sixty without drinking herself to death or worse.

Patrick wouldn't have seen her back then except that he had to drive through his hometown on his way to Arkansas. Sheila's trailer was on the main drag of the little town. Arcadia, Louisiana was known because in 1934 Bonnie and Clyde's bodies had been towed to the town in their car after they'd been ambushed by the Bienville Parish Police.

His mother somehow misunderstood they were horrible people and instead idolized them, especially Bonnie Parker. Sheila was a slight woman too with blue eyes and strawberry blond hair like the infamous woman. Smoking cigars and acting like she was tough, she always drew a rough crowd.

Patrick was her only child and she resented him. She would say he ruined her life and blamed him being born for causing her husband to leave her. She would lock Patrick outside when she had men over, sometimes until after midnight. It was that behavior that brought the police around.

Sheila Morales would say Patrick ran off but after a few years the police caught on to her lies. They would threaten her and say they were going to take him away if she didn't take better care of him. But Sheila never lost custody.

There were a couple of policemen that were good to

Patrick though. They'd stop by once a week and bring him something to eat or throw a ball with him. They saw him using an old soccer ball to shoot hoops and bought him a basketball.

Sheila didn't like them coming around. She would brag to Patrick that she was going to do something to those coppers if they didn't mind their own business. He couldn't remember a time when she wasn't mean. To make her point to Patrick she stuck a knife into his basketball.

That was when he started staying away from home more. He was ten at the time. He didn't know that Sheila wasn't capable of following through with her threats. He worried for the policemen who had shown him kindness and would go hiking in the woods to hide out. Eventually he found his way to the park and those police officers would sometimes stop and play basketball with him and the other boys. But more importantly, they'd stopped going to his house.

In high school, he ran around with a couple of rough teenagers. Things escalated when he was seventeen because one of the other guys started carrying a gun. Patrick was certain they would end up in jail together if he didn't get away from them.

Joining the Marines saved his life and Patrick didn't look back. He earned the money he needed for college and worked hard to become a police officer. For the first time in his life, he found where he belonged. Once the mayor appointed him as the police chief, he proudly led other officers, tirelessly they made the city a better place for all.

He never talked about his past or his childhood but around Nalani, who talked about her family and her life growing up, it was getting harder to keep those things to himself. The only thing he learned from his mother was self-preservation. It was a selfishness that he couldn't shake. Patrick Morales couldn't forget what it was like to have no one to depend on as a kid. He found it hard to trust anyone for anything real and those traits took marriage off the table for him. He had zero interest in finding a wife or having children.

Dedicating his life to helping others gave him a sense of worth. He hated it when anyone acted like he was a hero for doing his job. They had no idea what all he had to make up for and he was no hero. He was paying restitution for his bad behavior and some for Sheila's. It would take him a lifetime to do it.

Patrick took the last two empty bottles to the garbage and looked toward his bedroom where Nalani was sleeping. If there had ever been anyone he would change for, it would've been her. But he'd always known she would go back home to Hawaii.

Nalani had an entire island full of people that loved her, and he couldn't compete with that. Thinking of losing her sent him back to that dark place where he'd grown up and the only thing he could do was sit alone and drink. He didn't want her to know anything about that life or much less see him that way.

No. It was best that she goes now before it gets too complicated. This wasn't the place for sunshine. He would help her get home and then let things go back to normal. At least as normal as he would ever have in this life.

He stretched out on the sofa and thought about Nalani healing from all her injuries. She'd be well enough to surf in the ocean again. He could see her there in the waves with the sun glistening around her.

He didn't deserve her but whenever the sun was high and the sky was clear, he would think of Nalani Kahale, his sunshine.

Patrick slept hard but he dreamed of Nalani's beautiful

smile and the dimples that could make him do almost anything. In his dream, she'd walked up from the surf wearing a brown bikini and those luscious curves. He could almost touch her when he woke to noise in the kitchen.

The house was dark as pitch, and he quietly headed to the kitchen to see who had the nerve to break in to his house.

Chapter Thirty

Patrick had his gun in his hand as he crept across the room. As he filled the doorway and pointed his weapon, Nalani yelped. He'd been disoriented from sleeping on the couch again. It was five in the morning, and he'd never seen her up this early.

He quickly lowered his gun and apologized for scaring her.

"I was going to make a pot of coffee for you before I left. My brother got me an early flight this morning and I need to leave in a few minutes."

He looked at the coffee pot and then back at her. That was right. She was going home to Maui today. He wanted to grab her in his arms and keep her there. But it was too late.

"I'll drive you."

"That's okay. I've already packed, and Jensen ordered me a car."

"I'm not letting a stranger take you to the airport, Nalani."

She half smiled. He looked a mess but still Patrick Morales was the most handsome man she'd ever known. "Okay. Let me text him to cancel the car."

Twenty minutes later, Patrick carried the small bag that

Nalani's friend, Tenille, had brought over for her weeks ago. It had everything she needed but still he thought about how he could have gotten her a few more things to make her comfortable. Would it have made a difference?

They sat in silence all the way to the airport. When Patrick pulled up in the departure lane, he asked her to hold on. Nalani watched him get out of the car and go speak to the officer on duty. The man in uniform shook Patrick's hand and nodded happily.

When Patrick walked over and opened her door, he helped her out of the SUV and picked up her bag to carry it in for her. "I've got it," she said but he reached out to hold her hand.

"There aren't many perks to being the chief of police, but at least I can park here and walk you inside," he said. She saw the determination in his eyes and nodded his way.

There were so many things left unsaid between them, but she wanted to take every last second with him that she could. He walked with her to security and then he was allowed to walk to her gate.

Nalani didn't even know that was a possibility these days.

Patrick bought her a coffee for the plane ride and continued carrying her bag. The plane boarded early, and Jensen had bought her a first class ticket so she was one of the first allowed on board.

Still, Patrick held her hand and walked her to the line. She said goodbye and then he pulled her close and kissed her deeply. It was a kiss she would never forget. Especially when everyone in the waiting area clapped.

It was another one of those moments for them. At least that was how Nalani saw it.

Handing the bag over for her to carry for the first time all morning, he tipped his head at her. "Take care, sunshine," he said and then stepped back so she could hand over her boarding pass and get on the plane.

It was the single hardest thing Nalani had done in a long time and she wasn't sure she would ever get over Patrick Morales. As she took her seat in the front, she felt her phone vibrate.

Was he texting her? As she pulled out her phone, she saw it was Professor Helene Rolland. Nalani had left her a message knowing it would be a couple of hours before the professor got into her office. California was two hours behind New Orleans, but Nalani was anxious to know what she wanted with her.

Professor Rolland didn't give anything away in the text but instead, sent her availability that day and said she was desperate to talk to Nalani. Unfortunately, Nalani's flight had one stop over in Dallas, but it was short and she wouldn't have time to talk then either. She let the Professor know that it would be a solid ten hours before she could call her back.

Professor Helene Rolland sent Nalani her cell phone number and told her that she could call at any time or hour. Now Nalani was even more freaked out. If it had to do with her school records or the doctorate program then it would wait until office hours, couldn't it?

She stared at her phone and thought about how growing up, life was so uncomplicated for her. There was a lot of laughter in the Kahale family. They worked hard, even as kids, helping at the restaurant or helping around the house. It was nothing for her to go help one of her aunties or a cousin with their chores too. But they always sat around and talked after the restaurant closed or over big family meals. Of course, they had their problems or difficulties but it seemed like everything could be worked out or smoothed over by talking or talking and eating together.

Why couldn't she and Patrick talk things out? She'd promised herself to live life to the fullest when she got away from her kidnappers. But she hadn't prepared herself for falling in love. Especially with someone so far away from home.

New Orleans was an incredible place with tons of history. If she lived there, she could go back to school and finish her doctorate program. She would have followed her earlier dreams of teaching.

The small town of Maisonville had a calming vibe and she and Patrick could've spent their weekends together there. Her reading and him fishing or boating together. She would still live near water but also have the ability to carve out her own life.

She could show Patrick how wonderful it could be to end a day of hard work with sitting together around the table or an open fire pit outside and talking through the day's events. It would bring them even closer together but also with friends. Love of family and friends was everything. She could give him that. Or at least she could have given it to him if he'd given them a chance.

But perhaps she'd been wrong. He didn't feel the same way about her as she did about him. He wouldn't have shut down like he did or let her go if he'd felt the same.

Sure, he was older but she'd always gotten along well with older guys. She spent so much time with her oldest brother Keanu and their spirits matched. It was the same with Patrick and she gravitated toward the calm in his orbit.

The steward on the airplane politely interrupted Nalani's thoughts by asking her if her phone was in airplane mode and it pulled her back into the present. She put her phone away and pulled out a book to read. There was a full day of travel ahead of her and Nalani had to let go of the what ifs. Second guessing Patrick or stressing over the Professor would only make this harder and she'd made up her mind, hadn't she? She was on a plane headed home, so that was enough. At least for now because her parents needed her.

Still her mind kept drifting back to Patrick and New Orleans.

Back at the office, Patrick was irritable, and no one could seem to do anything right. At one point, he said, "If I want something done right then I have to do it myself."

Everyone stared at him as he went into his office and closed the door a bit harder than ever before. No one had ever seen the chief lose his temper. He was cool as a cucumber and straight as an arrow, no wavering in his behavior ever.

It wasn't until Mayor Regalia stopped in that anyone bothered to disturb him. "What's up, chief?"

"Paperwork, as usual," Patrick said as he finished signing another form and sat it and his pen down on his desk. "What can I do for you, Mayor Regalia?"

Alexavier had a seat in front of Patrick. "Just came over to get a good look at you."

"What the hell are you talking about?"

Alexavier Regalia was an amazing mayor and part of that was his ability to be everywhere and to know everything that went on in the city of New Orleans. It was a strange gift but got Patrick's attention on more than one occasion. "Are you going to tell me what this is about, or are you going to continue looking at me funny?"

"I heard our little Hawaiian girl got on a plane this morning headed back home to Maui, Hawaii."

"She isn't our Hawaiian girl. But yes, she was well enough to travel and headed home today. Her father is back in the hospital and her mother can't cope without her or something like that."

Alexavier raised an eyebrow still assessing his chief of police.

Patrick didn't have time for this nonsense. "Is that all?"

Standing up like he was going to leave, Alexavier buttoned his impeccably tailored suit jacket and then gave Patrick that politician smile that won him the election twice. "Unlike you, my friend, I understand big families and familial obligation." He crossed his arms and locked eyes with Patrick. "But from what I understand, Nalani Kahale is a force of nature, and she could handle her family, a relationship with a hard head like you, her own career and fry it all up in a pan."

Patrick rolled his eyes. The mayor was nosier than Patrick's next-door neighbor who had called him three times already wanting to know what was going on. Ironically, Miss Newsome used the words "Our Hawaiian girl," too.

"Nalani Kahale is an incredible woman. But she has a huge family that wanted her back home and she was simply waiting until she was well enough to travel."

"If that's what you have to tell yourself at night to sleep better then go ahead, my friend. Lie to yourself. But she was your person just like Olivia Dufrene is mine. She made you a better man and you will regret letting her go."

"It wasn't up to me."

"Are you sure about that?" Alexavier said and then tapped on Patrick's wooden desk like he'd dropped a mic. Then he turned and strutted out of Patrick's office leaving his door open.

Idiot mayor. What the hell did he know about Nalani anyway? He certainly didn't know about their relationship. Not that there was a relationship. Patrick growled under his breath.

The city was heating up with tourists already and there

were big parades the next weekend. He had more to do than worry about a relationship that wasn't going to work out. Nalani would get home and forget all about him.

He stood up and slammed his office door. It was time for him to move on and focus on his job. If he did that, he would eventually be able to forget her too. *Right?*

Chapter Thirty-One

"Miss Kahale, there isn't any easy way to say this but I need to ask you some personal questions and you may or may not want to answer them," Dr. Helene Rolland said.

Oren, the second Kahale son, had picked Nalani up from the airport and in less than a half hour at home, she excused herself to call Dr. Rolland. "Go ahead, professor."

Nalani remembered the robust woman who taught several of her graduate classes. She had light brown hair cut into a bob and always wore slacks, a tucked in blouse, and a blazer to class. It didn't matter if it was cool outside or a balmy ninety degrees, Professor Rolland never wavered from her uniform. She was steady as the sun and a great professor.

"I guess you know that it upset a great many of us when you quit the doctorate program without any warning. To be honest, I was very surprised by your behavior. I'd always found you to be an exceptional student."

Nalani honestly hadn't thought about how any of the staff would see her behavior. "Thank you, professor."

Dr. Helene Rolland cleared her throat. She was having a

hard time asking Nalani personal questions. "Um, okay, well, when I'd heard you left I went to your adviser, Dr. Lemay. He said that he wasn't surprised you quit at all because you'd failed his course. Which I found preposterous because according to your records, you have never made anything lower than an A. You certainly aced all my material.

"Then he confided in me that he caught you cheating, and you opted to quit instead of having him turn you in and having you kicked out of the program."

"What?" Nalani couldn't say anything else, and the silence was as awkward as the entire conversation.

"It was confusing because we have a duty to turn students in for cheating and there isn't any gray area where he can just decide to let you quit instead of having your record tarnished."

"I didn't cheat, Dr. Rolland. I have never cheated in my entire life." Nalani couldn't believe this conversation. She hadn't been able to face Dr. Lemay and his inappropriate sexual behavior, but she hadn't considered that he would make up a lie about her cheating and try to discredit her honesty and integrity. Were they going to now expel her after the fact? "That isn't what happened, Dr. Rolland. I swear."

"Miss Kahale, I never believed the story in the first place. But now, we seem to have a bigger problem."

What else could be worse than what she'd been through already? "Go ahead, Dr. Rolland, I can take it."

"My goodness, I can't seem to find my words. Miss Kahale, could you tell me the real reason you left? W-Was it because of Dr. Lemay?"

Nalani sat down on the floor of her bedroom. Her brothers had moved her furniture back to her parents' house after she'd been missing for three weeks and gave her apartment up. Everything was a mess and her heart hurt knowing she'd worked hard her entire life and now was living at home in her childhood bedroom as if she hadn't earned her bachelor's degree, a master's degree, and finished two years of a doctorate program. The shame of what happened was overshadowed by the cowardly way she'd handled the situation. But suddenly having a respected professor ask her what happened made Nalani question everything. Did Dr. Rolland suspect something? Had Dr. Lemay told someone? Did someone else see or hear him? No matter what, Nalani was suddenly compelled to admit what had happened to her. "Dr. Rolland, I left because of him, because of his behavior toward me."

"Okay, just to be clear, it wasn't because of him failing you? Correct?"

"Correct."

Nalani wasn't sure if it was a lump growing in her stomach or a fire raging but she wasn't going to hold back now. Earlier, when her plane landed on the island, she'd felt like she'd worked her whole life toward a goal that was pulled out from under her. It was infuriating to be right back where she'd started. Losing Patrick was the final straw, and she felt like she'd lost everything, every opportunity. Nalani was ready to go after the man who had set off the chain of negative events in her life.

"It was because he harassed me as a student and degraded me in front of others every chance he could and as I worked harder and harder to make him respect me, like me, and see me as a serious student, he took that opportunity to try and sexually assault me late one night in his office." Nalani hardly took a breath as the admitted for the first time out loud what had happened to her.

"Oh, Miss Kahale." Dr. Helene Rolland said, and her voice quivered.

There was a long pause and Nalani didn't know if she'd

shocked Dr. Rolland into silence but now that she'd said it out loud, she was ready to fight back even more.

"It's true and I have proof. I saved all the text messages that he sent to me. I even have a couple of handwritten notes that he slipped to me in class. He is a vile man and I wish I had done something about him then instead of quitting and moving home. But he had me so confused and upset that I didn't think anyone would believe me back then. I was ashamed that he'd tricked me so easily."

"You weren't the only one, Miss Kahale. He used his power over another student. She was failing his class and he changed her grade for sex. He taped the whole thing, and a janitor found the camera. I have it on good authority that he will be suspended until it can be sorted out. He said they had a consensual affair, and he changed her grade because she redid her paper and some extra credit work to bring up her grade. The young woman tried to press charges but ultimately left school, disgraced. I want to help her and you, Miss Kahale. Together, with your evidence, I think we could shut him down. I don't want this to happen to another unsuspecting woman."

The guilt of not trying to stop him when she had the chance felt like someone had punched Nalani in the gut. She held her stomach as the regret made her insides twist.

"Miss Kahale? Are you still there?"

Nalani nodded but couldn't talk yet. Dr. Rolland continued anyway. "There is supposed to be a detective assigned to this case. Can I give him your information so he can reach out to you? It could really help."

"Okay."

"Okay, then. I'm so glad you called me back. Thank you. This is going to change things for sure. Call me if you need anything, Miss Kahale."

As soon as Nalani got off the phone, she ran to her bathroom and vomited. She'd only had a cup of coffee, a diet coke and some pretzels all day but the realization that she was going to have to tell her family the real reason she quit school hit her hard.

One of the biggest injustices to sexual assault victims was that they weren't always believed and usually were forced to retell the deed repeatedly. Nalani had never had to talk to a detective before and the idea of telling him what Dr. Lemay did to her would be humiliating.

She sat on the cold tile floor of her bathroom and instantly wanted to talk to Patrick. In her past, she'd always turned to her family whenever she had a big decision or if something was wrong. She could certainly go to them now but still she wanted him. Patrick would know exactly what to do in this situation. But he wasn't there and he had made it clear that he wasn't a relationship kind of man.

He'd never loved anyone. He said he didn't think he could ever love anyone, too.

Nalani took a deep breath and forced herself to stand up. She brushed her teeth and rinsed her mouth. Having a strong partner would have been great, but she could handle this. She would handle this.

When she walked back into the family room, her mother was waiting on her. "Nala, can you drive me to the hospital?"

"Sure, ma."

It was hard to see how fragile her mother looked in this situation. The stress of having the family restaurant burned, her husband hurt in the fire, and Nalani kidnapped had been almost more than the sixty-year-old woman could take.

Her mother wasn't a wilting flower and could normally run circles around everyone. But she'd been with Nalani's father since she was a teenager. Nalani couldn't remember a single night that they'd slept apart in her entire life.

She would wait to find the right time to discuss her phone call with Professor Rolland.

When they got to the hospital, Nalani's dad held his arms out for her mother and then for her to come and give him a big hug. He was more gregarious and loved to have everyone around. "My girl. You look beautiful," he said to his wife and then looked at Nalani. "Hey, Nani," he said.

He always called Nalani, Nani which meant beautiful in Hawaiian. "Hey, dad," she said and then kissed him on the cheek. He was a tall man, bigger than normal like her brothers and always protective of his family.

"I heard they had to put you in here so you would stay away from the restaurant?" Nalani teased.

"Look at me, Nani. Do I look sick to you?"

She laughed at her father and then scolded him. "You know you have to take care of yourself. What would mama do without you? Keanu, Oren, Jensen, and Noa can take care of the restaurant. You know they won't let anyone make changes without your approval."

Her father grumbled. "You need to take care of yourself. You still have a cast on your arm."

Nalani rolled her eyes and laughed. Her dad didn't like to be wrong and wouldn't take criticism from anyone else but her. "My cast is coming off next week, but I do still have to go to physical therapy. I'll make a deal with you. I'll take care of myself if you take care of yourself?"

Her father agreed and then asked when they were going to let him out of there. "I'll talk to the doctor for you, dad. Just be patient. We want your heart to be strong like the rest of you."

Nalani kissed her father on the cheek again and he gave her a gentle bear hug.

"My girl. I'm glad you're home."

Nalani's eyes watered and she tried to swallow back her emotions. She was happy to see her family and wanted to check on everyone. But if she told the truth, she wished things had worked out with Patrick. She could see herself there, finishing her degree, teaching, and building a life with him.

How had Patrick become important to her so quickly?

Before her father could question her tears, her brother Oren walked in with a picnic basket full of food. He'd gone to culinary school and was an amazing chef. "I thought we could eat together like we used to and hang out," he said, and she wasn't certain but her dad looked like he was tearing up. What was going on with them? The Kahale's didn't cry.

They ate, laughed, and had serious discussions about what had happened to Nalani, her father, and to the restaurant. The nurses had to run them off, twice, and it was midnight when Nalani crawled into bed. She was feeling a lot better but the travel plus visiting with her family who talked nonstop for hours, wiped her out.

She looked up at the ceiling of her childhood bedroom and smiled at the crocheted cloth draped across it. Things hadn't changed there in ten years. She looked at the clock on her phone and wondered what Patrick was doing. It was seven in the evening in New Orleans, and he was probably still at work.

Just then, her phone vibrated. Patrick sent her a text.

Chapter Thirty-Two

I wanted to make sure you made it home safely, sunshine. He wrote.

Nalani read the words a few times, a little surprised to hear from him. Before she could respond, he called her.

"Hello."

Patrick sighed like he was relieved to hear her voice. Nalani couldn't help but miss him even more. "How is your father doing?"

"Obstinate as ever. Insisting they let him out of there." Nalani smirked. "But he looks good and will be fine once he rests a little more."

"How are you, sunshine? That was a long trip and I'm sure you spent most of the night at the hospital looking after your family."

"It's fine. I'm fine. Just got into bed. It's midnight here."

The thought of her not being in his bed got to him. He was such an asshole for not sleeping with her the last two nights she was there. He would give anything to have her there now. "The house is darker without you in it."

"I miss you, too," she replied. Why couldn't he have told her how much he wanted her when she was there in front of him? "I guess you are at home now?"

"Yes. Miss Newsome brought over some leftover casserole. I think this thing has canned tuna in it and maybe some potato chips."

Nalani laughed. "I bet it does." Miss Newsome admitted to Nalani that she wasn't a good cook but she'd always felt that cooking someone a homemade meal was a comfort.

"It's not so bad," Patrick admitted as he took a bite of the warm meal.

"My brother Oren is the head chef at our restaurant and always makes cooking look so effortless. We've cooked together but my stuff isn't as pretty as his final product."

Patrick loved the meal she'd prepared the night he missed her dinner party. He still owed her for that and probably an apology for a lot of things the last few days. "I really enjoyed that chicken dish you made and the pineapple cake."

Nalani remembered what a disaster that night had been. Miss Newsome and Dr. Bixby couldn't get out of there fast enough. They'd been inseparable ever since. Sort of like her parents. It was the kind of love she wanted. She wouldn't settle for less.

"You should try the fresh pineapple here. It's really the best."

"I'd like to do that."

Was he trying to say he wanted to come to Hawaii? Nalani was so relieved to hear his voice. She wanted to tell him about Dr. Lemay and ask his advice about talking to a detective. But this was harder than she'd thought it would be. They were thousands of miles away from each other and she may as well have been on another planet.

"Are you sure about that? It was pretty obvious that you weren't interested in Hawaii last night and the night before."

Patrick had hurt her, and it was the last thing he'd wanted to do. "I've been interested from the moment I saw you, sunshine. I was wrong for not telling you how much you meant to me every day. If I could go back and change my behavior, I would."

Nalani had tried to pick a fight with him. She missed him and missed the idea of what they could have been, but his response surprised her.

"How much did I mean to you? You told me that you didn't love me."

"I never said that, sunshine."

"Yes, you did. You said you'd never loved anyone and didn't think you ever could."

"I have never loved anyone before--" Patrick stopped himself from saying before you. She didn't deserve to hear that over the phone.

"Why can't you talk to me? What happened to you? Why do you think you have to always be alone?"

"You deserve better, sunshine."

"That's not what I'm saying, Patrick Morales. But I grew up with parents that adore each other. They can finish each other's sentences and they have all these inside jokes between them that none of us understand. The love around them is palpable. I want that."

"I want you to have that too, sunshine. But I didn't grow up around anything like that. I've never been in a long-term relationship."

"So what, you've sworn off love or relationships? You think you're too old to learn new tricks?"

Patrick laughed at her response. She was the light to his dark.

"Tell me about your childhood and family. I've talked about mine for weeks and you've met two of my brothers already."

"You don't want to know, trust me. It's been a burden I've carried my whole life." Patrick walked into his bedroom and saw the bed she'd made when she left that morning. He pulled off his shirt and climbed under the covers where she'd laid alone. He could smell her on his pillows and sheets.

"Don't tell me what I want, chief."

He loved her determination. It was undeniable the moment he saw her fighting to get untangled from the comforter those bastards had taped her in before they threw her out of the moving car onto the interstate. "Are you sure you aren't too tired to stay up and talk to me?"

Patrick Morales was one of the strongest men she knew which was saying a lot after growing up around the Kahale men. But at that moment, he sounded unsure of himself in a way that made her want to hug him so tightly and tell him that everything would be okay.

"I could stay up all night talking to you, Patrick Morales."

And they almost did.

He told her how his father left his mother after he was born. How Sheila Morales had zero mothering ability and mistreated him his whole life. About the time she was going to rob a store with one of her deadbeat boyfriends because they got the wild notion to follow in Bonnie and Clyde's footsteps. The loser boyfriend wanted to go out in a blaze of gunfire glory. Patrick was twelve and explained to his mother how the original ambush ended with Bonnie having 26 bullet wounds.

She changed her mind and broke up with the jerk. He went

on to rob the store anyway and was shot dead by an off-duty police officer that just happened to be there. It didn't change how mean she was to Patrick, but he finally realized that she would never be a mother to him.

He told her about joining the marines and going to Afghanistan. He'd originally thought he would stay for four years and earn college money. But the work he was doing overseas was too important and he signed up for four more years.

"Eight years is a long time," Nalani said. She didn't understand why he didn't like being called a hero, but she refrained from bringing it up again.

"It felt like I was there forever and then some days it felt like it flew by," he admitted. He told her how awkward it felt to go to college in his late twenties. "I didn't look that much older, but I felt like that old guy that goes to the bars and hangs out with twenty-one-year-olds."

Nalani laughed at him. "You dated college girls and felt like a cradle robber?"

"You are the first college girl I've dated."

"Technically, I'm not in college and we didn't really date."

"I want to change both of those things, sunshine."

"Uh-huh, tell me the rest of your story, chief." Patrick didn't know why he couldn't open up to her while she was living under his roof, but he felt like a damn show pony now and couldn't stop performing.

"I couldn't be a regular college student. I didn't feel productive enough, so I got into the police academy. Once I started with the NOPD, I took night classes." He told her about being promoted from within the department and how he really enjoyed mentoring other officers. Patrick had joined a group that were cleaning up graffiti and ran into Alexavier again there. He was just then running for mayor the first time and apparently kept an eye on Patrick's career. During Alexavier's second term in office, his police chief retired, and he told Patrick he was the natural choice to take over.

He spent all his time working and organizing the department from within to wipe out crime in the city. They were at the top of all the good lists now, like the safest city to live in or city with the lowest crime. He was most proud of his police officers who loved their jobs and enjoyed the structure he'd put into place when he took over as Police Chief. "Everyone wants to know they are appreciated, and it isn't just about money but our officers make a nice salary. The community knows the officers by name, and everyone works together to keep the peace."

"You put in a lot of hours, though. Do you think they can't do it without you? Are you trying to say it isn't a dangerous job?"

"I work a lot because I love what I do and who I work with not because they can't do it. And I don't feel like it's dangerous anymore, not like in most places. Do you not like my chosen profession, sunshine?"

"I want you to be happy, chief."

"You know there are some women who have a thing for men in uniform." He was flirting now, and she'd wanted to see that side of him again for a while.

"I like uniforms okay, but it's the handcuffs that turn me on," she said and kept a straight face trying not to laugh over the phone.

"Sunshine, I had no idea you had such a dirty mind." Patrick's voice was lower, and Nalani laughed nervously now because she was turned on talking to him.

He trusted her enough with his story, the background he didn't share with anyone. That had to mean something, didn't it? "You have no idea what goes on inside this head of mine."

"I sure would like to find out," he replied and then cursed, "Damn."

Nalani kicked off the covers on her bed because their conversation had made her suddenly hot. But now he sounded mad about something. "What?"

Chapter Thirty-Three

"Sunshine, I forgot about the six-hour time difference. I kept you up all night."

Nalani wanted to tell him he could keep her up all night anytime he wanted. Especially if he was in her bed, but she didn't. "I'm good. I have to meet my brothers at the restaurant in a few hours to see the new construction and make some notes for my dad. But then I can take a nap."

"Well, I gave you enough to think about today."

"Patrick Morales, none of us get to choose the family we are born into and I don't care if you never talk to your mother or know your father. Trust me, one overbearing family is enough."

"You're lucky to have them."

Nalani loved her family, and she did feel lucky to have them but she wanted to live her own life. The restaurant business was great, and she could surf every day of her life but she'd always wanted to teach and as she got older, becoming a professor was her dream. Could she find the strength to make that happen?

"Sunshine?" Patrick thought he'd lost her.

"I'm here. Just thinking about my family and how I want to tell them I want to finish the doctorate program." She couldn't tell him about the sexual assault yet. She had to figure out how to tell her family too. Perhaps she was worried for nothing. It might take that detective a long time to call her.

"I'm sure they will support you, no matter what you want to do."

"I can't do that here, though, and after what all has happened to the restaurant, my dad, and then me, I'm not so sure they will let me out of their sight."

Patrick understood how hard it was for her to stand up to her family. They loved her so. But they also were crazy protective and he understood that too. "Sunshine, that is a worry for another day. Get some sleep. I'll call you tonight. Okay?"

"Okay," she replied wanting to say more.

"Sweet dreams, sunshine."

"Same to you, chief."

When they hung up, she ached for him. Pulling up her covers again, she questioned how she could be this far away and still feeling that pull? Drawn to him in an unnatural way that actually felt more natural than she could understand. It was so hard because she wanted to be here too. Her family needed her, and she wanted to help her mom and dad because they'd always taken such good care of her.

Nalani's mind raced until the sun peaked through her curtains. It was no use, she couldn't sleep after that conversation. Patrick Morales had grown up in an impossible situation and didn't think he was lovable or think that he could love someone the way they deserved. The way she deserved. But that wasn't true. He was incredibly thoughtful of others. He just hadn't reached his full love potential yet.

Kicking off the comforter and sheet again, Nalani got up

and showered. She threw on a black and white striped bikini and covered it up with some blue jean overalls. She dug around until she found her sandals and then pulled her hair up into a messy bun. She would go to the restaurant and then get Keanu to take her to the beach.

She could tell her oldest brother anything and he gave the best advice. She would tell him about Patrick and how she felt about him. Then she would tell him about going back to school but if things went as usual, she would admit what happened with the lecherous professor that tried to ruin her life.

First she needed some caffeine and her mother always kept strong coffee brewing and a pitcher of tea. When she stepped into the outer room, the house was still dark. Her mother never slept in. As her eyes adjusted, Nalani saw her mother sitting at the counter with her cup of coffee and worry on her face.

"Ma? You, okay?"

Her mother nodded and took another sip of her coffee. Nalani made herself a cup and had a seat next to her mom. When she reached her hand out, her mother's skin was freezing cold.

Wrapping both hands around her mother's, she leaned in and kissed her on the cheek. "Mama, it's all going to be okay. Dad will be home in the next couple of days and the boys and I will make sure the restaurant is opening on time and ready to go. Promise."

"I needed you, my girl," she said and leaned in to kiss her daughter on the top of her messy hair.

"I'm here, mama. You don't have to worry about a thing." Nalani made small talk asking about her cousins, aunts, and uncles. After she finished her coffee, she set off for the restaurant to see her four brothers.

"Hey, shorty," Keanu said as he walked over and picked Nalani up to hug her. When she took a deep breath, Oren punched Keanu in the arm.

"She has broken ribs bro," Oren scolded him.

Keanu set her on her feet carefully. "I forgot, shorty. You okay? Did I hurt you?"

Jensen roughed up her already messy hair and then Noa looked her up and down. "You look like a homeless girl. That's all you could find to put on?"

Keanu shook his head. "She's ready to go surfing. Right shorty?"

As usual, her brothers talked at her and she couldn't get a word in. It meant they missed her. She'd missed them too.

She put her hands on her hips and looked around the restaurant. The kitchen looked done but the outer room for customers was a mess. "Ma isn't handling all of this too well. You boys need to get this place whipped into shape so I can bring her by tomorrow and ease her mind. You know she worries especially with dad not around."

Noa rolled his eyes. "What do you think we've been doing?"

Nalani locked onto her brother. "Clearly, not enough."

Keanu laughed and the other three brothers scowled at him. He always thought Nalani was hilarious. The other three usually couldn't tell when she was kidding. Oren was always the serious one. Moody like most chefs too and sensitive. "Ma has had a hard time of it. Maybe we should have a family dinner at the house tonight?"

Nalani hugged him. Oren was thoughtful and no doubt had watched over their mother while Nalani was gone. He showed her the upgraded kitchen appliances and then Keanu showed her how they'd expanded the outside covered deck. It overlooked the ocean and there were tiki lanterns all along the rim to light up the area at night.

The entire place looked incredible, and she was certain they would never have made the changes unless something drastic had happened. The restaurant had always been successful but now they could seat even more people. Business would blow up from there.

It would make her parents happy and perhaps the boys could talk them into retiring soon.

Keanu saw his sister's worried expression. "Want to go to the beach, Nani?" She nodded and he wrapped an arm around her as he led her outside to his jeep.

Her oldest brother was handsome and kind. He was a professional surfer for most of his life until he retired from the sport two years ago. He opened a few surf shops while he was a pro and people flocked to buy signature Keanu Kahale Gear.

He was loaded but still humble and helped at their family restaurant if he was needed. Mostly, he ate there and brought in a crowd who still wanted to see the locally famous surfer.

"You can't get that cast wet, yet, right?"

Frowning, Nalani told him no.

"That's okay, shorty," he handed her some sunglasses and pulled out two beach chairs from his back seat. "We'll grab some rays by the water, instead."

Keanu set up their chairs so their feet could touch the surf. Nalani shimmied out of her overalls, and he took off his shirt. The sky was bright blue but there were large white clouds in the distance. It felt like heaven here and Nalani had truly missed it.

She laid back with her head pointed toward the sky and breathed deeply. When she sat up, she saw her brother watching her. "Feel better?" he asked but he already knew the answer.

He reached out and squeezed her hand. "I wasn't so sure we'd get to hang out like this again, after those assholes took you."

"I always knew I would see you again."

"Yeah, but maybe not in this realm, right?"

"Right," Nalani agreed. Keanu was spiritual and always talked about how their spirits knew each other before they came together on Earth. He would tell her that was the reason you could meet someone for the first time and feel like you've always known them. She wasn't sure if she believed that but as soon as she saw Tenille in danger that night in the parking lot, she felt connected to her. Then they became close friends like they'd always known each other. It was incredible.

"Jensen and Noa came back and told us about the chief of police that had a thing for you. We all just call him *The Chief* but what is his name?"

"Patrick Morales," she said and her whole face lit up.

"Ah, you want to tell me about him?"

Nalani smiled. Keanu was the best listener. She explained how the chief stayed with her and would talk to her all night and day to keep her distracted from the pain.

"His neighbor was a nurse or something, yeah?"

"Yes. Miss Newsome was a nurse and very sweet."

"So where is this guy? If he is all smitten, then why didn't he come with you."

"Everyone can't just do whatever they want like you, Keanu. He has responsibilities. He's the chief of police in the city of New Orleans. That's a big deal."

"So are you, little sis."

Nalani knew he meant that comment. He'd always been

her biggest fan. She told him the truth about how things ended and how Patrick didn't have any family. "It's so hard to imagine being alone in this world. You know, like Tenille. It's sad."

"Yes, Nani, but you can't save everyone. I remember when you were younger, you wanted to save all the animals. A bird flew into the window of the restaurant, and you carried it around in a produce box for two days. We didn't have the heart to tell you it was dead."

Nalani remembered because when she tried to put it on a pillow in her bed, her mother broke the news to her. They both laughed. But she looked at him seriously. "Patrick doesn't need saving but I think I'm in love with him."

"And how do you think he feels?"

She shrugged and avoided her brother's stare. Keanu squatted in front of Nalani and lifted her chin to look at him. "He needs to make a big gesture now. If he loves you then I think he will."

"What if he needs a big gesture? I mean, he wasn't shown the kind of unconditional love that we were and maybe he doesn't know how."

Keanu shook his head and Nalani smiled because that was his sweet way of ending the conversation. She decided to hit him with the fact that she was ready to go back to school to finish her doctorate degree. "I'm not in a rush and I certainly don't plan to leave mom and dad when they need me. But I'm ready. I told myself when I finally got away from those kidnappers, I would live my life to the fullest."

Her big brother smiled looking out at the large waves crashing onto the shore. She waited but wasn't sure he was going to say anything. They watched as some young kids with their father tried to paddle out and surf the waves back in, but none of them were very good. "Their form is all off. Too stiff. I think they're afraid of the water," Keanu said under his breath.

For a minute she thought he was going to go out there and show them how to surf but he sat back in his chair, grounded to the idea that they would have to practice on their own because his sister needed him. "We've all wondered how long it would take for you to go back. It was never if, it was only when."

"It didn't seem like that to me."

"That's because you're young. We are older and wiser," Keanu said and then laughed when she pulled the hair on his legs.

"So I guess this is where I tell you what really happened to make me quit in the first place."

They watched as the kids and their dad carried their boards to a truck, packed up, and left. The beach was completely empty again which is why they always loved that spot.

Keanu's expression was serious as he waited on her to tell him what he'd waited two years to know. "Go ahead, Nani."

She managed to get through it all without too much emotion and when she looked up at her brother who was now sitting on the sand in front of her, she admitted, "I blamed myself because I basically let him get away with it. I'm a quitter. I dropped out and came home. And I'm most ashamed that I couldn't tell anyone the truth."

The anger on his face surprised her. Keanu was always the most levelheaded of her brothers. Nalani had never seen him angry, not really. He might have been disappointed or aggravated over a situation but at that moment, he looked like he would kill someone.

Chapter Thirty-Four

Keanu stood and demanded his sister to stand up, when Nalani was on her feet, he pulled her into his arms and hugged her until she couldn't breathe. "Your ribs, sorry shorty."

"It's okay. I'm okay. I'm stronger than I look," she said, and he kissed the top of her head. Then ruffled the hair in her messy bun with his hands.

"You sure as hell are and don't you forget it." Keanu locked onto her and this time he spoke seriously. "Don't you ever say you're ashamed for quitting school and coming home. This is your refuge. Your safe space and when you're here, we will always protect you. You know that right?"

Nalani nodded. He was going to make her cry.

"But don't ever think that you can't call any one of us if you need something. I will travel to the ends of the earth, Nani, to help you. So will Oren, Jensen, and Noa. Hell, any one of our cousins will too. Now tell me where that bastard is, so I can go take care of him."

That was all it took for her tears to flow. Swiping at her face she told him how Dr. Lemay was getting suspended because he'd hurt another student. He was under investigation and about Dr. Rolland asking her to speak with a detective.

Her brother turned to face the water again and this time she watched as he ran his hands through his thick black hair, and she saw his back muscles tighten and then release. "Alright. When are you supposed to talk to him?"

"I'm not sure. She's giving the detective my phone number."

"We'll do this together. Make him set a time to talk to you instead of just answering questions when he calls, okay? This should be more structured, so they don't try to spin this some way that isn't the truth as you know it."

Her brother loved surfing but in his retirement, he was a huge fan of true crime fiction and read tons of books about cases all over the country. She trusted him completely, which is why she asked him to tell the rest of the family. It was just too difficult for her to have to go over the details again with each of them.

Keanu gave her another hug and told her that he had her back. When he picked up their chairs so they could walk to his jeep, he stopped and stared at the sand for a minute. "Nani," he said, and she quickly turned to see two green sea turtles sunning themselves on the edge of the beach. They were huge and beautiful. Nalani's breath caught in her throat.

Her brother bumped his shoulder into hers lightly. "Hanu are a sign of good luck. You know that right?"

Nalani nodded and her eyes watered again. This was exactly what she needed after that heavy conversation. It was a sign. Things were going to be okay.

They drove straight to the hospital from the beach, and both brushed the sand off their feet and slipped into their clothes so they could visit with their dad. They laughed and talked about some of their surfing adventures as they walked into his room, but he was gone.

The nurse walked in after them and smiled. "The doctor set him free. You know your dad wasn't going to wait on anyone else. He showered and dressed immediately and made me go over his paperwork as we made our way to the front door of the hospital. I think it was one of your brothers that picked him up."

"Tall and slim, super short hair?"

"Yes, but I'd say more athletically built."

Nalani laughed, Keanu was always teasing Oren about being thin when, Keanu was just built like a surfer with muscle from head to toe. Oren wasn't thin, he just spent more time perfecting his cooking skills than surfing but he could hold his own.

"That was our brother, Oren. He's a chef you know. You can see him again if you come to our family restaurant. The Island Fish House. We reopen in about a week." Nalani winked at the young nurse.

"Thanks. Can't wait," the attractive nurse replied. She knew the Island Fish Company well, but she'd never seen the chef.

There was no mistaking how much the nurse liked their brother and Nalani grinned because she was certain they would see her at the grand opening.

"We will never hear the end of this from Oren if we don't get to the house to help dad get comfortable," Nalani said.

They rushed over to their parents' home but there weren't any cars there. Keanu tapped the top of his steering wheel. He was a little frustrated and made a U-turn on their parents' street.

"You know they are at the restaurant," he grumbled, and Nalani agreed.

When they got there it looked like a party because the parking lot was full of cars. Was their entire family there? As they walked into the main dining room, the whole place had transformed in the few hours they'd been gone.

"What?" Nalani couldn't believe it.

Oren, Jensen, and Noa walked over. They could see their parents, both with huge smiles on their faces talking to the rest of their family. It was loud inside and a madhouse with most of their relatives standing around grinning.

Jensen leaned in and whispered, "We called in the calvary and everyone showed up to help us finish."

Keanu nodded. But Nalani was still astonished. "Everything? It's all done?"

"We just have to stock the kitchen," Oren said and the look of pride on his face was heartwarming.

Nalani was relieved to see her mother so happy and her father was holding court in a circle of all his siblings, talking as fast as he could. It was a relief to see so many things in her life put back together so perfectly.

She was blessed to have this loud, wonderful family. "I'm going to go say hi to dad and mom and then I'm going home. I am wiped out," she said to her brothers. Nalani couldn't be sure, but they were all watching her a bit carefully. She was still in a little pain and hadn't rested since she got home. Keanu would probably tell them everything the moment she left.

At that moment, after staying up all night and confiding everything in her oldest brother, Nalani didn't care. He could take a billboard out with all the information as long as she could go home and sleep.

But she would need someone to drive her.

Chapter Thirty-Five

Nalani only had a few hours of sleep before the entire Kahale family descended upon her parents' house for dinner. She wasn't sure who brought what but there was enough food for an army and at least fifteen conversations going on at once all night.

She crawled into bed at midnight, swearing to not get up until noon the next day, but Patrick called her minutes later.

"Sunshine?" Patrick sounded worried. "What's wrong?"

She told him about her busy day and then how her father was released from the hospital. The giant family gathering afterward was as foreign to him as any family reunion, but he listened to her explain it.

He told her about the upcoming parade weekend and how busy the city would be until after Mardi Gras. These were black out days for the NOPD and no one could take off until after Fat Tuesday was over.

It was fascinating to hear about the parades, and she snuggled into her bed, loving that he'd picked up the routine of talking to each other after a long day on his own. He told her about Miss Newsome and Dr. Bixby getting engaged and they both marveled at how fast things had gone between the older couple. "Miss Newsome told me that when you know you know," Patrick said laughing about the blunt woman next door.

Nalani thought that was one of the truest statements she'd ever heard and told that to Patrick. She could feel his smile through the phone, especially when he agreed.

They talked about little things like their favorite foods and music but most of all they enjoyed getting to know everything about each other.

It excited Nalani that he was no longer hanging out at the surface but instead treading in the deep waters.

Two hours later, Patrick insisted she get some rest. She was so exhausted she was slurring her words but still she didn't want to get off the phone. "I'll call you when I get off work tomorrow, sunshine. Promise," Patrick said and he called her every single night.

The following week was busy from sunup to after sundown for both of them. The restaurant had its grand reopening and then the family and staff celebrated after hours each night either with drinks or drinks around a bonfire. The celebrating was getting out of hand, but no one wanted to call it quits.

The same went for Patrick Morales as the city filled with more tourists than they'd seen in years post pandemic. Hotel occupancy was at a hundred percent and still people kept coming. The celebration was grand but sometimes people got carried away with their drinking and partying hours after the parades ended and it kept him and his officers working impossible hours.

Still, they talked on the phone to each other for an hour or more, no matter how exhausted they were or overworked.

Another week went by, and Nalani had her arm cast removed and her ribs were healed enough that she was cleared by the doctors. She'd quit physical therapy after going three times because she'd started surfing with Keanu which she felt was all the therapy she needed.

She sent pictures of herself surfing or laying out on the beach and a few of the new restaurant during the day and more of it at night. She had selfies with her mom and dad and tons of candid shots of her brothers, friends, and cousins.

Patrick took pictures of his officers working the parades and a few selfies of him next to giant floats or with marching bands. He even showed her videos of men riding electric recliners in one parade and it fascinated her. He promised to mail her some Mardi Gras beads and she promised to send him pineapple.

It was late one night that she sat outside drinking with her brothers complaining over the fact that she was in love with someone who wanted to be her pen pal.

They laughed at their little sister, but they all knew not to tease her about the chief. She'd never been serious about anyone and if this didn't work out it was going to break her heart. They hoped to distract her as much as possible but there was no way to save her from it.

She'd been home for a little over two weeks and everything for the Kahale family was in order. The restaurant was open, and they had to turn people away each night because they were overbooked. Mr. Kahale's heart was strong, and he got a thumbs-up from his doctors that he could go back to work. Nalani's mother was happy and running around behind the scenes at the restaurant ordering supplies. Jensen and Noa both were dating several local women and Keanu was asked to judge some upcoming surfing competitions which was one of his favorite things to do.

Nalani had kept busy with the whirlwind schedule to help her family and talking to Patrick each night. She'd almost forgotten about that detective calling her. It was early Friday morning and she'd just gotten out of the shower when her phone rang.

"Ms. Kahale?"

"Yes."

"I got your number from Dr. Rolland. My name is Edgar Ramirez and I am in charge of the case against Dr. Lemay. I believe you were one of his students?"

Nalani's heart began to beat harder. She wanted to put her clothes on before she discussed that sexual predator, and she asked the detective to hold on. She towel-dried her hair and then put on some cut off shorts and a rock band t-shirt. She looked like a high school student, but she didn't care. She still hadn't unpacked all her boxes of clothes that her brothers brought over from her old apartment.

"Okay, Detective Ramirez, I'm back."

"You can call me Edgar," he said in a friendly voice.

"Okay, Edgar. Yes, I was in the doctorate program and Dr. Lemay was the committee chair and my adviser."

"And Dr. Rolland said he was inappropriate with you? Can you tell me what happened?"

This didn't feel right, and she suddenly remembered that Keanu told her to talk to the detective when he was there and not to do it alone. "To be honest, detective, I don't feel comfortable discussing this over the phone right now. Can we reschedule this for another time?"

Edgar instantly became aggravated as he tried to force the

conversation. "Ms. Kahale, we have a serious case here and either this man needs to get his life back or we need to charge him and move forward. I am asking you to simply answer a few questions."

Nalani didn't appreciate his tone but still felt guilty for not turning Dr. Lemay in when it happened. She agreed to answer a few questions and then she told him everything she'd told Professor Rolland.

"And you have proof?"

"Yes. I saved the text messages and the notes."

"How will anyone know they are actually from Dr. Lemay?"

"They are from his email account and anyone reading them can tell it's in his voice. The notes are in his handwriting."

Ramirez got quiet for a few minutes and then asked her if she would be willing to fly back to the school and meet with him. When she hesitated, he told her that the school would pay for her plane fare. "We want this to be over with as soon as possible, Ms. Kahale. I'm sure you feel the same way."

That didn't make sense to Nalani because things in the court system didn't move quickly according to her brother, the true crime expert. She wished Keanu was there so he could help her.

"Detective Ramirez, I don't need anyone to buy my plane ticket." She didn't know why but she didn't care for Edgar Ramirez, and it was time to let him know that he wasn't calling the shots. "If you want to take my statement and get a copy of the evidence then have the college pay for your ticket and come here to see me."

It should have been apparent to all of them that the last thing she wanted to do was return to the school or area. She didn't want to visit the state of California if Dr. Lemay lived there.

Edgar took a few minutes to respond, and she wondered if he thought that would make her change her mind. He didn't know her. She had an inner strength that most people never saw. Thinking back to her kidnappers, she knew they'd certainly been surprised by it. She never gave in to anything they said or did to her. Three weeks of sleeping on a concrete floor, half starved, and then tortured hadn't made her talk. This man wasn't going to push her around.

"Alright, Ms. Kahale. I'll be there Monday morning," he said and then hung up.

Nalani instantly wanted to rethink the whole situation. She'd kept this to herself for over two years and suddenly she had to discuss it three times in a matter of weeks. It was a lot to digest. She sat on her bed and tried to think clearly. She tried to compartmentalize what was happening and tuck the memories of how cruel Dr. Lemay was toward her even before the assault. She'd figured that was what people meant by attackers tearing down their victims. It put them in an unstable place trying to earn trust so they wouldn't see the nefarious behavior until it was too late.

She stood up and paced her small bedroom, trying to calm her nerves. Dr. Lemay deserved everything that was coming to him and although she didn't want to go to the college town, she would absolutely testify against him when it was time. But how was she going to explain Detective Ramirez to her family?

Nalani's family worked all over Maui. There was no place she could meet with him unseen. After Monday everyone would know something was wrong. Unfortunately, Keanu hadn't told their parents or brothers yet and now he was on the big island to judge that surfing contest.

All weekend long she tried to speak to her parents about the situation. But they were so happy and buzzing around from the restaurant to the house because things were finally settled in their eyes. She couldn't bring herself to upset them again. This all happened in the past and she was better than okay. But she understood this news would be too much for her mom and dad. If only her brother was home.

Sunday night she declined to hang out with the kitchen crew and wait staff after they closed. Instead, she went home and read all the emails she'd printed, and the notes Dr. Lemay had written to her. They were disgusting and put her right back in the moment when he'd ripped off her underwear and she pushed him off her.

The day after, she skipped classes and her advisee meeting because she couldn't face anyone. It would be hard to hear others praise him for whatever amazing thing he would do that day. It was so clear that he humble-bragged for attention but she could only admit that after he'd attacked her.

When she finally returned to class, he seemed to show up everywhere she went. Even though it wasn't his class, he would interrupt other teachers and ask if he could sit in on a lecture and then he stared at her the entire time.

Once he realized she wasn't going to turn him in then he began the ruthless harassment. Slipping her notes after a class or sometimes at the campus coffee shop where she would study. She tried to return to her advisee meetings since other graduate students would be there. He would say demeaning things to her under his breath but still a couple of them heard him.

It was the worst time of her life. Nalani shook her head because kidnapping wasn't a walk in the park but still the sexual assault and harassment by a professor, she'd idolized felt worse, more personal, like a betrayal.

There was noise in the kitchen, and she realized her parents were home. Telling them what had happened was going to be hard but it would fortify her for the meeting with Ramirez the next day. She had to do this.

As soon as her father saw her, his face lit up. "Hey, Nani. Home early tonight, aren't you?"

She grinned at her dad and then laughed as her mother fuss over him drinking a soda with his vitamins. "I needed to talk to you both about something and I'm afraid I waited until the last minute because we've all been so busy."

They instantly turned toward her. The worry on their faces was unmistakable.

Chapter Thirty-Six

Nalani smiled at her parents trying to set them at ease. "There is nothing to worry about. I just, well, first I wanted to tell you that I want to go back to college to finish my degree. I know I'm meant to teach and want to make that happen."

Her mother looked emotional, but her father stepped in to speak for both of them. "Nani, we always knew you would want to go back. It was only a matter of time before you told us when."

That shouldn't have surprised her since those were almost exactly the words Keanu said to her. But it still touched her heart how much her family understood and supported her. It was the reason this conversation was going to be so difficult.

She sat down on a barstool and her father handed her a Dr. Pepper which made her smile. Her mother didn't like them drinking soda because she said it had too much sugar. But whenever ma wasn't around, Nalani's dad would buy them.

"Going back to school to finish the doctorate program isn't the only news that I have to tell you guys." She looked at the can of soda and smiled. "But I guess you figured that out already, dad?"

"You looked like you had something on your mind, Nani. The weight of the world on your shoulders or something?" he said, sweetly.

"I heard you talking around the fire pit with your brothers, Nalani. You love that chief?" her mother said and her amber eyes glistened.

"I do love Patrick. We haven't known each other for very long and I'm not sure he feels the same way. But this isn't about him, Ma."

"We haven't met him yet. How can you love him?" Her mother wasn't going to let Nalani go without a fight. She'd always known her mother wanted her close, but it was easier to see now.

"Sit down, Mama." Nalani reached out and held her mother's hands as she sat next to her. "This isn't about Patrick."

Her father realized this was even more serious than he first thought. He stood behind his wife and put his hands on her shoulders. "Go ahead, Nani. We can handle it."

It was now or never. She took a deep breath and slowly began to tell them what had happened to her. It had helped that she'd already told Dr. Rolland, then Keanu, and a third time to Detective Ramirez.

She tried to spare them some of the gory details but felt it was important they understand how seriously it affected her. When she concluded her story telling them how the detective would be there tomorrow to take her statement, her father walked straight to her and wrapped his arms around her. Her mother swiped away a few tears and then wrapped her arms around Nalani too.

"So we are pressing charges against that professor." Her father said.

Nalani had to smile. Of course, her father saw it as a family action. "Yes. I believe the evidence I have is going to make the difference. I'm not sure what happens from there though."

Her father told her that it wouldn't matter because the whole family would be behind her every step of the way. He was curious where she was going to meet the detective and she told him that they hadn't made plans yet. Edgar Ramirez would call her when he got to town and they would decide then.

"Mama?" Nalani said. Her mother had been quietly listening but looked more worried than before. When she looked up at her husband he nodded as if he knew what his wife was thinking. They'd always been like that even when Nalani and her brothers were young. They didn't need to speak because they knew each other so well they could read each other's minds.

Clearing her throat, her mama looked deeply into Nalani's eyes. "Are you certain you want to go back to school after all of that happened there?"

Her mother didn't want her to go and Nalani would have to ease her into the idea. "I wasn't planning on going back to California."

The flight from Maui to Los Angeles was a little over five and half hours and easy for her mother. But going all the way to New Orleans felt like a full day affair and it would be more difficult.

Both her parents nodded as if they agreed with her decision to not go back to the same school. No one wanted to discuss where else she planned to go. This had been heavy talk and they needed to rest and contemplate all the news. They could discuss schools later.

As soon as Nalani climbed into bed, she noticed how heavy her heart felt. Telling her parents what had happened had been difficult, but she regretted more keeping it a secret for so long. She should have told them, told someone.

Now that she'd told her family and the wheels of justice were going to run Dr. Lemay down, she needed to tell Patrick. She lay awake until two in the morning when he called. "I apologize for calling so late, sunshine. Just a couple more days and things will quiet down around here."

He told her about some Mardi Gras shenanigans like people trying to climb poles in the French Quarter that had been greased. It was an actual event with music and everything. Sending her pictures of people dressed in costumes and musicians. It was wild looking to her. Patrick sounded more exhausted than she was, but still, she wanted to talk to him before she met with the detective.

Waiting until he finished giving her the view of Mardi Gras Weekend through the eyes of law enforcement, she asked him if he was home yet. After all, it was only eight in New Orleans and still plenty of time for craziness. She even thought she heard the muted sounds of a band playing.

"I'm actually sitting in the front seat of a cruiser. It was too loud to hear you outside so I thought I would take a minute to call you."

Nalani got quiet. This was a terrible time to tell him and yet, she felt the need to be honest.

"Sunshine? Is everything alright?"

"Yes. I just need to tell you something and I know this isn't a good time."

The noise in the background suddenly got louder and she

could barely hear him as he yelled to someone that he needed a few more minutes. Then it got quieter again and he was focused on her. "I always have time for you, Nalani. Now tell me what's wrong."

"There isn't anything wrong. I just haven't told you something, it happened years ago, and I need to do that now." She didn't wait for him to say anything. Rushing through what had happened, she told him everything. Then she explained that she was meeting a detective tomorrow.

"Why didn't you tell me this sooner?"

"I just wanted to forget it happened. Put it behind me, you know. I hadn't told anyone until Dr. Rolland called me and then Keanu a couple of weeks ago."

"Haven't we been telling each other everything all these late nights over the phone? I told you what happened with my mother, and you didn't think you could trust me?"

"I do trust you. Patrick, I love you."

"What?"

The crowd outside of Patrick's car was louder than before and she heard fireworks going off in the background.

"I have to go," he practically screamed those words at her and then he hung up.

No goodbye or I'll call you later. Nalani already knew what he thought about love, and she didn't expected him to say it back to her. But was he angry because she'd said it? She kicked off her covers and paced the room.

Telling his deepest secrets meant something to him and she should have realized he would think she hadn't trusted him the same way. Why didn't she wait to tell him later? Would he have still rushed to get off the phone?

Nalani climbed back into bed and stared up at the ceiling. Detective Ramirez would be on the island in a few hours. She would have to recount all the terrible things she told him over the phone again. Then she would have to show him and possibly discuss the emails and notes that Professor Lemay gave to her. It was going to be an impossibly long day until that task was done.

But at the foremost front of her mind was the conversation she'd just had with Patrick. The days during Mardi Gras were busy for him but the nights were crazy. He'd been lighthearted telling her about everything that happened in the city. She'd ruined the light conversation with her story.

She spent nearly a month with Patrick and cared about him. Then after returning home, they'd gotten even closer talking for hours on the phone. Recounting their life experiences and likes or dislikes. Of course, she'd fallen for him harder. She'd thought he'd also felt the same way, sharing his life with her. What was she thinking telling him how she felt when he'd clearly told her that he had never and could never love someone. Still, she hadn't expected for him to get angry. Perhaps she didn't understand him at all. She certainly didn't know where to go from here. Was it over between them? Would he let her explain? What if Patrick didn't want to talk to her again?

Nalani had no idea how much worse things were going to get.

Chapter Thirty-Seven

The morning began with a frenzied pace around the Kahale family home and Nalani wondered if it was too late for her to run away to Maisonville and live the quiet life. She wouldn't have to stay with Patrick at his lake house because Tenille would be happy to put her up at the boarding house.

She stirred sugar into her coffee and as she turned around to survey the crowd, when Noa tried to slip in and take her cup. Glaring at him, Nalani gripped her coffee mug and growled. Her brother raised an eyebrow. "Did you just growl at me?" he asked but Nalani sipped her coffee and refused to speak to him or anyone else yet.

Their dad was frying a giant skillet of spam and her mother was beside him making eggs. One of the aunts was cutting up some fruit as more of the family poured into the house with donuts and more.

Nalani had drifted off to sleep minutes before her alarm went off. That was when she heard the crowd in the kitchen and dragged herself out of bed. Her parents obviously told everyone already because each time another member of the family made eye contact with her, they winked, smiled, or gave her a nod of support.

They meant well, and she kept trying to remind herself of that whenever someone tried to talk to her. As she sipped her coffee, Noa, Jensen, and Oren made their way to stand near her.

The house was packed with people in every seat in the kitchen, dining room, and living room taken, but also, a lot of relatives were standing around the rooms too. Her parents didn't have a huge house and this was too much.

Finally feeling caffeinated, Nalani looked at Oren. "Who is at the restaurant if all of you are here?" It was really early in the morning but the guys usually got to the restaurant at dawn to start prep work for the lunch crowd.

Oren put his arm around her and gave her a hug. "Dad called a family meeting this morning and said for us to put out a closed for the day sign."

Nalani shook her head. In her entire life, he'd never done that.

Jensen added, "He said if he couldn't close for a family emergency then what was the point of owning his own business."

As usual, anything to do with her had to be over the top for the family. Couldn't they see that she didn't want to talk about this in front of everyone? Besides, it had been two years and she was doing better. She needed to talk to the detective and put this behind her.

She sure didn't need all of them to sit in the room as she answered questions or handed over evidence. Surely, they didn't think they were all going to accompany her to the interview? The more she thought about them being there, the more frustrated she felt. It could have been the sleep deprivation, but this was beginning to feel like a three ring circus.

Nalani put two fingers in her mouth and whistled loud enough for the next island to hear. At that moment her big brother, Keanu walked into the room, and she laughed. He had been on another island to judge a surfing contest.

"Hey," he said to her and then turned around to hug their mother and grab a piece of spam. He walked over to stand in front of Nalani, and she tried to keep her emotions in check.

"This is a lot of attention," he said to her, and Nalani tried to blink back tears. He locked onto her stare and asked, "Too much?"

Nalani nodded at her brother.

"Dad said someone was coming to talk to you about the incident today? You think they all plan to be there?"

Shrugging her shoulders, Nalani felt bad because she knew everyone just wanted to help. But she needed to handle this on her own.

When she looked up, all four of her brothers were watching her. Keanu leaned forward so they all could hear but no one else. "Let everyone eat, then we'll tell them you need to do this on your own, Okay?"

"Thank you," she said and leaned back against the counter watching everyone fill their plates. She was usually strong but this whole thing made her feel insecure and it was hard for her to understand. She was too nervous to eat but her mother insisted and handed Nalani a plate anyway.

It was eleven before the crowd thinned out. With the restaurant being closed, Nalani didn't have anything to do to keep her mind off the upcoming meeting. She mumbled under her breath that Detective Ramirez may not call her until tonight and that was when her phone rang.

The room got quiet as she answered. "Our family restaurant is closed today. I could meet you there and we can sit outside to talk."

Edgar agreed and when she got off the phone, she looked at her brothers. She appreciated them but she needed to take control and stand her ground. This was her family, she loved them, and could talk to them. "I'm meeting him in an hour at the restaurant, but I don't want anyone there. I just don't think I could stand for any of you to see the emails or notes--and I'm not up for discussing what happened again in front of any of you. Okay?"

The look on her mother and father's faces said they were not okay with it. "You should at least take Keanu," her father suggested.

Nalani smiled at her oldest brother. "You can drive me but that's it."

"I'll sit in my jeep," Keanu offered.

"Promise?"

"I promise, shorty."

Nalani smiled and then went to her bedroom to go change her clothes and grab her phone, computer, and notebooks. As she walked back out, all eyes were on her again. "Listen everyone, I'm good. I am ready to get this behind me. You don't have to worry."

Slowly each one made their way over to hug and kiss her. It felt like her own funeral or something, but she tried to smile.

As soon as she got in the car with Keanu, he sighed loudly. "That was intense."

"Imagine if I'd told them when it had happened."

Keanu shook his head. "We would've drawn straws to see who was going to go to prison for killing that dude."

"Exactly." Nalani shook her head. She couldn't help but

think of Patrick. This was what he had missed out on his entire life. Family.

They pulled up to the restaurant, but the detective wasn't there yet. Keanu made small talk and told her about the surfing contest that he had judged over the weekend and all the new talent coming up on the surfing scene.

It was great to talk about something other than herself. Nalani told him that when she was done talking to the detective that she would love to go out on the water. They made plans to invite their brothers and cousins and that was when the rental car pulled up.

At the same time, she received a text from Tenille asking her to call her as soon as possible. Had Tenille just realized she'd left town? She quickly sent a text that she was walking into a meeting but would call her as soon as she was done.

She tucked away her phone just as a slim older man stepped out of the driver's side of the car and looked over at the jeep and nodded. "Doesn't look like a detective," Keanu said under his breath.

Nalani shook her head. What was a detective supposed to look like? They were in Hawaii and the man had on slacks and a nice linen shirt. "I'll be back," she said and reached over to squeeze her big brother's hand.

As soon as she got out of the jeep, she shook Edgar's hand. He insisted she call him by his first name, as she unlocked the restaurant so they could go inside. She offered him a cold drink and they walked out to the back patio area that overlooked the ocean. It had always been a peaceful spot but the remodel made everything feel fresh and new.

Edgar wasn't as squared away as Nalani would have thought and so she pulled out the pages she'd printed for him and began the conversation. "Here are copies of the notes he gave to me and the emails he sent."

She handed them over and watched as Edgar Ramirez couldn't hide his surprise by the vulgar words the professor wrote to her. He cleared his throat after reading each one and there were twenty-two of them. Then he asked Nalani to tell him the story again, this time including the letters and emails. He wanted to have a timeline and order of the way things unfolded so he could present the case that way to the board when he returned.

Nalani had already told him the story in chronological order and didn't understand why he needed her to do it again adding the letters. They were graphic and his language offensive. What the professor wrote to her felt even more personal and it was harder to tell face to face reading out loud what the professor wrote. It instantly pushed Nalani right back to that impossible time. Seeing the professor for who and what he was behind the mask. He'd abused his power and made her feel small.

"It was after the night he harassed you in his office that he gave you the first note?" Edgar asked. He wasn't looking at her and she took the time to study him.

He was a bit prissy, and his hair cut was professional and short but also styled with product. Even with the wind coming off the water, every hair on his head was still in place.

Nalani didn't like the way he said Dr. Lemay harassed her in the office, as if it wasn't as big of a deal. "It was sexual assault not harassment," she corrected him. "He pushed me against his desk, ripped off my underwear and put his hands all over me without my consent," she barely blinked when she spoke to Edgar that time. She would never let anyone make her feel insignificant again.

Edgar looked up and into her eyes. He seemed to be weighing her words or perhaps his own. "And it was after that night that he gave you the first note?"

"Yes. I didn't go to class the next day because I needed to gather myself and think things through. You know what my recourse would be and how I should proceed."

"And still, you didn't think calling the police was warranted?"

"Of course, I thought calling the police was warranted. You have to know that I had no idea he would ever behave that way and once he locked his office door, I was in complete and utter shock. Then when I got away, I was too upset to talk about it. I didn't even tell my family or closest friends. I couldn't imagine having to discuss it with people I didn't know like police officers."

"I see." Edgar wrote more notes and then after a few minutes looked at her again to proceed.

"I went to my other classes the next day but avoided his class and my advisee group because he was my adviser, and I wasn't ready to face him. He sent me the first email that night."

Edgar picked up the printed email letter to verify which one she was talking about. She watched him write the number 1 and then he circled it on the paper. That seemed strange since it had the actual date that Dr. Lemay sent it to her.

"And once you had this in writing from him, you still didn't want to reach out to the police or the university?"

Nalani was getting aggravated at Edgar and wishing she had Keanu with her during this conversation. It was taking all of her self-control to not ask the detective whose side he was on. He was overall insensitive and proved why she hadn't gone to the authorities sooner.

"I was even more upset after his email because it proved to

me that he felt untouchable. It made me think he was unbeatable too."

Edgar looked down at his notebook avoiding her again. She didn't stop this time but instead stayed with her story adding which email was sent or when he handed her the filthy notes threatening to have her expelled if she didn't meet him in his office.

She felt worn out when she finished explaining every interaction, she'd had with Dr. Lemay up until the end of school. She'd already packed her things so she could leave town the day classes ended.

Pointing to some bullet point notes he'd made in his notebook; Edgar began questioning her. "You did take all your other finals, correct?"

"Yes, but most of them were papers or work I could complete off campus and send in by computer which I did before I left."

"And you failed Dr. Lemay's course, correct?"

Nalani paused for a moment wondering if this man even listened to her explanation. She wasn't the same frightened girl she was two years ago. "I think I've made it clear that he planned to fail me from the beginning unless I gave him sexual favors. I have never made less than an A in any class since kindergarten."

"What would you say if I told you that Dr. Lemay wrote that you did sub-par work for his class and after asking you to rework multiple assignments or come in for guidance that you refused."

"Well, I think it's obvious from those emails and notes what his idea of extra credit involved," Nalani said and stood up to finish her thought. "And I saved all of my assignments from his class. Trust me, Edgar, I know the subject matter inside and out and would dare anyone that is unbiased to look at it and say whether it is sub-par work or not."

"You're that sure, Ms. Kahale?"

"Positive," she said, still standing. "I'm done here."

Edgar looked insulted that she wanted him to leave. But gathered his things and stood to walk through the restaurant toward the exit behind her. Along the way, he had a few more words for her.

"This is highly unusual. I expect this to be difficult considering his position as committee chair and tenure. The fact that you didn't come forward while you were still enrolled is a problem and the board is going to have more questions. Are you certain that you want to go forward with these accusations?"

Nalani waited until they stepped into the parking lot and she'd locked up the restaurant to turn around and answer Edgar. She put both hands on her hips and looked up at him with a furious stare. The one that told her older brothers to back off because she was ready to explode. When she focused on him and then pointed her finger, Edgar seemed to understand and took a step back where he leaned against his rental car.

"I'm ready for a fight to make sure that vile man never has an opportunity to hurt another female student. You haven't mentioned the other woman or how this case is stronger since there is more than one of us willing to testify against him. But those emails and notes are real, and any expert out there can verify them. Have you even tried to find more victims? Clearly he's escalating since I left school."

Edgar fumbled to get into his car but before he closed his door, he mumbled that he wasn't at liberty to discuss anyone else.

Nalani stepped closer and he rolled down his window before closing his door. When he started his car, she stared at him. "You said you are presenting this to the board or committee several times, Edgar. Are you really a detective?"

He put the car into reverse, and she quickly moved out of the way so he didn't hit her. What the hell just happened? And who had she just given copies of all that evidence to?"

Chapter Thirty-Eight

The Kahale brothers didn't think they'd ever seen a woman madder than their little sister. She cursed and she stomped in the sand before taking her board out to the largest waves and riding them back in like a warrior.

"I would say we should kick someone's ass for her, but I think she can handle it," Oren said as he drank another pineapple shot. It was one of Nalani's favorite drinks, where he infused vodka with fresh pineapple, and he brought it to the beach along with a cooler of various alcoholic drinks.

Keanu had called everyone while she was inside talking to Edgar Ramirez, and they headed to the beach and set up a tent for her. One of the cousins brought a small barbecue and they grilled squid and burgers. But Nalani didn't want to eat. She wanted to surf and then she wanted to drink and forget this day ever happened.

They promised her to make that happen but wouldn't allow her or anyone else to surf irresponsibly. That meant, no swimming once they started drinking, so she cursed and surfed, sometimes yelling into the wind as she rode her board close to shore over and over again.

Noa took pictures of her and shared them with the group. She looked like a pro out there on that board and they knew she would have been as famous as Keanu if she hadn't chosen to be a book nerd.

By the time she'd worn herself out, Keanu carried her board for her and told her to sit by the fire. Jensen handed her a drink and Oren gave her a skewer of barbecue squid. They told stories of their childhood and how they didn't have very much back then but always seemed to have a great time.

Their family business grew over those years and they all were responsible for its success. Work hard, play hard was their motto and it gave them a closer bond than most people could understand. Tonight around the beach bonfire was only family, by blood or marriage and they all meant to support Nalani, however she needed it.

The drinks got stronger and the stories grew funnier as the night grew later. By the time Noa eased Nalani over his shoulder, careful to not put too much pressure on her tender ribs, she was never going to remember the ride home.

Keanu laughed as she sang her favorite childhood song, Baby Beluga and the Deep Blue Sea, all the way home. It took Jensen and Oren to keep her from waking their folks as they steered her to her bedroom and bed.

It was eight the next morning when she woke up and felt her head throbbing. "Oh my gosh, what have I done to myself," she grumbled as she went to the bathroom and stood under the hot water in her tiny shower. She threw her towel dried hair into a messy bun and slipped into a navy sundress she hadn't worn since she was in high school. She laughed because it looked better on her now, ten years later, and then rolled her eyes at how much bigger her bottom was at twenty-seven.

She slipped on her sandals and headed to the kitchen for coffee when she realized she didn't know where she'd left her phone. It would take caffeine for her to find it and she quickly made a cup. Everyone had to be at the restaurant by now, knowing that she would be too hungover to show up before lunch.

Halfway through her cup of Joe, she walked back into her bedroom to find her phone plugged into its charger on her nightstand. Gosh she loved her brothers. They were so dependable.

It was then that she saw she didn't have any missed calls or messages from Patrick and instantly her eyes watered. She swiped at them and sniffed her nose. There hadn't been a single night since she'd returned home that Patrick hadn't called or sent her a text except for last night.

That was when she tried rubbing her forehead to get rid of the deep headache that was growing inside her brain. She swore she would never drink pineapple infused vodka again and smiled because that was a lie. Then she rubbed her chest because her heart ached.

She wanted to act as if it wasn't that big of a deal that Patrick hadn't called but after telling him her biggest secret, had he just dropped her? Sure, she'd waited a little longer than she probably should have to tell him what happened. But were there really time constraints in a new relationship as to when you divulge your past?

Then she remembered telling him that she loved him. Had that scared the chief of police away?

Nalani picked up her bag, a change of shoes for later, and then slammed her bedroom door on the way out. She would go to the restaurant and see if they really needed her for the lunch or dinner shifts. If not, then she was going to Keanu's bungalow on the beach to sleep on his sofa for the rest of the afternoon.

When she walked into the restaurant, Keanu was sitting at the bar talking to Oren and their dad. Jensen and Noa were carrying food out to tables and three of her cousins and an uncle were talking to her mother near the kitchen.

When they saw her walking in, they all began to clap and cheer for her. She laughed but then had to hold her head. This was going to be the longest day in history. She sat down next to her dad and put her head on his shoulder.

"Nani, you didn't have to come in today," he said and Jensen and Noa both jeered for her. It was no secret that their father babied Nalani and, on this day, she needed it more than usual.

Oren offered her a drink of pineapple vodka and she made a fake gagging noise which made Keanu laugh. He handed her a glass of ice water instead along with some aspirin while Noa turned up the news on the television behind the bar.

They were showing one of the famous parades in New Orleans and talking about Mardi Gras. Nalani couldn't tear her face away. It made her miss Patrick even more as she stared at the screen. That was when they went straight to the story of how the party was going on but the celebrating was quieter than usual because of the horrible accident Sunday night. One police officer died, and the chief of police was still in a coma after saving a young girl in Sunday night's parade.

The glass of ice water hit the floor and splintered into a million pieces. Nalani covered her face with her hands, and it seemed like the entire restaurant held its breath.

Jensen was already on the phone calling Tenille while Noa

rang Miss Newsome. Nalani didn't know what to do, so she sat there waiting for news. Jensen handed her the phone, but she couldn't speak.

"Nalani?" Tenille said.

She managed to mumble unintelligibly.

"We don't know anything yet. He hasn't gained consciousness and the only person that's been allowed in there is Miss Newsome and the mayor."

"I-I will be on a plane this morning," Nalani said and then handed the phone back to Jensen.

Her family was already in motion. Oren cleaned up the mess while Jensen started looking at flights, her father handed her a wad of cash while her mother hugged her. Then Noa and Keanu took her to the house, helped her pack and stayed with her at the airport until she got on the plane.

Nalani barely remembered the stop over at LAX or boarding the next flight that would take her into New Orleans. When she landed and went to grab her luggage, a driver was there holding a cardboard sign with her name on it. She walked over to him, and he carried her suitcase to the town car.

"I was told you needed to go straight to the hospital, ma'am?"

She hadn't spoken all day and her throat felt raw with emotion. "Yes, please," she managed to say but then fell silent the rest of the way. Traffic was heavy and the driver explained people were on the interstate trying to get around the parades.

Nalani nodded but honestly couldn't think about anything except for Patrick.

As she stepped into the hospital, she realized she didn't know where she was going or know how she was going to get in to see Patrick. But as soon as she got off the elevator onto the floor where the ICU was located, Miss Newsome was there.

She grabbed Nalani into a big hug and held her tightly. "Oh, it's good to see you, my baby," the sweet woman said. When Nalani looked into her eyes, she could see she'd been crying.

"How is he?"

Miss Newsome shook her head and Nalani nodded.

"He's strong," Nalani said. "Stronger than most," she added.

"You're right. He sure is and we need to keep thinking positively," Miss Newsome added.

That was when an officer walked into the room next to the mayor. They called Nalani by name, and she was surprised they knew who she was. "Yes?" she said as she hurried toward them.

"Is he okay?" she asked, her eyes filling with tears.

Alexavier Regalia smiled warmly at her. "He's cut from a different cloth, Ms. Kahale. I have no doubt he is going to come out of this but in the meantime, he would be angry if we didn't take care of you." He looked over to see she had her suitcase. "You came here straight from the airport? What can we do to make you more comfortable? Do you have a hotel room yet?"

"I just need to see him and I'm not leaving this hospital until he does." She stared into the mayor's eyes, and he loved that type of sincerity.

"Then let's get you in there with him," he said and led her to the intercom on the wall where he asked the nurse to buzz them in.

The hallway smelled like disinfectant and the floors were the shiniest Nalani had ever seen. Everything looked so clean, and it reminded her that was because people in the intensive care unit were too sick to walk around.

Before they made it to his room, an alarm went off sending

nurses and doctors into immediate action as they ran past Nalani and the mayor. She gripped Alexavier's arm, and he held her before she hit the ground. It wasn't the chief's room but instead the elderly man next door to him.

"It's not Patrick," the mayor said and then again reassuring himself, "Thank God, it's not him."

Nalani's heart raced as they walked inside the darkened room where Patrick lay in bed. He was only hooked up to fluids and a few monitors but otherwise looked like he was sleeping comfortably. "He looks great," Nalani cried.

She picked up his hand and held it to her heart. It was warm and she'd missed his touch.

Alexavier brought a chair over for her and she sat down, still holding onto his hand. It was exactly how he'd sat next to her at the hospital. Tears rolled down her cheeks as she watched him breath in and out deeply. Then she laid her head down and sobbed.

She felt a warm hand stroking her hair and a gravelly voice telling her it was going to be okay. It took her a second but when she looked up, it was Patrick saying those words to her, but his eyes were still closed. "It's okay, sunshine. Don't cry."

Chapter Thirty-Nine

Alexavier ran to get a nurse and Nalani reached over and hugged Patrick tightly. "Oh, Patrick, I'm here. I'm here. You're going to be okay. I'm going to stay and make sure of it."

A nurse and a doctor stepped into the room and started examining the chief. He blinked a few times and then a little desperate said, "Sunshine?"

Nalani stepped closer so he could see her.

"I'm here," she said, and he saw her tears.

"What's wrong?"

She smiled because there he was in a hospital bed but worrying over her. "Nothing is wrong. Everything is great. I'm just so happy to see your face."

He grinned sleepily at her. "I'm happy to see your face too."

The nurse giggled at his response and the doctor who was trying to be all business, grinned uncontrollably. "Chief Morales, do you know where you are?" the doctor asked.

"Well, it seems I'm in the hospital, sir. But I don't know what the hell happened."

Nalani and Alexavier both laughed at him. He was going to be okay.

It took a half day to put Patrick Morales through all the cognitive tests and physical examinations to determine he was going to make a full recovery. His sprained ankle would keep him from being as mobile as usual and his concussion meant he had to be off work until the doctors examined him again in a couple of weeks.

Nalani helped Patrick up the stairs at his house and when she unlocked the front door for them to go inside, her mind flashed back to the day he'd brought her home with him. Oh, how the tables had turned.

"What are you smiling about, sunshine?"

"Just remembering the first time I came here."

"I was in a little bit better shape then," he admitted rolling his eyes.

He had a hard time relying on someone else and she wasn't going to miss this opportunity to take great care of him. Once she had him resting on the sofa, with his foot propped up, she turned off all the lights and closed the curtains.

"The nurse said limiting your exposure to bright lights would help speed up your recovery time," she said as she headed toward the kitchen. A few minutes later she came back with a large glass of water. "And you need to stay hydrated too."

He reached for her hand and tugged her toward him. "Sit down, sunshine. Keep me company." She kissed him sweetly and then told him she needed to get his dirty clothes from the other night into the laundry.

There was no way he was letting her go. Patrick wrapped his arms around her tightly. "No laundry," he said and kissed her again. It felt right to have her there and he loved how much brighter his home felt with her in it. It didn't matter if she turned off every light in the house and closed every curtain or window shade.

He kissed her warmly and she seemed to melt into him.

Nalani was grounded in that moment. The idea that he might never talk to her again had been difficult but knowing he was almost taken from this world had crushed her. She leaned into his warm body that she'd dreamed of so many nights while she was away from him.

Feeling a little desperate, she put both hands on his face and leaned back to look at him. He was still the most beautiful man she'd ever seen and this moment could get away from them easily. But she licked her lips and then leaned in and kissed him sweetly. He needed to rest.

However, she needed to know what happened so she could put things into perspective. Otherwise, she would worry about him constantly. "Tell me what happened, chief," she whispered as he began kissing his way up her jawline and behind her ear. She wasn't so sure she could distract him with conversation as well as he was distracting her with the promise of sex.

"I-I need to know, Patrick. How did this happen?"

He lifted her chin and kissed her cherry red lips. It was a promise. Taking a deep breath, he began. "I was sitting in that cruiser acting like an ass on the phone with you, when I saw some idiot teenagers shooting bottle rockets into the crowd. There was a large group, looked like family and friends, that had an area quartered off with old sofas and recliners. Clearly there had been a lot of drinking and very little supervision with the teens. A couple of officers went over to speak to them, and it got out of control. I saw an older man pull out a gun which was when I got off the phone with you and ran to stop him. I was too late because at the same time a little girl in that same group smiled at me, showing these big dimples right before she climbed through one of the street barricades."

"Oh my gosh," Nalani put her hand over her mouth. What an impossible situation for him.

"The officers tried to stop the old man with the gun, but he shot a round into the air as I jumped over the barricade. I came down on the other side hard twisting my ankle as I scooped up the little girl before she was hit by the next float. The crowd had heard the shot, and someone yelled *gun* which sent everyone into a frenzy. I saw an officer at the edge of the crowd go down as I handed the little girl to her mother. I knew what had happened but was only halfway over the metal barricade when the crowd slammed into it and me. The last thing I remember was falling toward the oncoming float and street."

"The officer that went down?"

"People don't realize when they shoot a gun into the air that it comes back down at a dangerous velocity. The bullet hit the officer and killed him instantly. Alexavier confirmed it, today."

"And you were hit by the float?"

"Not many people live to tell that tale, but I've done it twice," he smirked but Nalani wasn't laughing.

Patrick hugged her closely and kissed the top of her head. He'd worked in dangerous jobs for most of his adult life and he'd only been injured twice, both times by Mardi Gras floats. It was kind of funny.

Nalani snuggled next to him for a long while before she admitted, "I thought you were mad at me. That you didn't call because I hadn't told you what had happened to me at college."

"That was what I was referring to earlier about being an ass on the phone with you. I was upset that something like that had happened to you and had no right to be angry that you'd waited to tell me."

He lifted her chin and kissed her. When he leaned back to look into her eyes, he had a look she didn't recognize. "Sunshine, you have every right to keep whatever you want to yourself until I earn the right to know about it."

She carefully straddled his lap and kissed him. "I don't want there to be any secrets between us," she said and then told him everything that had happened with Detective Ramirez.

It was clear to him that she didn't trust Edgar Ramirez and Patrick was a big believer in blink reactions. "What made you not trust him, sunshine?"

"It could've been because of Keanu's comment that Edgar didn't look like a detective. Maybe it planted the idea in my head. But mostly, he didn't seem to have a particular way of doing things. You know, how you're methodical with everything like making the coffee or I don't know the way you ask questions. He wasn't like that. He was supposed to be there to take my statement but he didn't have things written down or lead the conversation. I did. But then I caught him twice saying he had to present the information to the board, not the DA, other policemen, or a judge. I don't know, anyone related to law enforcement, and I couldn't imagine who he was talking about."

"And he didn't show you his badge or credentials?"

Nalani suddenly realized that she'd met with a man who could have been lying about everything including his name. She shook her head unable to say out loud how ridiculous she felt, but Patrick understood her.

"Sunshine, you've never met with law enforcement and didn't know."

"I never considered the idea that anyone would impersonate a detective. Who do you think he was? An attorney or private eye? I was only trying to keep the professor from hurting anyone else. I guess I really messed up?"

The way her bottom lip pouted out a little bit when she was disappointed did something for him. He wasn't even sure she knew when she was doing it, but he wanted to kiss her all over and there was no way he could wait.

He surprised her by standing up and holding her tightly against his body. She wrapped her legs around him as he gripped her bottom tight to hold her in place.

Kissing her all the way to his bedroom, she finally stopped and stared into his eyes. "I'm supposed to be taking care of you and you're supposed to be resting."

Laughing at her bossy behavior, Patrick laid her across his bed, and smiled wickedly. "I'll rest so much better if you'll let me take care of you first." And he spent the next hour doing that.

Chapter Forty

The time difference had been difficult for Nalani to get used to again and she fell asleep at seven. Then she woke up at three in the morning. She laid on her side and watched Patrick sleep for a long time, thankful he was okay.

By four, she was up and doing laundry. He had distracted her and she hadn't cleaned and organized things the way she'd originally planned after they got in from the hospital.

A few hours later Patrick found Nalani sound asleep on his sofa. His entire house looked brand new after his girl went through it like a whirlwind. She'd dusted, swept, and mopped. She'd laundered his clothes and it looked like she'd even cleaned out and organized his refrigerator.

He sat at the far end of his dining room table with his computer so he could work and watch her too. She had no idea what it meant to him that she'd dropped everything to be there in his time of need.

He made another pot of coffee and two hours later when she woke up, he had a huge grin that lit up his face.

"Hey, sleepy head," he said, and she smiled back at him. The jet lag was worse than she'd thought, and she stumbled over to give him a kiss and to see what he was doing.

"You're not supposed to be working," she grumbled, and he playfully patted her bottom.

"Come sit, sunshine," he said and tugged for her to sit in his lap.

Had she ever sat in anyone's lap as an adult? She tried not to think too hard about it as he typed away on his laptop. "Recognize him?" he asked pointing to a picture of Edgar Ramirez.

"So that is his real name. Is he a detective?"

"No, sunshine. He works for the university."

"What?" Her shoulders sagged and Patrick pulled her close as he wrapped an arm tighter around her waist.

"When you said he told you he was presenting the information to a board that got me thinking that he had to be affiliated with the school somehow. It was simple enough to call the police department and verify that he didn't work for them. Then when I pulled up the college and plugged his name into the database, he was in several photos. You know people in academia love to celebrate themselves."

"Hey!" she scolded him. "I'm going to be one of those people one day," she said, and he winked at her.

"You sure are, sunshine," he agreed and kissed her.

"And all people in academia don't act like that."

He agreed with her again. "But this guy here is the public relations director and he has a vested interest in keeping the image of that little prestigious college squeaky clean. I think he thought he could intimidate you into dropping your charges or maybe he decided to see if you actually had evidence enough to convict the professor so they could plan their defense."

Nalani stood up and began to pace. She'd been tricked again by someone she trusted in authority and was frustrated at herself. "How could I be so naive?"

"There is a reason why impersonating a police officer is a crime, sunshine."

She turned and looked at him. Patrick was holding out the chair next to him and smiling at her. When she walked back over and had a seat, he handed her his cup of coffee. She sipped it while he typed some more information into the computer. When he turned it around, she saw an email sent to him. "I called the university police department to see if anyone had filed charges against that professor and they didn't know anything about it. They said that Dr. Lemay was still there in the history department and acting committee chair."

"What?"

"It's okay, sunshine. I then called the local PD and asked to speak to their chief. Did you know that in California there is no statute of limitations on sexual assault? If it happened today or ten years ago, you can still press charges. I explained how Edgar Ramirez posed as a detective to get your statement and that he flew to Maui to meet with you."

Nalani looked at Patrick. "Did I read that right? He already talked to his district attorney and they are going to arrest Edgar?"

"Yup. And I told him we would email the evidence you have on the professor this morning, and the notes you wrote down for Ramirez when he posed as a detective so they could arrest him too. Did you know that the chief there has twin daughters that are freshmen at the college? Both studying history? When I say he was thankful to help, I mean that he has a vested interest in cleaning that college up."

"I don't understand why Professor Rolland would call and lie to me."

Patrick turned his laptop screen around and began typing again. After a few minutes he looked at her. "I couldn't remember her name, so I just sent it to the chief. Guess we'll find that out as soon as he does. If she's in cahoots with Professor Lemay or Edgar Ramirez, then she'll be charged too."

Nalani jumped up and kissed Patrick all over his face. When she stopped, he was grinning like crazy and she marveled over how handsome he was and wonderful.

She cooked Patrick breakfast, insisting he needed to eat it so he would get better. Then over scrambled eggs he told her that he was sorry she would have to tell the story again to the real police but that he would sit beside her so she wouldn't be alone.

"Thank you," she said. It was funny to her that he'd never had a family but still he was supportive and caring just like her wonderful folks, brothers, and other relatives.

"What?" Patrick saw the way she was smiling at him. "You told me that you've never loved anyone and that you didn't think you ever could. It's not just a word. It's the way you care for someone and treat them. You show me that you love me."

"Sunshine, I don't want to hurt you."

"I'm not asking you for anything, Patrick."

He pulled her out of her chair and into his arms. "I want you to ask me for whatever you need. Don't hold back," he said.

Nalani crashed her lips into his. She wasn't holding back because she wanted him close to her. Leading him back to the bedroom, Nalani took her time showing him exactly what she needed. The rest of the afternoon, they laid on the sofa and watched movies. She made them popcorn and then talked on the phone to her family. She even put her father on the phone so he could talk to Patrick about freshwater fishing.

That night she cooked him salmon because high protein foods and foods rich in omega 3's were supposed to make him heal from his concussion faster. He laughed because she was going to follow every single item on the hospital list in order to get him well.

Over the next few days, Patrick made remarkable progress and his headaches were completely gone. He still had to wait to be cleared by the doctor and insisted on taking Nalani to his house on the lake in Maisonville.

They'd spent some great days there before and she agreed, but only if she drove them. She was going to make sure he followed the doctor's orders to the letter and limited his computer time too. He'd never had anyone take care of him. It took a little bit of getting used to, but he didn't admit that to her.

He tried to help her pack the SUV, but she insisted he rest until she had it done. "We might have our first real fight if you don't let me help you load the vehicle woman. I'm not helpless."

"Neither am I," she said and didn't even look his way. She was stubborn and adorable to him at the same time. But he secretly moved things closer to the SUV when she wasn't looking.

By the time they got to the cabin and unpacked, it was almost noon. He didn't want her to have to cook again and asked her to go to Miss Lynn's diner. Nalani loved that idea but before they headed out the door, Patrick's phone rang.

It was a California area code and he immediately answered. "Chief Morales?"

"Yes, sir, is this Chief Duncan?"

Patrick pointed to his phone and headed to the counter for his notebook and a pen. Nalani was right behind him reading each of the bullet points as he wrote them.

- Edgar Ramirez was arrested
- Ramirez told them about other women that had already come forward against Dr. Lemay
- Dr. Lemay will be arrested by tonight
- The DA is getting paperwork together to ask judge to not allow bail in his case
- Dr. Rolland was very agreeable, had been lied to by Edgar Ramirez, and offered to testify against him and/or Dr. Lemay

When he got off the phone, Nalani crashed into him, hugging him hard. "You did it, sunshine."

She shook her head. "No. You did."

He lifted her chin and kissed her lips. "We did it together."

Nalani and Patrick held hands as they walked into Miss Lynn's Diner. Two steps inside and Miss Lynn ran over to hug Nalani and to officially meet the chief. He'd been in the diner before, but he was a quiet man and Miss Lynn had pretended she didn't know who he was at the time. "You two make such a cute couple," Miss Lynn said after showing them to a booth in the corner.

The chief liked to sit where he could see the entire room, including the front and back doors. Nalani laughed because you could take the man out of the police department, but you couldn't take the police department out of the man.

After eating lunch, they each had coffee and shared a piece of warm apple pie. There was no getting out of dessert because there was something to the slower pace of this little town that felt warm and romantic. Life slowed down here, where you could smell the sweet scent of pie, and it made Nalani happy.

The beautiful waitress Olivia walked over to refill their coffee and to chat with them. She let them know that Tenille would be over soon. Tenille was at the boarding house helping one of Olivia's friends from her hometown who was relocating to Maisonville. He'd already started with the local police department and was renting a room there until he could find himself a house.

Nalani had already spoken to Tenille when she flew into town for Patrick, and once more when he got out of the hospital. It was Tenille's idea to get Nalani to apply for the doctorate program at Tulane. She'd taken the advice a step further by having all the application paperwork sent to Nalani's email. It was as if their roles had reversed where Tenille was looking after Nalani instead of the way it was in Hawaii.

Good friends looked out for each other and didn't keep score.

She and Patrick finished their dessert and said their goodbyes to the friendly ladies at the diner. Before they could get into the SUV, Tenille and Reaper pulled into the parking space beside them.

The women hugged each other, and the men shook hands just as a brand new silver jaguar screeched into the parking lot with a policeman coming in hot behind it.

In a blink, Patrick and Reaper had Nalani and Tenille pushed back out of the way behind them as a woman wearing a long lace wedding gown got out of the car. She had mascara smeared under her eyes and a giant mess of blonde curls half pulled out of some kind of fancy up-do.

When the police officer got out of his car, she immediately started yelling at him. "What in the ever-loving hell are you stopping me for? Obviously, I am in the middle of a crisis here." She waved her arms as she spoke and the officer looked like he was trying to be sympathetic.

"Ma'am, the car you're driving has been reported stolen."

The crowd in the parking lot looked at the car with streamers and bells tied to the bumper and a *Just Married* sign attached to the trunk, then looked back at the woman. She was wearing a wedding gown and certainly could belong with the car.

"As if," she said and stormed back toward the silver jag. The officer told her to stop. She didn't. He told her to stop again, and she turned around and glared at him. "It's my car. The asshole I just left gave it to me for my birthday last month. I was going to show you the title."

Tenille leaned forward and told Nalani, Patrick, and Reaper that the police officer was Olivia's friend from St. Marksville, Zachary Bowman.

"Looks like he's having a great first week on the job," Reaper added.

Officer Bowman stormed over to the hot-headed woman. "Look ma'am, I don't want to put you in handcuffs, but you aren't giving me much of a choice."

"I bet you want to put handcuffs on me. I swear, you men are all the same!"

Zachary Bowman looked like he'd had enough but the woman either didn't notice or didn't care. "My name is Marlow Ripley, and my mother is Senator Ripley--" before she finished her sentence she leaned over and threw up all over the officer's shoes and partially on that very expensive dress.

The chief and Reaper stepped up to ask if he needed some help, but he declined. Then he handcuffed the woman and put her in the back of his police car. He was a no-nonsense kind of guy and as Marlow Ripley cried, he didn't change his expression, just closed the door behind her. They watched as he took a giant roll of paper towels and tried to clean up his shoes and clothes. Then he tipped his head at the chief and Reaper, climbed into his car, and drove away.

Nalani looked at Tenille. *What just happened?*

Chapter Forty-One

Nalani and Patrick were quiet on the ten-minute drive to the lake house. She'd never seen anything like what happened in the parking lot. The only crazy thing that had happened at her family's restaurant, in fifty years was when they helped Tenille escape Peter Miller. But seeing that desperate woman in her wedding gown, yell at the officer, and then vomit all over him made Nalani have more questions for Patrick about his chosen career.

He held her hand as they walked inside the house. "Want me to build a fire?" he offered. February had some beautiful sunny days in South Louisiana but still could be quite cold, especially at the lake. A few minutes later, Nalani was wrapped in a blanket on the floor in front of the fire.

Patrick pulled cushions off the sofa and made them a more comfortable place to lounge on the floor. She smiled when he reached out and kissed the back of her hand as he sat beside her. "Why are you so quiet, sunshine?"

All the racing thoughts in her head finally narrowed to one. "It was hard watching that woman with the officer."

He nodded and under his breath added, "That was some dress."

"Right?" she agreed. "It should have been the happiest day of her life."

Patrick seemed to be weighing those words. After a long pause he gently squeezed her hand. "What's bothering you so much about that? The fact that she was left, or left someone at the altar? Or how upset and disoriented she seemed?"

Nalani shrugged. "All of the above. I've been in Maui almost my whole life. Even when I went to college I lived on campus or in an apartment close to campus and would go home for every break. I've mostly seen people at their happiest on vacation or celebrating something on the island. It made me think about you and how you've mostly seen people at their lowest or most unhappy moments."

"I can see your point--" he said but before he could add to his thought her eyes filled with tears and she stood up and walked to the back door looking out at the water. The wind had picked up and it was howling a bit against the glass doors.

Patrick walked up behind her, wrapped a blanket around her body as he pulled her back against his front. He felt her relax against him. His girl had a lot on her mind.

"How--" she started to speak and then turned around in his arms to look up at him. "How could you see stuff like that over and over again and then trust someone? You don't get into serious relationships because you know they can't last. You don't want to get married or have children because you've seen the worst that can happen. Am I right?"

Did she have any idea how beautiful she was? He stared into her dark eyes that seemed to absorb all the light around them. "Sunshine, I'd like to believe that I'm there to help people. The good guys and the bad guys need help. They just don't always know what that is and sometimes my only recourse is to take them to the station and put them in a holding cell. Let them and their lawyers sort it out."

"But what does that do to you on the inside day in and day out? I'm just now facing what happened two years ago with Professor Lemay. And to be honest, I feel guilty because it didn't go as far with me as it did so many other girls. Even when I think about the kidnapping, I feel lucky because Tenille had been through years of Peter Miller killing her family and unspeakable things. I was mostly locked in a room for three weeks. Sure, I was dumped on a highway, but you were there and watched over me. I get a second chance at the life I've always wanted. Why me?"

Patrick kissed her forehead before guiding her back to their pallet on the floor. This time they laid across the cushions in front of the fireplace and he pulled the blanket over them. He ran his hands through her thick dark hair and smiled at her. How could he make her understand? "Sunshine, you don't even hear yourself like I do. First of all, everyone has their battles to overcome but you have been through some of the worst things I've seen. And yet, here you are saying how lucky you are and wondering why you are so blessed."

He kissed her sweetly on the lips and when he pulled back the way he was looking at her made her feel adored. "Yes, there are people that have been through worse but there are a lot of people that have been through a lot less and have a terrible outlook on the world. I think the question is how do you always see the bright side of things and the good in a situation or people. It's fascinating to me."

"That makes me sound like an adolescent. Is that what you think of me?" She worried sometimes that being eleven years younger he would find her silly.

He stroked her hair again and shook his head. "I find you captivating." He kissed her on the lips. "And seductive." He kissed her cheek. "And irresistible." He sighed in her ear, and she wanted him more than ever before.

They made love by the fire and then again in the bedroom. It was hours later that she woke up to him staring at the ceiling. It was the early hours of the morning, and she could tell he hadn't slept.

Nalani curled into his side and kissed his chest. "What's wrong? Does your head hurt?"

Patrick leaned over and kissed her. "My head is fine. At least as fine as it's ever been."

Self-deprecating humor had never been his thing. She didn't like it. "You didn't answer my question earlier, you know."

"What question was that, sunshine?" He leaned over and kissed her again.

"Why haven't you dated anyone seriously? Have you avoided marriage and kids because you've seen the worst in people? Think it can't last?"

He pulled her hand to his mouth and kissed it. This affectionate behavior wasn't going to deter her for long and he had to answer her questions.

"I've never dated anyone seriously because I was waiting for you. Ditto to the marriage and kids' question." He winked at her and stared back up at the ceiling.

It was a great answer and she had to give him that because it melted her heart a little bit more to hear those words. But it wasn't the truth.

"The truth, chief. Didn't you take an oath or something?"

He laughed at her but naked in his bed, he couldn't keep any secrets from her. "Remember I told you that I wanted to become a police officer because they looked in on me from time to time when I was a kid."

She stroked his chest hair and nodded. She was putting him in a trance with every swipe of her hand and she had to know it.

"By the time I was a teenager, I was sick of living that miserable life with my mom. I went out and found myself some rough friends that took all the things they didn't have but wanted. At first it made me feel good because I had clothes, shoes, and plenty of food. But it quickly escalated to much worse. That feeling of bullying someone was addictive, and I was big for my age and angry. We were the bad guys and that went on for about a year. Late one night when I was out with a few of those guys, one of them pulled out a gun. It stopped me in my tracks. I knew there was no coming back from whatever he was planning, so I got out of the car and never looked back.

"I talked to a recruiter that next weekend and signed my letter of intent to join the marines. Two months later, I graduated high school and went straight to boot camp. It turned things around for me. I'm ashamed of what I did and the people that I hurt. It's why I don't like it when people call me a hero. I'm just a man who is trying to make up for my past and it'll take the rest of my life."

He felt the warm tears that fell from Nalani's eyes. "I'm sorry for upsetting you. I wanted to be honest and tell you who and what I really am. That is the reason I don't do relationships or more."

Patrick instantly felt a distance between them. Their bodies were still touching in bed but the cold seeped through him. He wished he could offer her more.

"I didn't mean to let you down, sunshine. Disappointing you was the last thing I wanted to do."

It took a couple of minutes for Nalani to pull herself together. Patrick had never seen love growing up like she had, and he didn't have a family that fussed and then made up on a regular basis. All he knew about people was the bad examples he'd had as a kid, then the structure of the military and now the sacrifice of being a police officer and the chief of police.

There was a lot she needed to teach him. She gathered the covers around her body and sat up in bed to look at him.

"If there is one thing I've learned by watching my parents, it's that you're going to disappoint me and I'm going to disappoint you sometimes. But then, we will make it up to each other and try harder. Love is sticking it out, no matter what. Through sickness and in health." She smiled at him turning on those dimples, "We've had enough injuries between us to cover one side of that, right? We should have a boat load of good health in our future."

Patrick locked onto her. It felt like she could look inside his soul. She had a way of seeing things and saying things that lit up his heart.

"Sunshine, I love you and I want to make you happy."

Nalani leaned down and kissed him hard on the lips. "I love you, too," she said. Then she pulled her sheet that was twisted around her and after a lot of tugging, laid down on top of his body, wriggling carefully until she was comfortable. "Patrick Morales, you make me happier than I've ever been."

He ran a warm hand through her thick hair and down her back. "Then say you'll move in with me, sunshine?"

She leaned up and kissed his chin. "I'll move in with you, chief. But you have to tell my family."

That got him laughing and then Nalani joined in. They had that forever kind of love, she just hoped he was ready to be a part of the crazy Kahale family too.

Coming soon
The next book in the Renaissance Lake Series
CHASING LOVE

About the Author

LISA HERRINGTON is a Women's fiction and YA novelist, and blogger. A former medical sales rep, she currently manages the largest Meet-Up writing group in the New Orleans area, The Bayou Writer's Club. She was born and raised in Louisiana, attended college at Ole Miss in Oxford, Mississippi and accepts that in New Orleans we never hide our crazy but instead parade it around on the front porch and give it a cocktail. It's certainly why she has so many stories to tell today. When she's not writing, and spending time with her husband and three children, she spends time reading, watching old movies or planning something new and exciting with her writers' group.

Connect with Lisa, find out about new releases, and get free books at lisaherrington.com

Made in the USA
Middletown, DE
23 September 2023

39172980R00166